The Third Floor

The
Third
Floor

By Leigh M. Rose

A Read Writers Publishing Book
Clay City, Kentucky

RWP

Cover Design by
Leigh M. Rose and James Mulcahy

Editorial and Sales Offices: Read Writers Publishing
295 Forge Mill Road, P. O. Box 710, Clay City KY 40312-0710

ISBN: 987-0-9858794-5-7
This book is printed on acid-free recycled paper.

Printed and manufactured in the United States of America

In Memory of:
My grandparents: Forest and Margaret Newkirk Rose
My aunt: Jewell Patton Rose
My cousin: Scott Harrington Rose

Preface

My dream was dark and shadowy. I remember the colors red and black. I was in bed beside my husband or boyfriend, it was never clear to me which, and we lived in a large old house we had just purchased. It was the type of house that always fascinated me as a child — large, dark, sad — haunting in some way. It was the kind of house in which I have always wanted to live.

I could hear wind whipping tree branches and I instinctively knew a storm was coming, but that wasn't what woke me. In my dream it was a noise that had awakened me; a noise that was not familiar to the large old house or the approaching storm. I sat up in bed and looked over at my significant other. He was still asleep. He hadn't heard the noise and I wasn't sure I had either, but I needed to investigate, otherwise there would be no sleeping for the next couple hours.

I didn't bother with a robe. It was late fall and my pajamas were warm. My feet were bare and cold on the hardwood floor as I walked down the long upstairs hallway from our bedroom to an unfurnished wing of the house. We hadn't lived there long and still needed furniture for several rooms. As I approached the end of the hall I could see inside the turret room. I loved those rooms in the old Victorian houses that had once been so prominent around Central Kentucky. As a child I had always imagined them as a perfect place to play.

I heard noises coming from the room. No, not noises, not the storm. Voices? Not an adult voice. It was young, a child perhaps. I approached the room quietly, carefully, on the chance that there was an intruder and not just voices echoing up from the street below. I neared the door and angled my body so that I could get a clear view of the room. That was when I saw her, and I took another step closer. Suddenly there was a blinding flash of light. I crouched and shielded my eyes. In that sudden flash, she was gone. And that is how my dream ended, and that is how my book began — with a dream so vivid it had to come to life on the page.

From the night I had the dream it was nearly three years before I decided to sit down at my computer and actually start writing. I'm not sure why it took me so long, probably a sense of priorities, putting everything else first when, in retrospect, some of those priorities weren't nearly as important as I perceived them. I did, however, win "Yard of the Month" in my subdivision one summer. A dubious honor at best, and one I hope never to repeat.

When I did finally place my fingers on my keyboard with the intent of bringing my dream to life, the story almost wrote itself, from opening scene of the first chapter to the last sentence of the Epilogue. I knew exactly where the story would go and how it would be resolved. It was just a matter of filling in events, dialogue between the characters that was true to their personalities, the situation, and of course, fitting in historical facts to tie it all together. Fortunately, I had always loved history and research and already had a good command of American and Kentucky history that made the research easy. For nearly two years I spent what little free time I had, evenings on the Internet researching, lunch breaks and layovers in airports, creating timelines for dates of events, developing names and characters, writing and rewriting until the woman with the newly acquired *big house* and the young girl came to life in front of me.

After I finished the book, priorities again got in the way and it was at least another three years before I would go back and start editing and revising some sections and get serious about getting it published. Editing was an interesting process. Not only because time away from the manuscript gave me time to rethink certain passages, and make changes that were more true to the characters and the story, but also because in re-reading the book I could see parallels between the main character and the change in direction my own life had taken.

19 October 1931

The little girl smiled and, with her doll held high in the air, twirled around the third floor turret room of the big old house. She was barely thirteen and still enjoyed playing with the doll her mother had given her when she was nine. Pretending made everything easier; she could go to magical places and be safe and loved and dance at beautiful parties and wear pretty clothes and meet interesting people from faraway places.

"What the hell have you done to my shirt?"

The little girl's peace was shattered by the angry voice and the heavy footsteps coming up the stairs. She clutched her doll and crouched behind the small rocking chair in the corner.

The man pushed the door to the little girl's room open so hard it slammed against the wall and knocked loose a piece of plaster from the wall.

"I'm sorry. I didn't mean to. I was ironing and one of the boys needed something and when I turned around ..."

"I don't want any damned excuses! Don't blame this on my boys!" He grabbed the chair and flung it across the room. She now had nothing separating them. He bent down and grabbed her by the arm and jerked her to her feet. She could smell the bourbon on his breath. "I should have thrown you out in the street a long time ago! You ruin one of my shirts again and I might as well kill you, you worthless little tramp!"

"Please, don't ..." But no sooner had the words passed her lips than the drunken man leveled a blow to the little girl's face so hard she felt as if her head might explode. Then another blow followed. This time blood poured from her nose and she fell to the floor.

With his fist raised, he bent down to deliver another blow, but was blinded by a flash of light. He looked up to see a figure, a person that appeared to be running out of the light and straight for him with fists raised.

"Leave her alone ..." the figure yelled.

1

Leslie drove east along Interstate 64, with the rolling hills of Kentucky's Bluegrass Region stretching in front of her. The sky was bright and clear and she could see the yellows and reds of fall color in the trees. Her father was career Army and the family moved frequently. But now with an interstate sign in the distance that read "Winchester 10 miles" Leslie finally felt like she was going home; and for a brief moment her thoughts trailed off to Mrs. Somers, her favorite teacher who had encouraged her to enter a technical field. "You're too smart to be a starving artist," Mrs. Somers had said, "It's a lot easier to be creative with a roof over your head and money in your pocket." Leslie had listened.

Leslie passed a truck and then saw the ramp for the first Winchester exit come plainly into view. A broad smile spread across her face. "Almost home!" She couldn't remember if the real estate agent had said to take the first Winchester exit to US 60 or the second exit. She hadn't written down the exit number and, not thinking she would need it, she had packed her GPS in her suitcase in the trunk. But Leslie didn't care; she could always stop and ask directions.

Winchester, Kentucky, where her parents grew up, wasn't exactly a small town, but it was by no means what she considered a city. No matter. What was to be her new hometown was big enough to have conveniences and still small enough that traffic wasn't a problem. Located a few miles east of Lexington, it would probably be just a few years before the only thing separating Winchester from its sprawling neighbor would be a line on a map. Nevertheless, she loved the town, especially the downtown area, what there was of it anyway. With the Victorian storefronts and the sidewalks which were elevated above the street level, she could only imagine what it must have been like to live there when people still rode in horse-drawn buggies and a streetcar made hourly trips from Main Street to Moundale Avenue.

Leslie couldn't wait any longer. She had to get off the interstate; she had to get home. She took the first exit. At the traffic light she knew to take a left on Lexington Avenue, but after that it would be guesswork.

As soon as she was off the ramp she realized her directions were from the second exit. But it didn't matter; at sixteen she had navigated most of Western Europe either alone or with a girlfriend from school. Winchester would be a snap.

Leslie's Mercedes popped up over the hill as she took the incline a little too fast. She hadn't noticed the rise in the road; she was paying more attention to where the dairy bar once was. As a child, she had eaten foot-long chili dogs there with her grandmother and grandfather.

"God, I can't believe it's gone. I really wanted one of those chili hot dogs." Leslie turned her steering wheel hard to the right and braked, just barely clearing the block wall at the edge of the parking lot. A horn blared as the car behind her zipped by. She looked in her rearview mirror. The car was already gone.

"With my luck I'll probably find out that guy is my neighbor." She sat in her idling car and considered her options. She had at least an hour to kill before closing on her house. She decided to go back to the convenience store at the intersection.

Taking a left out of the parking lot she noticed the trees in the cemetery were in their full fall glory. The bright oranges and yellows, with splashes of red mixed in, made the marble headstones seem to glow. "That would make a great painting," Leslie thought to herself.

Inside the convenience store Leslie looked at the hot dogs on a roller and at the prepared sandwiches in little plastic boxes. She selected a hot dog and added a liberal dose of mustard and ketchup, then pulled an Ale8 from one of the coolers lining the back wall. She had really wanted a chili dog from the old dairy bar, but this hot dog was better than nothing, she decided.

A young girl, with three red pimples on her face and dishwater blond hair pulled back into a ponytail, stood at the counter ready to ring up the items on the cash register.

"Will this be all, ma'am?"

"Yes, this is all, thank you."

"That'll be two ninety-six ma'am." Leslie handed the girl a twenty and waited for her change.

"Thank you ma'am. Have a good day."

Leslie smiled then took her food back to her car to eat. She took a long, slow drink from the Ale8. It was a soft drink invented in Winchester, and she hadn't had one since just before her grandmother died. It still tasted as good as she remembered. After a couple of bites of chili dog Leslie decided she wasn't as hungry as she had thought. She looked at her watch. Closing was at three; she still had forty-five minutes. Enough time to drive by the house for another quick look, and then find the lawyer's office. One more bite of hot dog. She was too excited to eat, but she knew she would be hungry later and didn't want her stomach to growl in the middle of signing the closing papers.

Leslie looked at her directions coming in from this side of town; they made little sense. In her two previous house-hunting trips to Winchester, Leslie had not driven around town other than to find a place to eat at night. Cathy, her real-estate agent, had driven, and she had always taken a different route through town.

"Let's see." Leslie had a habit of talking out loud to herself when she was alone and trying to solve a problem. "Burns, that sounds familiar. I think if I stay on Lexington Avenue it intersects with Maple." She put the key in the ignition and started her car, then pulled into traffic. "I think that friend of Grandma's lived on Wall Street. Shit, I just passed Maple." She took a right on Wall Street then back-tracked to Maple. "Should be right up here..."

Leslie's eyes widened and a broad smile slowly stretched across her face as she saw the house that was to be hers within the hour. She pulled up in front and parked at the curb. Cathy had placed a "sold" sign in front.

The house was built by retired Major Nathan Weatherly in 1887 and had remained in the family through two additional generations before passing through a series of owners. Looking up at it, she couldn't understand how anyone could let go of the house, but she was glad they had. Leslie got out of her car and stood on the sidewalk, gazing up at the structure. The house was in the Queen Anne style, with a large wrap-around porch and a round three-story high turret on its left side. Leslie had looked at other Victorians, but this one stood out because of its brick exterior and its position on top of a small hill giving it a command of the entire street. She was already planning to put a piano on the ground floor of the rounded room.

Leslie walked up on the porch and looked in the windows, each of which was bordered by colored stain-glass panels. Through the window she could tell the house had been cleaned and the hardwood floors waxed just as they had agreed in the contract. The house really wasn't dirty when she first toured it, just full of cobwebs and dust from disuse. She had hired contractors to inspect the house top-to-bottom. It had been well maintained over the years. Only the kitchen would require updating; the rest would just be a matter of the right paint, wallpaper and furnishings. The last owners had only lived there a couple of years before moving out. It had been vacant for nearly two more. Vacant until now that is; her furniture, what little she had, was coming tomorrow.

As Leslie turned she saw a woman standing at the foot of the porch steps and it startled her.

"I'm sorry. I didn't mean to scare you."

"That's okay; I didn't hear you walk up."

"Hi, I'm Barbara Rogers. I live in the white house over there." The woman turned and pointed to a large white colonial on the opposite side of the street. "Are you the new owner?"

"Yes, I am. I'm Leslie, Leslie Newkirk." Leslie shook the woman's hand. "Actually, I'm closing in about twenty minutes."

"Oh, how wonderful. I'll not keep you. I bet you and Mr. Newkirk are excited; it's a beautiful old house."

"Yes it is. I fell in love with it the first time I saw it. But there's not a Mr. Newkirk. It's just me; I'm buying the house."

"Oh really."

Leslie could see the surprise in the woman's face. She knew her new neighbor was, at this moment, trying to size her up to determine how a woman could afford a house like this without a man to provide the bulk of the income.

"Do you have anyone to help you move furniture?"

"No, actually I don't have a lot of furniture right now; I was in an apartment in Chicago."

"I see," said Barbara Rogers.

Leslie was amused. She knew that as soon as she drove off, Barbara Rogers would rush to the nearest house and, with pride, relay the "scoop" on the new neighbor.

"Well Leslie, if you need any help carrying boxes up the stairs or moving anything heavy just let me know, and I'll send my husband and my two sons over."

"Thank you. I appreciate that. I may need to take you up on your offer; there are a lot of stairs."

"I would imagine so, but you know I've never actually been inside the house; the last couple of owners weren't very sociable."

Leslie took this as a queue to invite Barbara Rogers over for a tour. She looked at her watch. "I hate to rush off but I need to get to the lawyer's office so I can close. Maybe you can come over tomorrow. I'll be moving in, but like I said, I don't have a lot of furniture."

"I would love to. Now I'll let you get going. Welcome to the neighborhood."

Leslie climbed in her car and looked in her rear-view mirror as she turned the ignition. She could see Barbara walking at a quick pace up the front sidewalk of another house a couple doors down from her own. Leslie made a bet with herself as to how long it would take before the stream of neighbors would start knocking on her door to get a look at the single woman from Chicago, who bought the big house on the hill.

Looking up at the house one more time before she pulled away, Leslie glimpsed something – some sort of shadow in a window on the third floor of the turret. She wasn't sure what it was, but for just an instant, it looked almost like the silhouette of a person. Rolling down her window she squinted to better focus her eyes. She saw nothing other than the reflection of tree branches in the windows as they swayed in the wind. Clouds were moving in front of the sun and the air felt as if it might rain.

2

Cathy, Leslie's real estate agent, was a bubbly, exuberant woman in her early fifties but could have passed for slightly younger if not for the graying hair. As tiring as Leslie found looking for a house, Cathy at least added a little fun to the process. Cathy was already inside when Leslie arrived at the lawyer's office and was all smiles, almost to the point of giggling. But then who wouldn't be; she was about to collect a commission check from the sale of a half-million-dollar home, which, in a different economy, would have sold for even more.

The couple selling the house was seated opposite her, along with their agent. "Ms. Newkirk, right on time." The lawyer stood and greeted her. "Here, have a seat. We have a big stack of papers, but it won't take long. Just a few signatures and you'll be ready to move in."

Cathy leaned over and squeezed Leslie's arm and let out a little laugh. Leslie felt her stomach tighten. In just a few minutes the house would officially be hers. She looked across the table at the couple and smiled. "It's a beautiful house. I feel very lucky that you put it on the market."

"Thank you. We hated to sell it but we had to move." The woman looked at her husband.

Leslie noticed that the woman seemed nervous and had shifted her body closer to her husband's. Cathy didn't know all the details behind the reason for the sale, and Leslie wanted to ask why they had moved, but she also felt she shouldn't pry into their personal business. She just assumed it was more house than they could afford.

"Shall we get started?" the lawyer asked. The entire process took fifteen minutes – she was a homeowner.

The couple shook her hand. "I hope you'll be happy in the house," the woman smiled. "All the neighbors are nice, and the street is usually very quiet."

"I'm sure I will." Leslie thought it odd that the woman would comment on the neighbors, especially when Barbara Rogers had remarked that the previous owners weren't sociable.

"Would you like me to go over there with you and make sure you get in okay?" Cathy asked.

"No, I have my keys." Smiling, Leslie held them up in front of her and shook them, making a jingling sound. "I have your cell phone number; I can give you call if I have any problems getting in. But if you could give me directions to the hotel from here, I would appreciate it. I want to get some rest. The movers are bringing my things tomorrow." Cathy walked her to her car. Leslie only half listened to the directions, her mind kept trailing off. She was too excited to concentrate and she knew she could always dig the GPS out of her bag.

Just before she got in her car, Cathy gave her a hug so tight Leslie felt like the air was being squeezed out of her lungs. As she drove off Leslie debated with herself; should she stop by the house? There was nothing she could do, except perhaps get some idea where to set her few pieces of furniture when the movers arrived, and maybe empty her backseat, which was loaded down with boxes full of tubes of paint, brushes, and drawing pads. She looked up at the darkening sky, which was threatening to open up with a torrent of rain at any minute. "I hope this doesn't last long; that's all I'll need tomorrow – moving in a rainstorm." She looked at the house keys in her hand and smiled. "It's all mine." Leslie got in her car and drove off in the direction of her new home.

She saw the first drops of rain hit her windshield just as she pulled under the porte-cochere which once served as access to the front entrance for people arriving in carriages. It was one of her favorite features on the exterior of the house. The first time she had driven under the red brick arch with Cathy, she imagined what it must have been like to have lived there one hundred years ago and watch Winchester's fashionably-dressed elite arrive for dinner parties and balls.

Leslie walked up the steps and across the porch. She put the key in the door, and then, with a firm hand, slowly turned the lock. She felt the tumblers click, then turned the brass knob and opened the door. Thunder rumbled overhead just as she stepped across the threshold of her home. "Looks like the storm is going to be a doosey." The floorboards creaked under her feet as Leslie took a few steps into the foyer. "Hello, is anyone here? If there's anyone here come on down and congratulate me, I just bought this house." She was used to living alone, but being in the large empty house by herself felt a little unnerving. "Just checking," she called out. Come on, Leslie, you can't get jittery in your own house just because it's big…and empty…and dark…and no one has lived in it for two years.

What little light was entering the foyer quickly faded as storm clouds covered the sky, causing Leslie's eyes to strain in the semi-darkness. "Light switch – I know there's one here somewhere." Finding it, she pushed the on button and the foyer instantly filled with light from the leaded crystal chandelier overhead. She looked down and saw her reflection in the freshly waxed floors; it was like looking into a mirror that reflected only in sepia tones. She wondered if the movers had pads to protect the floor. Leslie walked into the room to her left, the room that contained the first floor of the round turret. She tried to visualize what it would look like with furniture and area rugs, and the baby grand piano she planned to buy. She knew the furniture from her apartment wouldn't work in here or anywhere else in the house; everything she had was too contemporary.

Much like her furniture debacle, Leslie was full of contradictions, and she knew it. Her mother had always said it was because they had moved so many times when she was a child, and never had a chance to settle down. But Leslie's standard reply was simply that she is flexible. She had no romantic notions of living in some bygone era. She was far too logical for that; she knew life wasn't easy back then unless you were a rich white man, and hey, you could have died from almost any aliment. However, the other side of her personality was in love with the picturesque quality of the early part of the twentieth century. She disliked antiques, but she loved old homes. She disliked most modern art, but that was mostly due to the egos of the artists. She had once commented to a particularly arrogant and self-absorbed painter who was showing his work at a prominent gallery in Chicago, that her six-year-old niece could do as well. But, Leslie scoffed at the mass-produced landscapes as well; she could not comprehend that people bought them just because they matched the living room sofa. She was a composite of opposites, but she didn't care. Her motto: "Keep them guessing; it makes life interesting."

Leslie ran her fingertips across the wood mantel above the fireplace; the swirls and deep grooves of the carvings were smooth and had an almost fluid quality. The intricacies of the craftsman's work made the dark wood seem delicate. She marveled at its complexity and beauty. The green marble beneath the mantel was cold and hard to the touch, but when it was viewed in combination with the wood it had a warmth, like a forest in summer.

Instantly, Leslie's attention shifted from the fireplace and into the present when she heard a sound come from upstairs. It was a hollow thud, like something small and heavy had been dropped. Her body tensed, and she turned to face the entryway and took two steps back-

18

ward all in the same movement. Her heart pounded in her chest. She heard another clap of thunder overhead and saw lighting flash. She took a deep breath and tried to stand perfectly still.

Pepper spray. She thought she had some in the car. Leslie debated whether to check out the house, get the spray and check out the house, or just leave. Considering how long the house had been vacant, she knew it was possible someone had gained access to it. Perhaps neighborhood kids, or some homeless person off the street? She doubted Winchester had a large contingent of homeless.

She took another deep breath, and with slow deliberate steps, she walked across the floor of the drawing room until she was standing in the middle of the foyer. She heard no more noises coming from upstairs, only the wind and rain beating relentlessly against the house. Remembering there was a door in the kitchen that opened onto the back porch, Leslie decided to make sure it was securely locked before proceeding up the stairs to inspect the upper floors. She was somewhat relieved when she found the door tightly bolted shut and the screen door on the back porch locked from the inside with a small hook. The door leading down to the cellar was also secure, but with both an interior and exterior access, this would be the most likely way for an intruder to enter the house. She made a mental note to herself to have the contractor she hired install heavier exterior doors with stronger locks.

Leslie walked back into the foyer and listened carefully; still no sound from upstairs. Turning, she placed her left hand on the banister and began her slow climb up the stairs. She tried to make each step as delicate and light as possible, but some of the boards creaked and popped under her feet. When she reached the landing she paused; there was still time to change her mind, go get the pepper spray or get Barbara Rogers' husband and sons to explore the house with her. Again the thunder rumbled, this time louder than before. The storm had moved and was now directly overhead. Leslie listened carefully. She turned her head, first to the left, then the right. Had she heard something else, another sound other than the thunder? It sounded almost like a cry or a sob. It had to be the wind whistling around the corners of the house. The knuckles of her left hand were white from gripping the banister. Leslie continued her climb up the second flight.

When she reached the top of the stairs, a long hallway stretched to her left and right. There were five bedrooms on the second floor and two bathrooms. She was breathing harder. God, I'm going to hyperventilate if I don't calm down, she thought. Check out these rooms first, they're closer – that was her plan. She felt inside the pockets of her leather jacket. She had her cell phone, a pack of gum and a tissue, nothing more. Leslie pushed the door to the room fully open until its knob touched the wall, nothing in here. She then worked her way down the hall, opening the doors to each room. Lastly, having inspected the master bedroom and bath, she was almost confident that she was alone in the house. Only the small third floor, with one additional room and the turret room where she planned to set up her art studio, remained to be searched.

"Here goes." Leslie gripped the railing, but not as tightly as before; she had relaxed somewhat and no longer felt her heart pounding in her ears. Still using the same careful, light steps she ascended the stairs. The third floor hallway was wide, not as wide as the second floor, but still wider than most contemporary homes. In addition to the two rooms there was a door allowing access to the attic. Cathy had said that the previous owners hadn't known about the attic when they bought the house, but found it later by accident. Apparently, it had been boarded over decades earlier.

The attic door bolted on the hallway side, which was a relief; no one could have shut themselves in the attic and still locked the door from the hall. She couldn't remember if there were lights in the attic and didn't want to go up there without a flashlight. She then slowly opened the door to the first room – nothing. All that remained was the turret room where the door was already open. Even with the storm, the tall windows that covered the exterior walls allowed light to fill the room. When Leslie first toured the house, it had been a bright sunny day. Sunlight had poured into the room, making it perfect for painting.

Again nothing, the room was empty except for two statuettes, one sitting on a window sill, the other lying in the floor beneath the window. She bent down and picked up the one on the floor; it was about twelve inches tall and heavy, possibly bronze. Thunder rumbled overhead and lightening cracked outside. She could tell it had struck somewhere close by. She saw the figurine on the sill vibrate slightly. Leslie exhaled in a sigh of relief. A half-smile formed on her lips. She had solved the mystery of the noise in her house. Suddenly, she felt foolish. The previous owners had left behind these two small statues of women dancing. One had obviously been sitting too close to the edge, and the thunder rattled it off its perch.

She stood up and turned the statues over in her hand, examining them in the light from the window. They were definitely in the art deco style and probably vintage. "I'll just take these babies downstairs so they don't rattle off the sill again." She looked out the window; the rain was letting up and the wind had died down. The adrenaline she burned from her search of the house had left her feeling tired, and she suddenly wasn't in the mood to carry boxes of art supplies up two flights of stairs. "I'll just set them inside the front door and then carry them up here tomorrow. Leslie grinned to herself, "Or better yet, let the movers do it. That's what they're getting paid for."

Leslie took the statuettes downstairs and set them on the mantel in the drawing room. "There you go ladies; you look like you were made for this room. I'm glad they left you behind." She then smiled, and headed for her car and the boxes in the back seat.

3

It was after six by the time Leslie finished unloading her car and surveying her new home to determine where the movers should place her few pieces of furniture. The long drive was starting to catch up with her and her legs ached. She could tell it had been over a week since she had been to the gym. She hated missing her workouts, but with packing and moving and saying goodbye to friends there just hadn't been enough time. Mental list: What else do I need to do? Call Mom and Dad. She knew they would be worried by now, wondering if she had arrived safely. Her mother had offered to fly to Chicago and then drive with her to Kentucky, but Leslie had said no. She had a good relationship with her mother, but seven hours alone in a car with her was too much.

Leslie parked her car under a light in the hotel parking lot, retrieved her two small bags from the trunk and entered the lobby.

"Hello. Can I help you?"

"Yes, I have reservations. My name is Leslie Newkirk." She watched as the younger woman looked through her list of arrivals.

"Here you are. Are you staying for only one night?"

"Can I hold the room for a second night? Movers are supposed to bring my things tomorrow, but just in case they don't show up in time I want to have some place to sleep."

"Sure, that won't be a problem. If you could just let us know by noon tomorrow. Are you moving to Winchester from out of town?"

"Yes, from Chicago."

"Really? Chicago sounds exciting. What brings you to Winchester?"

"My grandparents are from Winchester, and I used to visit a lot when I was growing up."

"Well, welcome home," the young woman smiled.

Leslie smiled; she was only half listening as she signed the registration form. She was amused by the girl as she continued to chatter about how exciting it must be to live in a big city like Chicago. "Thanks." Leslie took her key card, and then walked down the hallway to the elevator. The hotel was just off the interstate and older than others near by. Signs of the wear-and-tear of years of guest traffic were obvious in places, but it had a small restaurant, which was the primary reason for her selection. She knew she would be too tired tonight to drive around town looking for a place to eat, and she remembered there weren't a lot of options in town. A shower, room service and then channel surfing until bed time; that was the plan for the evening.

The room was typical of any hotel. It had a king-size bed with a head-board that was bolted to the wall, dresser, TV, desk and chair, and an armchair shoved into the corner. Nothing special, just the same flower print bedspread and mass-produced art on the walls. Leslie tossed her bags on the end of the bed, then rubbed her arms. The room was cold; the heat probably hadn't been on all day. She closed the drapes, and then read the labels over the knobs and buttons on the heating unit. "Let's see, low heat should do it. God, I have got to stop talking to myself," she said, rubbing her arms again to warm them. "Maybe I should get a cat."

Leslie set her priorities: warmth, food and comfortable clothes, then a call to the parents, in that order. There was a green three-ring binder lying on the desk with Guest Services embossed in gold across the front cover. Leslie flipped to the room service selection. Their dinner menu was limited to only four entrees: spaghetti, fried chicken, fried catfish, and grilled sirloin steak. She decided to risk the fried chicken; unless it was over-cooked it was hard to screw up chicken. She picked up the receiver of the phone and pressed three to place her order. "Yes, that's right. I'd like a pitcher of ice tea and plenty of artificial sweetener, the pink stuff please; and a slice of apple pie for dessert. No, no ice cream. Thank you." Leslie hung up and checked her wallet to make sure she had enough change for a tip. Placing three ones on the dresser behind her, she unzipped her bag and pulled out her favorite sweat pants and shirt. The pants were a faded navy blue with straight legs and a hem at the bottom that was starting to unravel. They were soft from years of wear, and as she slid her hands inside the pockets to straighten them she saw a tiny hole near the seam of the left leg. "I'll have to fix that before it gets any bigger," she said to herself. Leslie knew she should probably throw them out; she would have thrown out other clothing long before now. But they felt so good, and she liked the way they fit. Leslie finished changing into her sweatshirt and socks, then stretched out on the king size bed to call her parents while she waited for her dinner to arrive.

"Mom."

"Leslie, is that you?"

"Yes it's me. You can say congratulations now; I closed on the house."

"Oh that's wonderful. We were starting to get worried; we hadn't heard from you and you had so far to drive."

"I'm fine. I got a really early start this morning so it wasn't bad at all. The time went by fast."

"Let me get your father on the other phone."

Leslie could hear her mother calling for her father and sounds of papers shuffling on the other end of the line. "Dad, are you there?"

"Hi honey. So your mother said you own the house now."

"Yep, that's right. It's all mine! You and mom need to come up and visit after I get the bedrooms set up. I'm going to have to buy more furniture."

"Now don't go broke trying to do everything at once," her mother cautioned.

Leslie laughed. "Mother, don't worry. I'm in no danger of going broke, and I have no intention of buying everything at once. I have to find the right furnitue to fit the house."

"Joyce, if our girl says she's loaded, then she's loaded. Don't worry about her." Leslie smiled. She could hear the pride in her father's voice.

"Dad, you're exagerating a little, again." Both her parents knew she was now in a position where she didn't need to worry about finances, but she had purposefully not told them any details of her financial situation, mainly because she didn't want the other relatives to know. Every family has a deadbeat or two, and she knew if word got around she had some money put away, the family deadbeat would show up on her doorstep.

Leslie's train of thought was broken by her mother's voice. "Did the closing go alright? Did they wax the floors like you wanted them?"

"Oh yeah, they did everything. The house is beautiful, but it's going to look pretty empty with just the furniture from my apartment."

"Are you going to have to buy all new things?"

"For the most part. The table and chairs I have can go in the kitchen. They'll be fine in there. Pictures, vases — those things can stay, but everything else will have to be replaced."

Her father interrupted, "When are you going to start furniture shopping?"

"Probably right away. I at least want to get the downstairs furnished and the master suite and one other bedroom. I might wait a while on the other three."

"My lord!" Her mother replied. "I know you told us how big this house was, but it just boggles my mind when I stop and think about it"

"Our girl has herself a mansion," her father interjected.

"Mom, Dad, someone's at the door. I think its room service with my dinner."

"Now don't open the door if you can't see who it is."

"I know mother. I've got to go; I'll call you tomorrow morning when I go back over to the house."

"We love you and we're so proud of you."

"Thanks, I love you guys, too. Good night."

Leslie's dinner was warm when it arrived; she took this to be a good sign. She tipped the waiter and bolted the door after he left. The smell of the fried chicken filled her nostrils and made her stomach rumble. She removed the plate, silverware and iced tea from the large round tray and arranged them on the desk. "Remote control – where'd I put it?" Her eyes scanned the room. She saw it sticking from underneath the silk shirt that she had tossed on the bed when she changed. "There you are." Leslie then positioned the armchair beside the desk so she could prop up her feet and watch TV while she ate. Removing the aluminum foil from the baked potato Leslie split it open with her knife, then added a generous portion of butter and sour cream. Steam rose from the potato as she mixed the inside with her fork. The chicken was a little dry but she didn't care, it still had a good flavor. Leslie leaned back in the chair and pointed the remote at the TV and surfed channels until she found the local news. She wanted a weather report, so she would know what to expect tomorrow. They were predicting storms throughout the night but that the rain would clear in the early morning and then sunshine for the remainder of the day, Friday.

Leslie sighed and closed her eyes. She thought about the work that lay ahead of her. I'm never moving again, she told herself. She had done more than her share growing up. Her mother had recommended she call her cousins to help, but Leslie felt that she would be imposing. Her parents hadn't lived in Winchester since they both graduated high school and her father joined the army. And as for Leslie, she had only spent time with the other relatives when she had visited her grandparents during the summers. That had been over fifteen years ago. She felt it would be better to borrow the neighbor's sons if they offered again, rather than call up a relative and say, "Hi, I'm your cousin you haven't seen in god knows how many years; remember the time we sneaked off to the railroad tracks and you got caught and I didn't? Well, I just moved here and I need you to help me carry boxes to the second and third floors of my house." And then there was the issue of the family bum.

Leslie finished her dinner and set the tray outside the door for housekeeping to pick up. Pulling the blankets over her legs, she then settled into bed. There was a good movie on one of the cable channels, a romantic comedy, and she was tempted to watch it. But, tomorrow would be a busy day and she knew she needed a good night's sleep.

4

Leslie was up and in the shower before her wake-up call. She felt as if it was Christmas Day and she was counting down the minutes until she could open her presents. Only her present was a Victorian mansion. Leslie dressed in old jeans, sneakers and a University of Kentucky sweatshirt she had purchased during one of her house-hunting trips. "Just like a native," she said out loud as she smiled and looked at herself in the mirror.

After drying her hair, Leslie went downstairs to the restaurant for breakfast. She had two biscuits covered in gravy; hash browns and sliced fresh fruit. She tried the scrambled eggs, but they were overcooked.

There were only two other people in the restaurant. Probably all the business travelers had already eaten and left, giving the waitress time to socialize with the patrons, which Leslie tolerated. She was in such a good mood; not even a chatty waitress could spoil it. As she refilled Leslie's glass, the waitress asked why she was in Winchester, and Leslie again had to explain that parents grew up here and now she had bought a house and decided to settle here. The waitress raised an eyebrow upon hearing the name of the street. "Oh, that's where the rich people in town live. You must be rich."

Leslie was a little surprised; she was a caught off guard by the directness. "I wouldn't exactly say rich," Leslie replied, "but I had some money put away so I just decided to put it into a house. If you take care of them they go up in value – well, most of the time. I guess these days you are ahead if they just hold their value."

"Well honey, you ain't going to have to worry about that where you're going to be living."

Leslie smiled as the waitress walked away, coffeepot in one hand, water pitcher in the other. Leslie paid her check then left a five-dollar bill on the table. The waitress was older than she, and her brown eyes had the look of someone who had worked hard all her life. She looked at the five lying on the table and added another five to it, feeling grateful for her own good fortune and sympathy for the waitress who obviously worked hard for less.

Leslie went back to her room and threw her sweats and clothes from the day before in her bag, then double-checked the bathroom to make certain she had packed all her toiletries. She made another turn around the room, looking for the odd sock, bra, anything she might have dropped on the floor. Confident she had packed all her belongings, she flipped off the lights and left her room.

Now that she somewhat had her bearings, her home was only a short drive from the hotel; of course, everything in Winchester was only a short drive from everything else. Leslie pulled into the driveway and looked up at the third floor window, where the day before she thought she had glimpsed the silhouette of a person. She saw nothing other than the reflection of the sycamore limbs on the glass. The left corner of her lip curled upward in a half smile and Leslie made a short quick snorting sound chastising herself for being spooked.

5

Pulling through the porte cochere and into the back yard, Leslie parked her car in front of the garage door. The garage was a short two-story building at the rear of the lot. It was original to the house, with the same brick construction, and it could easily accommodate two cars. The building had originally functioned as a carriage house for the owner's tack and two horses. On the interior, one half of the structure had a second floor with an iron spiral staircase, allowing access to what probably had been a hay loft. On the opposite side of the structure, the two stable stalls were surprisingly still intact. Leslie was also shocked to see old tack still hanging in the rafters. She had asked Cathy if she knew why, after passing through several hands outside the original family, things like the tack would still be here. Cathy had no idea, and only said that, from what she had been told, after the last of the direct descendants died off, the estate settled with some distant relatives, and they just left everything as it was. Cathy was of the opinion that most people didn't realize the expense of maintaining a house of this size and age, and they usually never stayed long enough to sort through anything that had been left behind.

Leslie tried to enter the house through the rear, but remembered she had left the screen door on the back porch latched. As she walked to the front of the house a large muscular man climbing from the cab of a moving truck greeted her. "Hey there. Are you..." He paused and looked down at the paper on his clipboard. "Mrs. Leslie Newkirk?"

"Ms. Leslie Newkirk, and yes, that's me. You guys are right on time; I didn't expect you this early."

"You're our first stop and there ain't much in your load." The muscular man looked up at the house. "This is a mighty big house you got here. It's pretty. I like these big old ones."

"Thank you. I like it too."

"Well, if you'll walk us through it real quick and show us which rooms are which, then we'll get started unloading. Now remember, we don't put furniture and things back together, but we will put it in the

29

right rooms for you."

"Yes, I know. That's fine," Leslie nodded her head, acknowledging that she remembered the terms of the moving contract. Leslie pointed out the parlor, dining room, den, kitchen, and then started up the stairs to show the three men the master suite and first guest bedroom.

"You sure got a lot of stairs in here, lady," one of the men commented as they climbed the second flight.

Leslie turned and smiled, "It could be worse you know."

"How's that?"

"I could have more furniture."

The man chuckled and adjusted the baseball cap on his head. "Well, you're right there."

Leslie completed the tour of the house, then led the men back downstairs and positioned herself near the front door out of their way. The men worked fast; time was money for them. When they weren't sure where a box belonged, they stopped and asked, and Leslie obliged by identifying the location and pointing in the correct direction. She was surprised that her few furnishings equated to dozens of boxes. It hadn't seemed like so much when it was going into the truck. Still, the large house would look bare without enough furniture to fill even one downstairs room.

The men were almost finished when Barbara Rogers suddenly appeared on the front porch as if she had just beamed down from a hovering spacecraft. Leslie hesitated, "Barbara, hi. It is Barbara, right?"

"Yes, that's right; I'm in the white house across the street."

"You'll have to excuse me, I'm not always so good at remembering new names, but I do get the faces right."

"Oh, that's quite alright." Barbara looked out at the sky. "It turned out to be a nice day for moving. When that storm blew through last night I was afraid it would rain on you all day today."

"Yes, I was pretty lucky."

Barbara turned back to Leslie and smiled. "I know you're busy right now and I'll not stay here and get in your way, but I just wanted to offer again to send my husband and boys over here to help move furniture, lift heavy boxes, just whatever you need help with."

"Thank you. I really appreciate the offer. Actually, I might need a hand with something." Barbara's face beamed at Leslie's reply. "I might need to borrow a couple hand tools so I can put my bed together. I have a little toolbox, but I'm not sure which box it's in. And I was hoping to spend the night here tonight."

"Say no more. I'll send Jim and the boys over when they get home, and they'll get everything all set up for you."

Leslie hated to ask for help; she wanted to do as much as possible of the work around the house herself. She liked the feeling of being completely self-sufficient. "I don't want to impose; I can probably manage if I can just borrow a couple tools."

Barbara Rogers held up her hand. "No, I insist and I want you to come to dinner tonight. I know you won't be able to get your kitchen set up by the time you're hungry, so please join us."

"I wouldn't want you to go to any trouble."

"Oh, no trouble at all. I'll just throw something in the crock pot."

Leslie had already planned to order pizza and sit in the floor of her living room with a roaring fire in the fireplace; however, she remembered she didn't have fireplace utensils, and she didn't have the other primary ingredient – firewood. Reconsidering, she accepted Barbara's offer. "If you're sure I won't be imposing."

"Of course not, we'd love to have you. And my husband Jim will be home in about an hour; he was leaving work early today. I'll send him over with his tool box to help you get your bed put together so you can spend the night here."

"Thank you. I was holding the hotel room just in case, but I'm a little excited about staying here tonight."

"I understand completely. Jim and I were so excited when we bought our house; it was a real step up for us from where we were living." Barbara squeezed Leslie's arm.

"The movers should be finished soon; when you and your husband come back I'll give you both a tour. Of course, there is not much to look at yet. I have very little furniture."

Barbara's eyes widened. "Oh, I'd love that. I think I told you I've never seen the inside of the house." Barbara leaned closer to Leslie and lowered her voice as if there were someone listening who might take issue with her comments. "I think I may have mentioned it before but the last owners weren't friendly at all. Now their son was a friend of my boys, but he always acted a little nervous. I think he may have needed medicine to calm him down, you know A.D.D. or something like that. And the girl, I don't know much about her; she was in college, so she wasn't around much."

Leslie pushed her hands into the front pockets of her jeans and knitted her eyebrows. "I see. What do you suppose was the problem?" By asking the question, Leslie knew she had just scored points with the new

31

neighbor.

"I'm not sure. At first they seemed friendly enough, but they just wouldn't associate with anyone else on the street. Once or twice we saw vans full of electronic equipment and people coming and going at all hours of the night. Mr. Connor lives next door to us. He got my oldest son a part-time job at Channel 27, and he said it looked like sound and video equipment."

"Did they work in advertising?"

"I think he is a doctor and she works at the University of Kentucky in one of the administrative offices, but I'm not sure."

"You said your two boys were friends with the previous owners' son? Did they say anything about them?" Leslie noticed Barbara hesitate for a moment.

"Actually, it was my oldest son who was friends with their son, but no, not really. I think he didn't want to talk about his friend's parents in front of us." With this Barbara raised her eyebrows and straightened her back as if she had just imparted a cache of information.

Their conversation was interrupted by one of the movers. "Ma'am, where do you want this box; its labeled sculpting supplies?"

"That goes in the round turret room on the third floor." The man moaned and headed up the stairs.

Leslie was relieved when Barbara said she was in the way, excused herself and trotted off across the street to her own house. Watching as the movers unloaded the last of her boxes, Leslie began to formulate a plan of attack. First, she would tackle the kitchen. It was big and roomy with lots of cabinet space and had a large butler's pantry. Her dishes and cookware would easily fit in the cupboards with plenty of space left over.

Her grandmother's china would have looked good displayed in this house. She didn't know what had happened to it after her grandmother died; just that a distant cousin had carried it off. And that was exactly how she remembered it – carried off. There was no will, and even though her grandmother had over the last two years of her life left verbal instructions as to how she wanted her affairs handled, they were never followed. Of course, it had been years since her grandparents died, but Leslie became angry each time she allowed herself to think about how a few of her grandmother's relatives managed to get what few valuable items and family heirlooms her grandmother had, leaving nothing for the rest of the family.

Her mother and father had grown up here, but chose to move away. Her brother was younger and had spent fewer summers in Winchester with the rest of the family. He didn't notice the detachment that she felt. Leslie, on the other hand, always knew she belonged here, but didn't quite know how to fit in with the others. It was like being a part of something that was just out of reach. Still, Winchester was more of a home than any other place she had lived and she knew she could make it work in time.

6

Leslie put one hand on the cabinet and pulled herself up off the kitchen floor. She looked around the room, admiring her work. Cardboard boxes and packing materials were scattered across the floor and her table was leaning against the far wall with the legs lying in a neat stack beside it. "One down – and several to go." She had finished unpacking her dishes, pots, pans and glassware. All that was left was to pick up the debris and reattach the legs to the table. She looked at her watch; it was almost six. Barbara Rogers had invited her to dinner at six. Likewise, Barbara had promised to send her husband and a tool box to help put the bed together, but then they hadn't shown up. Leslie wondered if the invitation to dinner still stood.

As Leslie began stuffing bubble wrap and newspaper into a large empty box, she heard her doorbell chime for the first time. It wasn't the sharp electronic sound like the doorbell in her apartment in Chicago. This sound was a deep throaty chime that resonated through the big house. Leslie was startled for just an instant; the sudden sound had caught her off guard. Then she smiled and let out a small laugh. "My first door chime." She put down the box, and with a hop that betrayed the levity of her mood, she jumped over a small pile of bubble wrap that was blocking the kitchen door, then hurriedly walked down the foyer to the front door.

When she swung open the door, Barbara and a tall stocky man were standing on her porch smiling. "Hi, Barbara."

"Hello, I'm back again and this is my husband Jim." Jim switched the small red metal toolbox he was carrying from his right hand to his left, then extended his arm to shake Leslie's hand. "I'm sorry we didn't get back over here sooner. Jim had planned to leave the office early today, but was held up."

"We're here to put your bed together and anything else you might need reassembled." Jim smiled again.

"Oh, thank you. I still haven't found the box that has my hand tools. Not like I have a lot of them, but I do have the basics. I guess now that I own a house that is one of the things I'll have to start acquiring."

"Well, whatever you need, feel free to come over and borrow it," Jim offered.

"Thank you." Leslie stepped to the side of the door. "I'm being rude; please, come on in. I'll warn you it's a mess right now, but I'd be happy to show you around if you would like to see the house."

"I'd love to see it. I think I told you the other owners never invited anyone else from our neighborhood over. Not even for coffee."

Leslie smiled, "Yes, I remember you said that." Leslie led them through the downstairs rooms pausing long enough in the kitchen for Jim to reattach the legs to the table. She could tell Barbara was scrutinizing everything she saw. Leslie felt compelled to explain to Barbara and Jim that she had lived in an apartment in Chicago and would soon need to begin shopping for furniture. Barbara offered to show her around Winchester and Lexington and assist in the shopping. As politely as possible, Leslie explained that she would most likely work with a decorator.

After assembling Leslie's bed, the three climbed the last flight of stairs to the third floor and the round turret room. In there they saw easels, a large drawing table, and several boxes of various sizes labeled as art supplies. Barbara put her hand to her cheek. "Oh my, you're an artist? "

"Well, I don't know that I would call myself an artist just yet, but I draw, paint and have started experimenting with sculpting."

"Do you have any of your work here?"

"I have a few things, but they're still boxed up."

"Well, you are just going to have to give me a show of your work."

"Barbara quit, you're embarrassing the woman."

"Nonsense, Jim. I'm just excited to meet a real artist from Chicago. And imagine, living right here across the street from us."

Any time she received this type of attention, Leslie always felt a mixture of pride and embarrassment. She looked up, seeing Jim Rogers scratch the back of his head and smile. She interrupted the gesture as some sort of apology for his wife. As they made their way back down the stairs to the foyer, Leslie silently chastised herself for allowing them to come over. She could have slept on the mattress on the floor or made an earnest search for the tools. Now she was certain that throughout dinner she would have to listen to Barbara's prattle about having an artist in their midst.

At the foot of the stairs Barbara asked, "You're still coming to dinner aren't you?"

Having no good excuse prepared, Leslie responded with a hesitant, "Sure."

"Good, I hope you like roast."

"Yes, just let me just lock up here." Leslie turned on the chandelier in the foyer, so she wouldn't return home to a dark house, then followed Jim and Barbara across the street.

The Rogers' home looked exactly as Leslie had envisioned. The furniture was traditional, with dark cherry-stained wood and satin upholstery work in the formal living room. The artwork was what she often called suburban chic – everything matched the sofa or whatever was the dominant piece of furniture in the room. In the dining room, over the buffet, was a landscape in a gilded frame with a light over top illuminating the print. They probably had paid a high price for the mass produced piece, she thought to herself.

Barbara had set the table in the dining room for dinner. "Now don't think I'm trying to impress you or anything, we just don't eat in here often with all the rushing around with the boys' activities. I thought it would be nice to sit in here for a change. And this way we won't be crowded around the breakfast table."

Leslie smiled, "My jeans are a little dusty from the unpacking – I don't want to get your chairs dirty."

"Oh, don't be silly. Here, sit down beside Mark."

Leslie nodded and smiled at the tall teenager seated in the chair beside her. Mark was the older of the two boys and at seventeen was already nearly six feet tall and comfortable in his long frame. His movements weren't at all awkward, as was the case with many boys his age. Thomas sat opposite Leslie; he was Mark's junior by almost three years. His frame was smaller and he seemed just a little clumsy, like a puppy that hadn't yet grown into its feet. Both boys were well mannered and polite throughout dinner. They seemed to know when to join in the adult conservation and when to keep quiet. Leslie wondered if they were always this well behaved, or if it was only for guests.

Barbara's roast was simple, just as she had promised; it was just something she had thrown together in her crock-pot. But when Leslie bit into the meat, the flavor was anything but simple. The roast had absorbed the flavors of the vegetables and spices it had been cooked with, creating a sensation on Leslie's palate that literally made her mouth begin to water. It was not only tasty, but the delicate texture and slow cooking had given the beef an amazing flavor. She couldn't remember when she had eaten anything that had tasted as good. In its simplicity it rivaled any of the food she had eaten in some of the better restaurants in Chicago.

"You will have to teach me how to cook this roast and get this flavor. It's wonderful." Barbara, with mock humility, insisted that it was just an exceptionally good cut.

After everyone finished, Barbara left the table to retrieve the dessert. Just another little thing she whipped up. Leslie could tell it was a favorite with this family; both sons and Barbara's husband were seated in a posture that betrayed their excited anticipation. When her hostess reentered the dining room, she was carrying a round pedestal, clear glass bowl with straight sides, which contained a layered dessert that Barbara announced was a trifle. To help his mother, Mark retrieved the dessert dishes and forks from the kitchen and placed them in front of his mother, so she could serve her masterpiece.

Neither boy made a sound while they ate the dessert. Thomas finished first and asked for seconds. Barbara commented on their growth rates while she spooned another large portion onto her youngest son's dish. While they ate, the conversation slowly turned back to Leslie's new home and her plans for it. "That is a lot of house for just one person to maintain," Jim Rogers commented.

"The ghost can help you." Thomas snickered.

"Shut up, stooge!" Mark snapped.

Jim frowned and deepening his voice corrected his sons. "Boys, that's enough!"

"Yes sir," they said in unison.

"What's this about a ghost? Is my house supposed to be haunted?" Leslie's interest was sparked. Considering the age of her house, she would have been surprised had it not come with at least one or two ghost stories.

"Oh, don't pay attention to that. It's just something the last owners made up to get attention for themselves. I think they just got into debt over their heads and couldn't make the payments. This ghost story stuff was a way to save face."

Mark interrupted his mother, "No, Mom it is haunted, Chris saw it. It's a girl and she..."

Barbara interrupted before her son could continue, "Mark, don't be silly; I know you and Chris were friends, but I'm sure he just thought it was fun to tell ghost stories about his house." Barbara turned to Leslie and smiled. "Chris is the Andersons' son, and he and Mark were good friends."

"Chris doesn't lie," Mark said as he crossed his arms across his chest and slid down in his chair, a sulking expression clearly readable on his face.

Leslie looked around the table. Thomas was slouched down in his chair giggling and Jim and Barbara were visibly annoyed. Mark, on the other hand, was obviously upset, and Leslie could tell he believed what his friend had told him. She wasn't frightened by the discussion of a ghost in her house; every old house has some sort of story to go along with it. She did, however, find the Rogers' reaction interesting. Perhaps the Andersons had been problem neighbors. She decided to change the subject and try to catch Mark alone some day to quiz him.

After dessert, Mark and Thomas excused themselves from the table. Both boys went to the basement to watch television, while Leslie and her hosts had coffee in the living room. It was almost nine when Leslie realized the time. "Oh, wow. I didn't know it was so late. I don't want to wear out my welcome the first time over."

"Of course you didn't. We've enjoyed it."

"We most certainly have," agreed Jim.

The three exchanged pleasantries and made commitments to join Leslie for dinner in her home as soon as she acquired enough furniture to seat everyone.

7

Leslie walked across the street and up the steps of her porch, and then slid the key into the lock. She smiled when she heard it click. She turned and waved to Jim and Barbara. They had waited in their doorway to make sure she got inside with no problems. Locking the door behind her, Leslie stood in the foyer with her hands on her hips and looked first into the parlor on her left and the dining room to her right. She sighed, "I didn't think I had this much stuff in that apartment." Walking into the kitchen she checked the back door to reassure herself it was still locked. Then she confirmed all the windows were latched and the cellar door was secure before going upstairs.

After turning on the lights in the long hallway, she then turned out the chandelier in the foyer from a switch at the top of the stairs. Leslie was tired and her back ached from unpacking boxes of kitchen items. At least she could sleep in her own bed. Finding the box containing her linens, she quickly made her bed and placed the toiletries from her travel bag on the vanity. One of the previous owners had updated all the fixtures in the bathrooms, which included a contemporary version of a claw-foot tub. While she brushed her teeth she began making a mental list of what needed to be done the next day. Unpack boxes, grocery store, food, cleaning supplies, unpack more boxes. "Good thing I don't have to go to work every day, otherwise it would take me a year to get this finished on my own." She thought about writing everything down but was too tired to bother. The only thing she wanted right now was a good night's sleep. Leslie fished through her overnight bag and pulled out a night-light. She thought, until she adjusted to her new surroundings, a night-light would be a good idea. Plugging in the little light, she switched off the overhead and climbed into bed. She was asleep in minutes.

8

It was after eight and bright sunlight shone through the large windows in the master bedroom. Leslie, though still groggy, felt herself slowly becoming aware of her surroundings. For just a second she wondered why the sun was so bright in her apartment. Then she remembered she wasn't in her apartment anymore. She was in her house – her house in Winchester. She rolled over on her side and looked out the window. There was a gentle breeze blowing through the brown sycamore leaves as a squirrel raced across its branches. It was Saturday, and she didn't want to get out of bed just yet. But she had no television to watch, the cable installers wouldn't arrive until Monday, and she had no morning paper to read. She felt her stomach growl, and remembered that not only didn't she have a paper and TV, she also had nothing for breakfast. "Guess I'm getting up whether I like it or not."

As Leslie climbed out of bed, she rubbed her arms to warm them from the cold. "Got to find my bathrobe." She brushed her teeth, as was her habit each morning to do this before anything else. Picking her sweatshirt off the bathroom floor, she shook it before putting it on, and then walked down the hallway. Her legs felt weak and stiff as she descended the stairs; finding a gym was a high priority. Once in the kitchen, out of habit, she opened the refrigerator; it was empty, but she already knew this. Her stomach rumbled again. Leslie looked at her reflection in one of the windowpanes of the back door. "Ooh, bad hair day." Hungry, and not wanting to take the time to shower before venturing out in search of breakfast, she decided to simply run a brush through her hair, change into her favorite sweatpants and look for the nearest restaurant where her appearance wouldn't matter.

Most of the streets were virtually empty as she made her way through the neighborhood. It seemed the entire town had decided to sleep late today. Leslie made a couple wrong turns but regained her bearings. She knew there was a pancake house near the interstate, but she wanted to find an old restaurant she remembered from her childhood, if the chain was still in existence. But like the little dairy bar across from the cemetery and Ale 8s, it was one more connection to a home.

When she had announced to her friends in Chicago that she was packing up and moving to Winchester, Kentucky, they said she was crazy. They said she would go nuts living in a small town. They told her to at least look around Lexington or Louisville, but her family connection was here. It was here where she had spent most of her summers, splashing in the Kentucky River at Boonesboro, setting pennies on railroad tracks for the train to run over, watching movies at Leeds Theater and yes, eating chili dogs and drinking Ale 8s with her grandparents.

Leslie was disappointed to find the restaurant, Jerry's, was gone. She knew it was a long shot it would still be there after all these years, so she drove in the direction of the city's by-pass. There were a few places there where she could get a quick breakfast and then hit the grocery store and the big box store if she needed to stop there as well. She was confident that between the two she could find what she needed for her house, or at least it would be a good start.

At the grocery store, Leslie filled up her shopping cart almost to the point of overflowing. She looked like she was either preparing for a blizzard or feeding ten kids. Other than dry pantry staples like spices and salt and pepper, she had either given most of her foodstuffs away to neighbors or thrown them out when she emptied her apartment. She had felt it would be easier to start from scratch than bother with moving everything.

All of her purchases fit in her trunk, with the exception of the broom she bought. That went in the back seat with the bread and eggs. By the time she left the grocery store, traffic had begun to pick up. "I guess Winchester just woke up." She tried to remember if there was anything else she needed to do before she went home. If there was she knew she would probably remember after she pulled in the driveway. As Leslie headed home she saw a man selling house plants out of a tractor trailer truck. He had an open-sided canvas tent set up with what seemed to be hundreds of plants of all sizes and varieties. Leslie slowed down to look. Other than her two favorites that had made the trip with her in the car, she had given away all her houseplants. She debated with herself for a moment then decided it would be better to wait until after she bought new furniture; besides, she still had enough to do without adding re-potting plants to her list.

It was a short drive home; she was beginning to develop a sense of direction in her new surroundings. She was certainly more confident about taking turns and going through side streets. This time she found her own street on the first try. As she approached the house she saw Mark, the Rogers' oldest son standing on the sidewalk with another boy. She waved and smiled as she passed them and pulled in her driveway. Leslie parked her Mercedes in front of the carriage house and walked to the back of her car. As she started to gather up her groceries, she remembered she had never unlocked the door to the screened back porch. "Shit!"

Leslie shoved one hand into the pocket of her sweat pants and walked to the front of the house. She paused to stand under the arched porte-cochere. Mark was still on the sidewalk dribbling a basketball; the other boy was gone. "Mark. Hello Mark." Leslie waved.

Mark returned her wave.

"Hey, how would you like to make five bucks?"

Mark looked in her direction then crossed the street. "Sure. What do you need?"

"Actually, I have a trunk full of groceries, if you would like to help me carry them inside." She noticed Mark glance upward; he was looking at the upper floors of the house. "I just want some help getting them in the kitchen; I'll have to figure out where to put everything after that." Mark glanced up again.

"Sure I'll help, but you don't have to pay me."

"No, I insist. Hey, I don't want to be known as the neighbor who mooches free labor." Mark smiled. "I left the screen around back latched so we'll have to go through the front."

Mark hesitated. "I'll just meet you around back." From the porch Leslie watched as Mark, with his basketball under his arm, disappeared around the corner of the house. When she reached the back door, he was already standing at the foot of the porch steps with an armload of groceries. "Wow, you beat me." She held the screen door open for him as he stepped onto the porch.

"I like your car," he said as he passed by her. "It's sportier looking than most of the Mercedes you see around here."

"Thank you. When I bought it I didn't want something that looked like an old lady would drive. Not that I'm actually that old. But I like sporty cars."

"How old are you?"

Leslie was surprised that he would ask such a blunt question. She laughed.

"I'm sorry. That was rude wasn't it?"

Leslie smiled. "I'm thirty-four. I guess that seems like old-as-dirt to you?"

"Not really. I have a part-time job at WLEX, so I'm around a lot of people older than me." Mark set down the bag and then went back to the car for another armload. "Well, that's everything."

"Here let me get you your money."

"You don't have to pay me – really."

"I insist. Actually, I have so much work to do around here, any jobs like this will be a big help." Leslie handed Mark a five-dollar bill, and then she paused. "Mark, can I ask you a question?"

"Sure."

"It's about last night. It was something you and your brother said during dinner." She saw Mark's face flush, but she didn't waste time in asking her question. "So what's the ghost story about my house?"

"I better go; Dad wanted me to help him in the yard."

Leslie put her hand on his shoulder. "Mark, really, I'd like to know." Mark knitted his eyebrows and pursed his lips together in a sort of pouting scowl.

"Mom and Dad really don't like me to talk about it."

"It's okay, it can be our secret. I would just like to know."

Mark took a deep breath and looked around the kitchen.

Leslie noticed that the boy seemed nervous. "Would you feel more comfortable if we went out on the porch?"

"No, that's not it. It's just..."

"If you're not comfortable talking about it I understand, but I really would like to know. I've always loved ghost stories."

"It's not a story," Mark snapped.

Leslie raised her left eyebrow in surprise. She hadn't expected such a strong response from him.

"I'm sorry, it's just that Thomas bugs me about it every chance he gets and then if I say anything to him, Mom and Dad get on my ass."

"Mark, anything you tell me isn't going to go any further. I won't mention it to your parents."

Mark hesitated again. "Can we go outside?"

"Sure." Leslie opened the door and they both walked out and sat on the porch steps. She could tell he was agitated. Perhaps he really believes in ghosts and was afraid to be inside her house, she thought, or perhaps he was just afraid of getting in trouble with his parents. "I would offer you something to drink, but I don't have anything cold. My refrigerator was completely empty before I went to the store."

"That's okay; I'm not thirsty. Did you like living in Chicago?"

"Yes, I liked it a lot."

"So, then, why did you want to move here?"

"When I was growing up my Dad was in the army, and every time I would start to feel settled in some place we would have to move."

"Did you have a lot of friends?"

"Sort of. I met a lot of people, but it always seemed like just when I was starting to make friends and feel like I fit in, we would move. Just a lot of hellos and good-byes."

"Do you still have relatives here?"

"I still have some, but I don't know them that well anymore. I'm going to try to reconnect with them. I guess for me, since I do have family here, I feel like I have roots to the town, like I belong here. I love Chicago, but I don't belong there."

Mark was silent for a moment. "What made you buy this house?"

"Honestly, I just loved the way it looked. I love big old Victorian houses, and I was lucky enough to make enough money to buy it."

"It is pretty neat looking." Mark paused. "You know Chris used to hear things in it."

"Chris is your friend who lived here?"

"Yeah. Some of the other guys at school laughed at him when he told us about it. But I think they were just scared. Chris had a sleep over once, and other than me, only one guy came. They all made excuses about their folks making them work around the house the next morning – stuff like that."

"So you slept here?"

"A few times, until Mom and Dad stopped letting me stay over."

"Why wouldn't they let you stay?"

"They didn't like the Andersons; they thought they were weird. They didn't even know them. Mom is a real snob. You should hear her when she gets around some of her country club friends. I don't know why she thinks it's such a big deal. It's a pissy little country club anyway."

"What about your dad?"

"He isn't much better. He likes to brag about what he shot on the course and then smoke cigars in the clubhouse with a bunch of old farts. I mean, god, he doesn't even smoke for real. He just thinks it looks cool."

Listening to Mark, Leslie knew her first impressions of her new neighbors had been correct, but she didn't want to get into that now, not with their son. If Mark needed an adult to talk to, she could be that. For now, she just wanted to know more about her house and the supposed ghost. "You said Chris used to hear things in the house. What kind of things?"

"Well, he said the first time it happened he thought he heard his dad and his sister arguing about something. He thought maybe she had been out late and hadn't called, you know. But when he got up to check, his parents were in bed asleep and Karen wasn't even home. She was still at school in Lexington."

"Could they have been arguing on the phone and hung up by the time Chris got up?"

"No, it was the ghost!"

"Did he ever see it? The ghost, I mean?"

"He told me he did, and then as soon as he would see her, she would just vanish."

"Did you ever see her?" Mark was silent for a moment.

"Yeah. I think so."

"You aren't sure?"

"It was only for a second. We were outside; we had been skateboarding up and down the street all morning. You know, just horsing around. We sat down on the sidewalk out front, and I don't know why, but I just happened to look up and I saw her standing in the window."

"In the window?"

"Yeah, up on the third floor in the round room." Leslie felt a chill go through her, like the small hairs at her hairline suddenly stood up. She thought of the day she had closed on the house. The noise she heard, the statues she found in the turret room, and then the split second that she too thought she saw someone standing in one of the windows. For a few moments there was an uneasy silence between the two of them. Mark still starring at the ground, picking at the corners of his fingernails, he asked, "You've seen her too, haven't you?"

Leslie turned and looked at him. "Let's just say I saw something in the window Thursday when I stopped by before my closing, but the logical explanation is that it was just the reflection of the tree limbs. Storm clouds were rolling in and the wind was picking up; the tree branches were moving so much that it was most likely the reflection in the glass. The glass is leaded, it distorts things."

Mark stopped picking at his fingernails and looked into Leslie's eyes. "If you believed that you wouldn't have paid me five dollars to help you with your groceries just so you could ask me questions."

Leslie was surprised by Mark's response. She didn't realize she was that transparent to a seventeen-year-old. "I guess next time I want to ask you questions, I'll just ask. I like a good ghost story and every old house has at least one."

"Yeah right. Tell me that again when you get spooked off like everyone else that's lived here."

"Is that why the Andersons moved?"

"Yes. Mom and Dad think that they couldn't afford the house and just told people there was a ghost because they didn't want to admit they were bankrupt. But that's not true. They had these people come in with all kinds of equipment to try to find the ghost." Mark laughed. "Chris and I had fun calling them the Ghost Busters. One of the guys got pissed at us."

Leslie noticed this was the first time she had seen Mark actually smile. "So the Andersons didn't file for bankruptcy?"

"God no, they're loaded. Mr. Anderson is a surgeon at the UK Medical Center. He does transplants and stuff. And Mrs. Anderson, she's a professor at UK. Both of them make like six figures."

"Where do they live now?"

"Lexington. They moved over to the other side of town off Man-O'War Boulevard and built a huge house. Chris said they built a new house so they wouldn't have any ghosts in it."

"Have you seen them since they moved?"

Mark hesitated.

"Yes, but don't tell my parents. I'm not supposed to drive into Lexington by myself, other than to go to work or the mall; and they really don't want me around Mr. and Mrs. Anderson."

"Do you think there would be a problem with me calling the Andersons and asking them some questions?"

"I don't know. They are really nice, but you might freak them out. Just make sure my parents don't find out I've been over there or I told you all of this. I get bitched at enough already."

"Don't worry, it'll be our secret. I'm really not ready to be labeled as the crazy new neighbor."

"I think you believe you've seen her, too."

"Let's just put it this way: as far as I know, I haven't seen anything out of the ordinary, but I have reason enough to feel I need to investigate this a little further."

Mark stood up to leave. "I better get home. I have to help Dad with some stuff." Leslie, still seated on the porch steps, looked up at Mark. He suddenly seemed very mature for his age. "Ms. Newkirk," he said, "this house creeps me out a little, but if you need me to walk around in it with you and look for...you know...her, then I'm okay with that. I mean

I'll do that for you, if you ever get scared."

"Thanks Mark, but I wouldn't want you to do that if you are uncomfortable being in the house. And certainly I don't want to interfere between you and your parents, but if you ever need someone to listen, just remember I'm right across the street."

Mark looked up. "I hear my dad calling; got to go. Thanks for the five bucks."

"Thanks for the help and the info." Mark quickly disappeared around the corner of the house. Leslie stood up and walked to her car and closed the trunk lid. She watched as Mark pointed in her direction and showed his father the five dollar bill she had given him. Jim Rogers waved and smiled, then put his arm around his son's shoulder as they walked to their open garage.

9

The remainder of her day was uneventful. Other than the normal creaks and pops associated with all old houses, there were no unexplained noises, no shadows in the windows, nothing that didn't have an obvious source or logical explanation. She had managed to unpack all but a couple boxes. These were just keepsakes, things from her childhood, old letters and mementos from college. She decided to store the boxes in the attic as the cellar was too damp. She made a shopping trip to Wal-Mart and bought plastic storage containers to protect the trinkets from mice. One by one, she carried the three plastic boxes up the stairs to the third floor. By the time she set the third and last box on the floor in front of the door leading into the attic, she could feel beads of sweat on her back and forehead. She was tired, but this was the last little job to complete before declaring herself finished and ready to buy furniture.

The attic was the only part of the house she hadn't examined. The contractor she hired to inspect the house had said the floor and beams were sound, and there was no evidence of any roof leaks. The entire house was in good condition. The lock on the attic door appeared to be part of the original hardware. Shaped like a square flat box, possibly made of brass, the lock had filigree on its surface and sides. A small oval ceramic handle turned the internal mechanisms that opened it. The door creaked when the pressure from the latch was released. Leslie turned the doorknob and slowly opened the door. She wasn't sure why she opened it so slowly, or what she was expecting to see other than a dark empty room. Or possibly a bat?

With her flashlight, Leslie searched for a light switch. It was on the wall, far to her right. When she flipped on the switch, a half dozen exposed bulbs hanging from cords throughout the attic flickered to life. She took a couple steps, testing the boards before applying her weight. If she fell through the floor, no one would find her for days, and then only because her mother would call the police when she hadn't been heard from. After taking a few more steps, and satisfying herself that the contractor was correct in his assessment in the soundness of the floor, Leslie relaxed.

The attic was large and ran the entire length and width of the house, with the exception of the turret room. Cobwebs hung from the rafters and everywhere the dust was thick. The bare bulbs provided limited light, so Leslie used her flashlight to inspect the corners and further recesses of the attic. There were deteriorating cardboard boxes stacked around the walls, along with some wooden crates and a couple old trunks. The storage and packing materials gave an indication as to the time period of each. From the information Cathy had given her, the Andersons had discovered the attic access while doing some minor repairs. Apparently the door had been walled up years earlier and the attic concealed. The Andersons had left the attic contents undisturbed and let everything in it go with the sale of the house. Now she was introducing Rubbermaid into the mix, which seemed very out of place.

There was a dress dummy in one corner. The type women once used when sewing their own clothes. Her eyes scanned the room; she felt like a child on a treasure hunt. The first items she found were lighting fixtures stacked in a far corner. She wasn't sure, but they looked like gaslights and probably had been original to the house. She would have to do some research to determine when the citizens of Winchester first had access to gas lighting and made the conversion to electric.

"I wonder if there is anyone in town who has pictures of this house from years ago?" she asked herself. Leslie walked up and stood beside one of the trunks. It was about three feet high, with a rounded top like a treasure chest in old pirate movies. There was a brass plate on top with a name engraved in it, but it was too tarnished and dusty to read. On its side were thick leather handles, and on the front there was a heavy lock. She tried the lock – it wouldn't budge. In the process of unpacking, she had located her small toolbox and thought about going downstairs to get it so that she might pry open the lock, but she didn't feel like making the trip up and down the stairs. Again, she would save that project for later. Who knows, maybe there is a key up here somewhere. There were a couple pieces of furniture; a dresser with a mirror and a wingback chair. Fortunately the chair had been covered with a drop cloth, so the fabric wasn't in bad shape. She examined them closer and decided that, with some help, she could get these downstairs and use them somewhere in the house.

In another corner of the attic she found some children's toys from the turn of the century. There was a porcelain doll lying in a tiny doll bed. Beside it was a wooden rocking horse, its painted black spots still visible. In addition, there was a pair of ice skates with leather uppers and thick rusted blades, and a ball and bat. She couldn't understand why anyone would leave these things, or why any of the other owners hadn't taken them out before walling up the attic. If nothing else, they could have sold the items. "I've hit the jackpot," she said aloud to herself.

Leslie wished she had someone with which to share her find. Suddenly she felt very alone in her new home and new town. She had been too busy the last few days to really think about the fact that, other than some relatives she hadn't seen in years, there was no one here that she was close to. Other than the neighbors whom she had just met, and the jury was still out on them, she knew no one in Winchester. Leslie sat back on the dusty floor. "I need to join a club or something." Her eyes slowly surveyed the attic again. Lexington has an art league that seems pretty active, she thought to herself. That will be a good place to start. I'll check on it tomorrow.

She missed Beth. Beth would be the perfect person to help sort through the attic. To her it would be an adventure, a party in the making. "I have to call Beth; she'll love hearing about the stuff I found. I'll tell her and she'll have Angie with her on the first plane out of Chicago." Leslie stood up and dusted off the seat of her jeans. At least I can afford to fly up to Chicago if I want, and Beth definitely has the money to make the trip here when she pleases. Leslie decided she would call Beth immediately and start making plans for her to visit Kentucky. Then, she would call the Lexington Art League, get their office hours then drive into Lexington and sign up.

But before leaving the attic, Leslie bent over and picked up the porcelain doll; she hesitated for a moment. As Leslie returned the doll to its resting place, from the corner of her eye, she saw a flash of light outside the attic door. Instantly she spun around and with her flashlight in hand rushed to the open door and into the hallway. She stopped quickly; the short third floor hallway was empty. She wasn't sure what she had expected to see. Cautiously, she walked into the turret room. Again nothing, with the exception of a couple of loose sheets of sketch paper that had fallen from her drawing table to the floor, everything was just as she had left it. Leslie looked up at the light fixture overhead. Other than a barely detectable sway of the chandelier, nothing appeared out of the ordinary. All the bulbs looked intact, and there were no apparent scorch marks on the wall sockets from electrical shorts.

Leslie picked up the sketch paper and returned the sheets to her table then walked to stand in front of the window. Across the street she saw one of the Rogers' cars idling in the driveway while they waited for the garage door to open. It must have been the headlights from the car. Leslie looked at her watch; it was after six. God, how did it get so late? No wonder I'm hungry. Looking up across the tops of the trees, she could see the last rays of the sunset filling the evening sky with oranges, purples, blues and yellows. This was one of the things that was always so vivid in her memories of this area, its brilliant sunsets. It was difficult to see here because of the dense trees and houses, but from the open fields of her grandparents' small farm they had been extraordinary. Despite her loneliness, she was glad she was here.

10

"Well, I was beginning to think you had run away and forgotten all about us."

Leslie could hear the laughter in Beth's voice, and she knew Beth was delighted to hear from her. "You have to come down here. You won't believe all the stuff I've found; this house is amazing."

"And you say the attic still has things in it the owners just left?"

"At some point someone walled it up and just left everything."

"Oh god, that is just like a scene from a book I read one time where a woman moves back home to take over ownership of a big old spooky house that had been in her family for generations and finds a skeleton rolled up in a big oriental run in the attic. The body had been there for like seventy years. Maybe you have a body in your attic."

"Stop it. I have to sleep tonight and alone unfortunately."

"Okay, I'll be serious. I wonder why they would just leave their things. I could understand the gaslight fixtures and maybe the children's toys if they had outgrown them, but you say there are trunks full of stuff?"

"Well, I'm assuming they are full because they were too heavy to be empty. But, yes, and in the third floor turret room, the day I closed, I found two art deco statuettes. They are beautiful; I have them setting on my mantel downstairs."

"Wow, sounds exciting, just like a treasure hunt."

"I knew you would say that. That is why I haven't gone through any of the boxes or trunks. I'm saving it until you get here; that is, if you can come down anytime soon."

"Are you joking? How about this weekend? I could fly down Friday afternoon; you could pick me up at the airport in Lexington. It isn't too far from there is it?"

"No, not at all. I can get to the airport in 30 minutes, maybe 40 tops; depending on traffic. You have to remember, we aren't talking about cities the size of Chicago."

"I know; so how is life in the sticks? Met any interesting characters yet?"

"I wouldn't exactly call this the sticks, and yes, I have met my neighbors across the street. They had me over to dinner the night I moved in."

"Oh my, how suburban of you."

"Oh please, Beth, I'm not the suburb type, which is why I bought a Victorian mansion that is rumored to be haunted."

"Leslie, this story just keeps getting better! Did you say haunted? Have you seen a ghost? I bet there is a body in the attic. Do you have a cellar? There could be an entire family under the cellar floor. Sorry, I'll stop."

"Yes, I have a cellar, and no, I personally have not seen a ghost. However, my neighbor's oldest son, Mark, told me it is haunted. And his parents got a little upset with him when he mentioned it."

"Oh really, why was that?"

"I'm not sure, Mark helped me carry groceries in the other day, and I was able to get him to talk a little. But he's still cautious with me. However, I did find out that his parents didn't like the former owners, but Mark is still friends with their son. And from what I gather from him, the family who owned the house may have believed it was haunted. Or at least they wanted people to believe it was haunted."

"Interesting. So should I wear a protective charm when I come to visit or burn incense or something? I know, I'll dig out my Ouija Board and we can have a séance."

"That sounds so middle school."

"I know, won't it be fun?" Beth's voice had by now almost converted to a squeal, and Leslie was joining in the laughter. She had never really believed in ghosts; she preferred to think she was open to the possibility. "After all," she would say, "no one really knows what is after this." Leslie listened while Beth rattled on with stories about ghosts and spirits. She found her best friend's excitement amusing, but then Beth was almost always amusing.

After nearly an hour, they had finalized their plans. All that was left to do was for Beth to go online and book a reservation. "I'll call you tomorrow with the flight number and arrival time. You say Delta is the main airline in and out of there?"

"Yes, I believe so. At least that is what I flew when I came down to house hunt. Are you going to bring Angie with you?"

"I don't know, maybe. I'll see if she can get away. It might be more fun with just the two of us. You know how Angie gets sometimes when we are having fun."

"Yeah, she gets annoyed when you have a little too much fun for your

53

own good."

"Yes, her mother hen instinct kicks in."

Leslie could picture the expression on Beth's face. She could see her rolling her eyes skyward and cocking her head to the left in mock exasperation. "Just let me know what you are going to do."

11

Leslie laid her cordless phone on its base, then she stood up from the sofa and walked to the fireplace. She had built a fire before calling Beth, but now it needed stoking and more wood. The four bundles she had purchased at the grocery store were more than enough for now, but she would need to buy at least a truckload to last her through the winter. The living room, or parlor, and the study both had wood-burning fireplaces. The dining room, along with the kitchen, master bedroom and one of the spare bedrooms had gas logs, probably installed for convenience by one of the previous owners. The fireplaces in the other upstairs rooms, as well as the third floor turret room where she was in the process of setting up her art studio, had all been blocked off with decorative cast iron plates.

She wasn't sure what she would do with all the fireplaces. Probably for now she would just leave them as they were. When she toured the house with her agent, her first question had been, "Do all the fireplaces work?" She had been delighted to discover they did. Growing up, she never had a fireplace in the houses or apartments where her family had lived. Army bases weren't big on amenities. Her grandparents' old farmhouse had three chimneys and five fireplaces, one chimney and fireplace in the kitchen area and one chimney on each end of the main section of house, and each had first and second floor fireplaces.

As she stared at the flames, she remembered how her grandfather would come into the kitchen through the back door and pull off his barn boots, setting them on some old newspaper her grandmother had left in the corner of the pantry. Then he would crumble cornbread into a glass of fresh milk and eat it with an iced-tea spoon, while he read the Lexington Leader, the afternoon paper at the time.

Leslie had inquired about buying the old farm, but the family had sold it years ago and the current owners weren't interested in selling. She asked Cathy to keep an eye on it and alert her if it ever went on the market. Leslie returned to her seat on the sofa and poured herself another glass of red wine from the bottle on the coffee table. The reflection of the flames danced through the red liquid in her glass like fiery fairies drifting in a red sea. She pulled a knitted cotton throw over her feet and legs and opened a book she had started reading weeks earlier but had been too busy to finish. After reading the same paragraph three times, she knew that trying to concentrate at this late hour was pointless. Leslie laid the book on the floor beside the sofa, and pulling the throw up around her neck, she slid her body down into the overstuffed cushions to watch the fire.

Drifting into light sleep, Leslie's dreams were a hodgepodge of images, some from the Winchester she knew as a child, some of Chicago, others were pictures flashing in and out of her mind like sound bites from a movie. Everything was blended together into a story without a plot. As visions of her past and present flowed through her unconscious brain, she could hear someone in the distance, almost as if they were miles away, crying in soft, delicate, vulnerable sobs. Slowly the sobs became more real as if they were external to her and part of the waking world, not just flashes from her subconscious.

Leslie, now fully awake and aware of her surroundings, stretched to right herself on the sofa, and then felt a sharp pain shoot through her neck and shoulder. She pulled her hand from under the throw and rubbed the aching muscle. The logs in the fireplace had burned down to glowing embers and the room was nearly dark. She looked at her watch but couldn't see the numbers in the darkness. How long have I been asleep? Sitting upright she rubbed her eyes and tried to focus more clearly before climbing the stairs to her bedroom. The stiff muscles of her neck pulled as she turned her head from side to side.

With the fire having burned itself out, the air in the large, high-ceiling living room was cold. Leslie shivered and pulled the throw over her shoulders as she stood. Other than the crackle of an ember breaking apart, the house was completely silent. As she walked into the foyer to check the lock on the front door, Leslie thought she heard a muffled sound coming from inside the house. She turned quickly and stood motionless with her back to the door, listening for the sound. Again she heard it, but this time it had a vague familiarity. Leslie strained to remember. The sound…it was the same in her dream. Perhaps she hadn't been dreaming at all. Perhaps she had heard it all along.

Leslie looked down at her feet; she was wearing only socks. Not good if she had to run from someone on waxed hardwood floors. She thought for a moment then remembered she had left her sneakers beside the sofa. Still hearing the sound, she slowly walked into the living room and quickly put on her shoes. Sitting on the sofa, she considered her options. She was certain the sound was coming from somewhere upstairs, which she could choose to investigate herself or she could call the police and have them search the house. But, when they found nothing, she would be labeled a nut, and next time, if there really was an intruder; they would be slow to respond. She didn't own a gun, so searching the house with a weapon in hand wasn't one of the options. Maybe I'll buy one tomorrow, she thought. But what good would that do? She couldn't, or rather she wouldn't, walk around the house with a pistol on her hip or in her pocket.

Leslie stood up and lightly walked to the fireplace. She silently removed the poker from the stand holding the fireplace tools. She gripped the wooden handle tightly and tested the weight. It could do some damage if needed. Armed with the poker, Leslie again walked into the foyer. She listened; the sound was fainter now but definitely coming from somewhere on the second or third floor. As she ascended the stairs, she was careful where she placed her feet on the old floorboards. She didn't want whoever was in her house alerted she was coming to confront them.

Her hands were trembling and her knees felt weak as she reached the top of the stairs. She silently chastised herself. God, I should have called the police. Standing now in the wide hallway of the second floor, she listened. Again the house was silent – the noise had stopped. They know I'm looking for them. Leslie could feel her heart pounding in her chest, pumping blood laced with adrenaline throughout her body, instinctively telling her to flee.

Again there was the sound, somewhere to her right, at the end of the hall, the end of the hall where her bedroom was. Here goes. Leslie swiftly and quietly walked down the hall with the poker held tightly in her hand in a striking position. When she reached her bedroom – nothing. She listened for a moment. She could now hear more clearly; the sound wasn't coming from her bedroom; it was on the third floor. It was the sound of someone crying. With her back against the wall and the poker ready to strike, Leslie forced her legs to carry her up the short flight of stairs to the third floor hallway.

As she reached the top of the stairs, she could see directly into the turret room, her studio. There, in the darkness with only the faint glow of a half moon to illuminate the room, she saw the small figure of a girl sitting on her knees with her arms crossed resting on the window sill, her head bent and lying on her arm. Leslie's mind raced. If this girl is in my house there could be someone else in here, too. They could be in there waiting for me. Why didn't I call the police when I had the chance? Across from her, she could see that the door to the attic was still bolted shut; the door to the other room was open and it appeared to be empty. If anyone else is up here, they are either in one of the bedrooms on the second floor or in my studio around the corner where I can't see them.

Leslie took two deep breaths to try to slow the pace of her heart. The adrenaline surging through her body screamed at her to run, but she had gone too far, she knew she couldn't. Walking down the hallway with careful measured steps, she approached the room. She knew that whoever might be in the room with the girl could try to rush her and catch her off guard. What if it's more than one person? She decided to stay to the side of the door, not directly in front. This way she wouldn't be in a direct line with whoever might come running out.

Stopping about two feet from the door, Leslie took a defensive stance. "Hey! You in there! What are you doing in my house?" There was no response from the girl. "What do you want? How did you get in my house?" Leslie's fear was now turning to anger. The girl was ignoring her. Leslie took two more steps forward. "Look at me!"

She saw the girl lift her head and look out the window. "Damn it! What are you doing in my house?" The girl turned and looked in Leslie's direction. Even in the moonlight, Leslie could see tear stained cheeks. She took another step toward the door. Still the girl did nothing. With her heart racing, Leslie made the decision to enter the turret room. She took a deep breath then lifted her foot to take another step forward, but just as she crossed the threshold there was a surge of light in the room. Not bright and intense like the flash of a camera, but just dull and yellowed and not so bright that it prevented her from seeing her surroundings. And all around her she could feel the sensation of a static charge in the air, like the crackle of clean towels being pulled from a dryer. Leslie blinked and the light and the girl were gone. She ran into the room. "Where did you go?" Leslie spun around. The hall was dark and empty, the closet door in her studio was open, and with the exception the boxes and canvases she had placed there, it was empty. She knew that no one could have gotten past her in the doorway. She looked around the room again.

Suddenly her thoughts went back to the day before, and to her conversation with Mark. "A girl," he had said, "looking out the third floor window." Leslie felt the blood rush to her head and a cold chill run through her body. "Shit, I didn't see this. I did not see this. This is not real." She felt like she was going to hyperventilate.

12

Leslie checked every room, every window, and every door to convince herself her house was secure. She thought about sleeping downstairs in the living room but decided against it. At least in her own room, even though it was near the stairs to the third floor, she could lock the door and barricade herself inside. But can't ghosts walk through walls? Leslie went into her kitchen; she suddenly felt as though she needed a drink. Her hands were shaking as she filled the glass with ice from the dispenser. Just as the last cube clinked against the side of the glass, Leslie heard a cabinet door slam behind her. She jumped and spun around, throwing ice cubes across the kitchen. The glass fell from her hand and shattered against the floor.

With her back pressed against the wall she immediately realized what she had done. When she had reached for the tumbler from the cabinet she only partially opened the cabinet door. The hinge hadn't caught, and its own weight had caused it to slam shut. Leslie rubbed her eyes and her forehead. "Shit!" Then she started to laugh at herself. "Okay, girl. So your house came with a pet ghost; it's got to be cheaper than a dog and at least you won't have to go out in the cold and walk it."

Looking at the clock on the microwave, she knew it was too late to call Beth even for a story like this one. Leslie swept up the broken glass and ice, and then mixed herself a strong drink of vodka and tonic water, after which she cautiously climbed the stairs and locked herself in her bedroom for the night.

13

When morning finally came, Leslie awoke exhausted. It had taken what felt like hours to fall asleep. She rolled over in bed and looked out the window at the squirrel running across the sycamore limb. I wonder if it is the same squirrel every morning, she thought. I'll have to give it a name. For a moment she forgot about the events of the evening, then as the sleep cleared from her head everything, the crying, the search of the house, the girl, the bright light, it all came back. Leslie sprang up in bed and looked around the room. She was alone and everything was as she had left it.

She felt under her pillow and wrapped her fingers tightly around the small slender canister of pepper spray. Leslie started to get out of bed but stopped. A forgotten fear from childhood suddenly came to the forefront. What if something grabs my feet? She sat there, pepper spray in hand, looking over the edge of the bed, staring at the floor. This is stupid; the rails of this bed aren't high enough for anyone to get under it... which means it will hurt that much more when something tries to pull me under it. She sat for a moment, thinking. Okay, this is dumb, but I don't really care at this point. Leslie drew her legs up under her, then perching on the edge of the bed, she leapt out into the room.

She landed with a thud, and feeling her ankle give slightly, rolled over onto her back. "Stupid!" She peered under the bed, rubbing the aching joint. She was annoyed with herself. There was nothing under the bed — not even dust.

Leslie stood up and carefully flexed the tendons in her ankle. It was loosening up and didn't appear to be sprained. It was almost nine, eight in Chicago; Beth was probably awake by now but still in bed. Leslie dialed her number.

"Hello?"

Beth sounded groggy. "Beth, it's Leslie, are you awake enough to talk?"

"What time is it?"

"Nine, I mean eight. I can call back later, but I really need to talk to you." Leslie could hear background noise like glasses and things being moved on a nightstand. She heard something heavy fall and Beth respond with an expletive.

"Okay, I'm back."

"What happened?"

"Oh, I just knocked over my damn water glass; I'm getting a towel now to clean it up."

"Sorry."

"It's not your fault, there is just too much shit on my nightstand. So what has you so fired up at eight in the morning?"

"God, I don't know where to start!"

"The beginning is always nice. Is this a short story or a long story? If it's a long story I'm going to turn on the coffee maker."

"I don't know, medium I guess. Okay, here goes, but please don't think I'm crazy because right now I'm not sure if I should be scared or trying to find a psychologist?"

Beth became more attentive. "Scared? What happened?"

"I saw it! I saw the ghost!"

"What? Did a race horse pee on that bluegrass you were smoking?"

"Beth, I'm serious. It scared the hell out of me. It is taking me some time to get used to being in a house this big by myself, and then when I heard the noises last night, I thought someone had broken into the house. Then I went upstairs to the third floor, and she was in there. She was in my studio just staring out the window, then there was a dull flash of light and she just vanished!"

Beth could tell her friend was shaken. With a more serious tone she tried to calm Leslie. "Look, are you sure you saw a ghost and not some kid that had sneaked into your house? I remember you said it was vacant for a while. Maybe some of the neighborhood kids found a way in or one of them has a key."

"No, I mean yes, I think so; she was sitting there. I heard her crying and then poof – gone!"

"How easy would it be for someone to play a joke on you? You know, like somehow reflect an image into the room?"

Leslie thought for a moment. "Pretty easy actually. Anything you would need could be bought at Radio Shack or over the Internet. It's not that expensive anymore or that high tech. But that doesn't make sense. Why would anyone want to scare me? I just moved here."

"Hey, why do people do any of the weird things they do? Because they get off on it."

61

"Why are you trying to be so logical? I'm normally the logical one. I thought that by now you would have told me to call Ghost Busters and Miss Cleo."

"Because you're there in the haunted mansion alone until I can get there."

"So you believe I saw a ghost?"

"I don't know. I've never seen a ghost. But you did see something, and as soon as we hang up I'm calling and I'm going to get on the first flight into Lexington today."

"I'm fine, really. A little nervous, a little tired from not sleeping but otherwise fine. You really can wait until the weekend. I'll be fine."

"Leslie, you might as well stop talking now because I'm coming."

Leslie was quiet. She didn't want to disrupt Beth's week but she was grateful for her friend's persistence. "Thanks, Beth."

"I'm glad you called me. Where are you right now?"

Leslie was embarrassed, but she admitted she was barricaded in her bedroom with pepper spray and a poker from the fireplace. Beth was shocked; she had never known her friend, who had traveled around Europe as a teen and even into the Eastern Bloc when the Berlin Wall was still up, to be afraid of anything. "Leslie, I'll call you back with my new flight numbers as soon as I know something."

"That's fine. I'm just going to dig myself out of my bedroom and go downstairs and try to eat breakfast. Then I'll come back up here and shower and try to stay busy."

"What's the weather like down there?"

"Sunny and a little warm, but the breeze is crisp. But not Chicago crisp. So short sleeves or long sleeves during the day, either one would be fine but definitely sweaters at night. And remember, the house is big and old so it is a little chilly in here at night."

"Actually, I wasn't asking so I would know what to pack. Besides, you know what Angie says about how I pack."

"Of course I know. Two days worth of clothes for you is a week's worth for someone else."

"I live to over-pack. That's my motto. What I was going to suggest is that while you wait for me to arrive, you could do something in the yard. Just something that will keep you out of the house most of the day. Now, are you on your cell?"

"Yes, why?"

"Why don't you talk to me on the phone while you take a stroll around the house, just so I'll know you are okay? Look under beds, in closets, go in the attic – the works. It will make us both feel better. It will be like having me there with you, and at the same time, I'll know you're alone and safe. And don't argue with me – you may have been the brainy one in school, but I have loads of common sense when I choose to use it."

Leslie agreed. Having Beth on the phone did make her feel better and less alone as she walked through the house. She started first with the third floor. Her studio was just as she had left it. There was no indication of last night's apparition. After the second and first floors were secured to her satisfaction Leslie inspected the cellar and the old carriage house, all the while talking with Beth and making plans for furniture shopping. Beth was from old Chicago money and had grown up in a house larger than the one Leslie had just purchased. Leslie trusted any recommendations Beth might make on decor. "Feel better now?"

"I think so."

"Would you like me to stay on the line while you go back upstairs?"

"No, I'll be fine. I know, without a doubt, that the house is empty – there is no one else in here with me, so I don't have to worry about someone having broken in. The alarm is turned on and I'm all set. All I have to do now is take a shower and kill some time until you get here. Maybe I should use another word besides 'kill'."

"I would stay away from words like kill and dead. Since you are going to be in the shower, do you want me to leave a message on your answering machine when I get my flight booked?"

"No, I'll take the phone in the bathroom with me and set it beside the shower. I feel like I'm being ridiculous, but I don't trust the answering machine. The ghost might erase it."

"You're right, you are being ridiculous, but then I didn't see what you saw last night. Call you in a few."

Leslie laid the receiver on its base, stared at it a moment then picked it up again. She was still on edge and didn't want to be too far from a phone. She also dropped her cell phone into the pocket of her pajama pants so she would have a backup. Walking back into the kitchen, she began cleaning up a few scattered remnants of the glass she had broken last night. She dumped the remaining shards in the trash can, then stood in front of the refrigerator with the door open, trying to decide what to eat.

She was hungry but the nervous energy that had built up inside her made her feel more like pacing than eating. Cereal. Cereal was a good choice, it was fast, easy and she wouldn't feel guilty if she couldn't eat and washed it down the garbage disposal. She poured the nonfat milk over the flakes, and sat down at the table. Realizing her back was to both the outside door and the door to the hall, Leslie moved to a different chair. She couldn't see the small television she had mounted under one of the cabinets, but it was better to cover her back than to watch an old episode of CSI.

She ate a few more bites, then pushed the bowl away and looked at her watch. It was fifteen after ten. Beth should have called by now. Maybe she was checking other airlines, or maybe she couldn't get a good flight and isn't coming until the end of the week like originally planned. She looked at her watch again – sixteen after. "This is driving me nuts. I need to do something." Leslie washed the remaining cereal from her bowl down the disposal; then with phone in hand she climbed the stairs to her bedroom and changed into jeans and a sweatshirt. The shrubs and bushes in the backyard had become overgrown during their two years of neglect. Cleaning these out should keep her busy most of the morning.

She had bought a rake, hedge clippers, a shovel, and an ax at Lowe's the day before. Leslie couldn't remember ever having seen the inside of one of the stores until yesterday. The few hand tools she owned had been purchased at Sears and other department stores. Walking into Lowe's was like going into another world. She was in awe of the endless rows of tools, fasteners, hardware, plumbing, lumber; anything she could possibly need was there. "This must be like home improvement heaven," she had said aloud to herself. Then she looked around to see if anyone had heard her. She silently wished she had a friend in town with which to share some of her new experiences.

Leslie retrieved her new rake from the old carriage house, and stood in the center of the backyard with one hand on her hip sizing up her project. "I guess I'll start at the corner of the house." Just as she took the rake in both hands and bent over to pull leaves away from the latticework, her cell phone rang. She rushed to pick it up. "Hello."

"Leslie. Good news. I managed to change my flight. I'll be there tonight."

Leslie exhaled a sigh of relief. She really didn't want to spend another night alone in the house, at least not until she understood exactly what she had seen. "That's great. What time do I need to pick you up?"

"My flight will arrive in Lexington at nine forty-five. I'm flying Delta and it is flight number forty-five thirty-two. Got all that?"

"Hang on I'm outside raking. Let me go in and write it down."

"Raking? As in leaves?"

"Yes, as in leaves. The last owners kept the front yard in pretty good shape, I guess for curb appeal so it would sell, but they pretty much let the back go, so I'm cleaning it up."

"Taking my advice and staying out of the house?"

"Well, it needs to be done, but yes; I thought this would help me burn off some nervous energy and some calories, since I haven't joined a gym yet."

"Good girl, stay busy but don't wear yourself out. I want to stay up and see if we can see Casper."

"Casper?"

"You know, Casper, the Friendly Ghost."

"Beth, you watched way too much television when you were growing up."

"What can I say? Mom and Dad did the cocktail party circuit and the nanny fancied the gardener. I had to have something to do other than wander around an empty house by myself. Just call me Ms. Pop Culture."

Leslie smiled. She loved that Beth's conversations could always make her forget, even if just for the moment, whatever was bothering her. "Okay, I've got it all written down. I'll wait for you at the bottom of the escalator in baggage claim. It's not a big airport, just follow the signs. I'll be the one with the forklift to carry your luggage. Is Angie coming?"

"No, she can't get off. They have a big-deal client coming in and she has to be there. She said to give you her love and to tell you she hates to miss the party."

"I don't know that I would classify this as a party. I don't get rattled easily, but last night I was really freaked out. I seriously thought about going to a hotel, but I can't do that. I just can't let this scare me out of my own home, especially if it's just someone playing some kind of sick joke."

Beth's voice took on a comforting tone. "Don't worry; we'll figure this out."

"Thank you." Leslie turned off the phone and looked at her watch. It was only half past ten. She had roughly eleven more hours to keep herself busy. Leslie returned to her yard work and began bagging the leaves she had raked from around the porch. In just a few minutes she had managed to fill two trash bags. She knew tomorrow was trash day so she carried the bags to the end of her driveway and set them on the curb. She saw Mark sitting on the front porch step and waved. "Hi there, how are you doing?"

"Okay. I was just fixing the wheel on my skateboard."

"I used to skateboard a zillion years ago. Are you any good?"

"I do okay. Nothing fancy, like jumps and stuff." Mark picked up his board and walked across the street. "Do you want to try it?"

Leslie looked at the board. "It's tempting, but maybe later. I don't bounce like I used to." Before Mark could skate off Leslie asked, "I hate to keep bringing up a touchy subject, but I just wanted to ask. When you say your friend saw a ghost here in my house did he tell you what she looked like?"

Mark look squarely into Leslie's eyes. "You saw her didn't you?" His words sounded more like an accusation than a question.

"I didn't say that. I was just curious. Like I told you the other day – I like a good ghost story."

"Yeah right. I know you saw her. I can tell; you're not a good liar."

Leslie remembered the times as a child when her mother had warned her she might as well tell the truth because she would know if she were lying. "What would you think if I told you I saw her?"

Mark shrugged. "I don't know, but I wouldn't mention it to my mom and dad if I were you."

Leslie watched Mark's body language. He was tall but not awkward in his teenage body. In her few encounters with him he seemed thoughtful and introspective, not at all the type who might stage a haunted house for kicks. But she reminded herself of his part-time job at the TV station. He had access to audio-visual equipment, and even if he wasn't capable of setting it up, he most likely knew someone who could. "Why does talking about a ghost upset your parents?"

Mark shrugged again and flipped one end of his skateboard in the air by forcing down the other end with his foot. "I don't know."

"Now you're not doing a good job lying."

Mark looked up. Leslie had pulled his attention away from his skateboard. "I really don't know why it bugs them so much, but they just always said Mr. and Mrs. Anderson were strange and they didn't want my brother and me being influenced by them."

"They never liked them?"

"Well, they did when they first moved in the house, but then after a few months, when they started talking about what they saw and heard in the house, Mom and Dad just got an attitude about it. Mr. and Mrs. Anderson shouldn't have told anyone what was going on."

"What exactly was going on?" Mark didn't answer. "Mark, I saw something last night that scared the shit out of me. Is that honest enough? And as of right now, I don't believe in ghosts. Right now I'm thinking someone could have put some audio-visual equipment in my house and is trying to scare me because they either have too much time on their hands or they just get off scaring people. I used to work for a software company. I know something about electronics, and I know what I saw can be generated on a home computer."

"Are you accusing me of doing that?"

"No. I'm just saying I'm not convinced I have a ghost, and you are the only person I know that I can talk to about this. "

Mark flipped up his skateboard again. "I really need to go; my friends are waiting for me. If you want, I'll come over later and talk to you then, but I just don't want Mom and Dad to find out." Leslie felt guilty that she had put Mark in a situation where he felt he had to lie to his parents.

Turning her head and looking in the direction of the bulging trash bags Leslie replied, "I tell you what – I'm cleaning up the backyard to-day. When you finish with your friends why don't you stop by and carry the bags to the curb for me. I'll pay you a few dollars and we can talk then. That way you don't have to lie about being over here. Is that cool?"

Mark gave a sideways grin. "That's cool, but you don't have to pay me."

"This time I'll insist on paying — I'm not so old that I can't remember what it was like being a teenager and always needing more money than I had."

"I could help you with the yard. I just need to go right now, but I'll come back in a couple hours."

"That's fine, but let me show you what I'm doing because I might be in the shower when you get back." Leslie walked Mark around to the back yard and explained her plan for cleaning out the hedgerows and old flowerbeds. Then she showed Mark where the lawn tools would be in the old carriage house. He waved as he skated off down the sidewalk. Leslie watched until he turned the corner, then looking at her watch, decided she would sweep out the floor of the carriage house before going inside for lunch. Just as she turned to face her house, Leslie looked up to the third floor windows. For just a moment she thought she saw someone in the window. Leslie instantly broke into a run. She knew the front door was still locked so she ran to the backyard and up the steps, slinging the screen door open and letting it slam behind her. She raced through the kitchen, catching her shoulder on the door facing. The impact caused her to momentarily lose her balance, but she quickly recovered and skid-ded across the foyer floor. She grabbed the banister and sprinted up the stairs two and three steps at a time.

Her footsteps echoed down the second floor hall as she raced to the stairs leading to the third floor. Whoever was here this time she would catch them – she knew she would. As Leslie bolted onto the third floor and looked directly into her studio, she saw the young girl standing in front of the window. Leslie, breathless from her race yelled out, "Hey, you, don't try to get away, I've called the police." The young girl spun around, and holding her arm above her head as if shielding herself from something, she fell to the floor and then was gone.

14

Leslie ran into the room and skidded to a halt where the girl, only a second before, had fallen. Leslie bent over, her hands resting on her knees, gasping for breath. Her side ached and she felt lightheaded. She willed herself to breathe slower. There was no way she wanted to hyperventilate and pass out now. "I am not going crazy – do you hear me? I'm not! And you're not going to run me out of my house you son-of-a-bitch!"

Her heart still pounding from her race up two flights of stairs, Leslie began frantically searching the room. She felt around baseboards, window seals and door jams. She ran her hands across the walls, looking for anything out of the ordinary. Anything that would prove someone was creating these images. "Damn it!" She stood with her hands on her hips, staring at the crown molding running along the edge of the wall and ceiling. "It has got to be up there. The optics are probably hidden in the plaster molding." She looked around the room. There was a stool in the corner but it wasn't tall enough to stand on and reach the top of the wall. She knew she needed a ladder but didn't have one. The Rogers probably have a ladder. I'll borrow one from them.

Leslie heard her phone ring. She hadn't bought one for the studio and the closest one was in her bedroom. She ran down the stairs and around the corner to her bedroom. "Hello."

"Leslie, are you alright?"

"Mom, hi; yes I'm fine, I just had to run to get the phone. I was up on the third floor."

"With a house that big you should have a phone in every room. It's a safety issue you know."

"Yes, I know Mom. And I will put phones in all the rooms. I just haven't had a chance to do that yet. But I have my cell with me. Beth is coming down for a visit, and I'm sure we'll go shopping and get some things for the house."

"Beth? I've met her haven't I? Isn't she the one with the blonde hair and the family that is well off?"

"That's her."

"Well, be careful about letting her influence you to buy too much all at once. She's not used to having to save for anything or worry about paying bills. You don't want to run through all your money and then have nothing to live on."

"Don't worry, Mom. I think I can handle it." Leslie was both amused and annoyed. Even though she had shared with them some of her finances, they still did not comprehend. "So what are you doing calling in the middle of the day? Is everything okay?"

"Oh, everything is fine. I just wanted to talk to you about your second cousin Mike and his wife Sheila. They live right there in Winchester near a golf course and are very nice, not at all like his brother Tony. Anyway, I told his mother Ruth to have him give you a call, and maybe the three of you could get together for dinner or something."

Leslie knew her mother was expecting a complaint about giving out her number, followed by a string of excuses as to why she couldn't meet her cousin, but instead Leslie simply replied, "That's fine. I remember Mike. He was nice when we were kids. I'll call him and maybe invite them over after I get some furniture." Leslie knew she had moved back to Kentucky to reestablish a connection with her family, even though her parents, after years of moving with the Army, had opted for retirement in Florida. Florida wasn't home for her. Winchester was the connection.

"Honey, your dad wants to come up and see your new home. He has been bragging about it to his friends. And of course, I want to visit you, too."

"So in other words, you want to know when you are going to get an invitation to visit."

"Well, yes."

"Don't worry, Mom. I'm not trying to exclude you and Dad from anything. I finally got all my boxes unpacked, and you'll get an invitation as soon as I buy a bed for you to sleep in."

"Well, where is Beth going to sleep?"

"On the futon in one of the spare rooms. One of our plans is to furniture shop this week."

"Okay, well, I'll let you go then. I just wanted to let you know to expect a call from your cousin and maybe Ruth, too."

"Where's Dad?"

"He's playing golf."

"Tell him I said hello."

"I will honey, and you take care and don't let Beth talk you into anything too expensive. I know you want your home to look nice, but your father and I don't need anything fancy to sleep on when we visit, just so long as it's got a mattress and not that futon thing."

"That's why I haven't invited you yet. I promise to invite you up, as soon as I get at least one guest bedroom set up."

15

Leslie walked out her front door and across the street to Jim and Barbara Rogers' house. She rang the doorbell and waited, all the while turning to look up at her third floor windows. Nothing: no faces in the window, no silhouettes, no shadows. She rang the doorbell again, and then looked at her watch. It was almost noon, so she knew if they weren't at home then they could be out to lunch after church. But then, Mark was home. If they were in the habit of attending church on Sunday, then why was Mark home? Leslie felt her stomach rumble; her appetite had returned, and with it a headache that made her feel slightly nauseous. She had done too much on an empty stomach and needed to get some food in her system. But she was nervous about being in her house alone, and she hated that feeling. Never had she ever been actually afraid. She was the one who would climb the highest in the tree, take the biggest jump with her bicycle, travel around Europe, and move to a large city alone.

Now here in her own home, she was afraid that each time she rounded a corner whatever was in her house would be standing there, waiting for her. As she walked back across the street, she said aloud to herself, "It's a projected image and the optics are hidden somewhere in that room; there is no other explanation." Leslie locked the door behind her and stood in the foyer looking at the staircase in front of her. "Not now. No more right now." She walked past the stairs and down the hall into the kitchen to make lunch for herself.

After eating and then watching two old movies back-to-back, Leslie realized that not only had she relaxed, but there had been no more noises inside her house in over four hours. She looked at her watch; she still had almost five hours until Beth's plane arrived. She wasn't sure what to do to pass the time. Normally that wasn't a problem for her, but she felt her nervousness returning, and along with it an impulse to pace the floor.

She decided to start with a shower, anything to hang onto the feeling of relaxation. Leslie stayed in the shower, letting the warm water flow over her body until she had exhausted the supply of hot water. Her thoughts trailed off, planning activities for Beth and herself. They would have to hit a couple of the nightspots in Lexington. A friend from Chicago, who traveled to Lexington occasionally on business, had told her about a good club on Vine Street. She couldn't remember the name; maybe she had written it down in her planner. Leslie also remembered Columbia Steak House on Limestone. She wasn't sure why she remembered it, just that she had eaten there with her grandparents a couple of times, and it had been pretty good.

Leslie brushed out her hair and walked over to the windows of her bedroom to look out onto the street. She saw Mark on the sidewalk and remembered he hadn't come back after they had spoken this morning. She watched as he walked into her driveway and disappeared from view. Leslie quickly took off her bathrobe and put on a pair of sweatpants and a sweatshirt, then hurried down the stairs.

Leslie looked out the front door first. Mark was nowhere in sight, then she went to the back. Mark looked up when he saw her step out on the porch. "Hi there, Ms. Newkirk. I hope you don't mind. I didn't think you were home, so I just went ahead and started working."

Leslie looked at the yard with amazement. Mark had already cleaned debris from under every bush, pulled the dead flowers from the flowerbeds and trimmed back the hedges. "Wow, how long have you been working?"

"About three hours. I was just finishing up. I wasn't sure what else you wanted done so I thought I'd quit now, but if you have something else for me to do..."

"No, this is great. I'm sorry I didn't know you were out here or I would have helped."

"That's okay, Ms. Newkirk. I kind of like doing yard work sometimes. Just don't tell my dad, or he'll want me to do it all the time."

Leslie smiled. "Don't worry, your secret is safe with me, and please, just call me Leslie. Ms. Newkirk makes me feel old."

Mark returned the smile as he tied the garbage bag shut. "Last one!"

"Wait there; don't go anywhere. You can come on in if you like; I'll get some money for you. How much do you charge?"

Mark hesitated a moment then walked up the steps and followed Leslie into the kitchen. "I don't know; whatever you think its worth."

Leslie's eyes scanned the kitchen. "Let's see, I think I left my billfold in my bedroom. There's some soda in the refrigerator, just help yourself. I haven't really decided where I need to keep things. In my apartment, when I would lay something down, like car keys or my billfold, it wasn't that big a deal. It's a lot different in a house this big. I'll be right back."

Even if Mark was still basically a kid, just having someone else in the house made her feel more secure. She took the stairs to the second floor without hesitation, and as she reached the end of the hall and her bedroom, she paused to look at the flight of stairs that led to the small third floor. She contemplated her options. What if she saw the "thing," which was how she had begun to think of the girl. Mark was here; he could run and get help if she needed it. Leslie put her hand on the banister. Mark was waiting on her to bring his money. She debated with herself. Did she really want to risk seeing it again and lose the relaxed feeling she had for the first time since late last night? Her curiosity got the best of her.

Trying to be as quiet as possible, Leslie slowly walked to the top of the stairs. Reaching the top step, she paused and looked directly into her studio – nothing, nothing other than her art supplies. She felt the knot in her stomach relax as she turned and walked back down the stairs to her bedroom.

"Sorry I took so long Mark." Leslie opened her billfold and pulled out three crisp twenties. "Is sixty enough?"

Mark's eyes widened slightly. "Oh yeah, that's fine, thank you. I'd take less."

"When someone offers you money, don't ever tell them you'll take less. They might actually take you up on it."

Mark folded the bills and stuffed them in his back pocket. "I'll remember that. And thanks again." Mark turned to leave.

"Mark, I have a question for you, actually maybe several questions. Would you sit down and talk to me for a few minutes?"

"Mom is going to have dinner ready soon, and unless we're at practice or work or something she's pretty picky about being on time." He's probably nervous about being in the house or worried about the questions I might ask, Leslie thought to herself.

"I promise I won't keep you long. It's just that right now you are probably the closest thing to a friend I have here in town, and you are the only one I know that can answer some of my questions." Mark looked directly into Leslie's eyes. She could see the worry in them.

"Sure. What do you want to know?"

"Thanks. Do you want to sit in here or outside?"

"Here is fine. I'm not afraid to be in your house, you know," Mark declared.

"Great. Neither am I." Looking at the empty bottle in his hand, "Would you like another Ale8?"

"Sure." Leslie opened the bottle with an opener. Ale8 still bottled their soft drinks in glass bottles with press-on caps. They had other bottle styles, but they weren't as fun or nostalgic. Leslie opened one for herself and set both on the kitchen table. "I would drink these all summer long when I visited my grandparents here in Winchester. And it was the first thing I did when I got back: drink an Ale8."

Mark laughed.

Leslie paused. "Okay, I'll stop beating around the bush. Did the Andersons really leave the house vacant for almost two years because they thought it was haunted?" Mark stared at the green bottle in his hand and traced the letters with his index finger. "Mark, I would really like to know. Please."

Without looking up Mark replied, "Yes, they were positive that the house was haunted. After they started seeing the ghost, they tried living here for a while, but they said it was too much to deal with. They were scared; so they moved out after the researchers couldn't help them."

"Researchers? What researchers?" Mark slouched down in his chair.

"I don't know where they were from, but they investigated paranormal activity. Mrs. Anderson found them through some friends of hers at the University."

"What do you know about paranormal activity?"

"Not much, just what I've seen on TV, and then what Chris said his mom and dad talked about with those people."

"What did his parents say?"

Mark shifted in his seat. "I don't remember a lot of it, just that they said it was probably the spirit of someone who died here at the house, maybe tragically, and their soul couldn't rest."

"What did you think when Chris told you all of this?"

"At first, I didn't believe him. I thought he just had a warped way of trying to impress people. So I just laughed it off like the rest of the guys. But Chris just wouldn't let up about it, and I had been over here a hundred times with him and never heard anything." Leslie watched carefully the expressions on Mark's face for any indication that he might be part of the joke someone was playing on her. "Then one night I saw it. It scared the crap out of me."

Leslie caught Mark's slip up. "I thought you told me you had never seen it?"

For the first time Mark took his eyes off the green Ale8 bottle. "I mean I didn't really see it, I just thought I saw something."

"Where were you when you thought you saw something?"

"Chris and I were up on the third floor."

"The other day you told me you were outside and looked up in the window and thought you saw something." Mark shifted nervously in his chair. Leslie had caught him in a lie, and Mark knew it. Now she just had to determine what the lie meant. Was it a prank he was covering up, or was he afraid to talk about the ghost? "I think I need to go. My mom is going to jump all over me if I'm late for dinner."

"Mark please, I need some answers and you are my only friend here." Mark knitted his eyebrows and shifted back down in his chair.

"Okay, but please don't tell my mom or dad."

"I promise."

"My mom and dad don't believe any of this. They think Mr. and Mrs. Anderson were making it all up, so that they could write a book or something. I think they were afraid that the Andersons would make a joke out of everyone here in our neighborhood. Mom and Dad are real uptight. Dad's not as bad as Mom most of the time, but he likes to be Mr. Big Shot at the country club. Mom is like the worst about what everybody wears, and who is or isn't the right sort of people."

"Why are they like that?"

"I don't know, but I get tired of it sometimes. My brother Thomas is going to be just like them. He's already a snob."

Looking at Mark, she suddenly felt sorry for him. She could see how he felt out of place in his own home. She wanted to give him some words of comfort, but first she needed information. "I'm sorry, Mark. It sounds like your parents weren't very understanding when you thought you saw the ghost."

"I did see her. She was like from here to that door away from me." Mark pointed to the door leading to the screened porch.

"When you talk about it you keep saying she?"

"That's because it's the ghost of a girl. You know. You've seen her, and you can't tell me you haven't."

"Yes, I've seen her, but I still think somehow, someone is just playing a practical joke on me."

"When Mr. and Mrs. Anderson first started hearing her upstairs, they thought Chris and I were playing a joke. Even when Mr. Anderson saw the ghost for the first time, he still thought we were the ones doing it. He thought we had one of our friends from school dress up."

"What made him change his mind?"

"I don't know, I guess he just realized that we didn't know how to do the kinds of things he was accusing us of, like setting up projected images, that kind of stuff. And even if we did, you can't buy that kind of equipment on our allowances."

Leslie smiled with understanding.

"Well, if there is any equipment in the house and someone is doing this, then I'll find it. A friend of mine is flying down from Chicago tonight, and we are going to start searching the house. And if I find anything, I'll have whoever is responsible arrested. All I'll have to do is trace serial numbers on the electronics." Leslie thought it was important to share this information. If there was someone responsible for the apparitions, then she wanted word to get back to them. Mark was most likely innocent, but she knew he might talk to others.

Even though she was by nature skeptical, on the outside chance ghosts did exist and one was in residence in her house, she saw her only options at this point to be either to sell and lose a bundle or learn how to share her studio with a spirit.

"Judging from their past reaction, I don't think it would be a good idea to tell your parents I'm seeing ghosts, too."

Mark rolled his eyes. "I'll say. So what are you going to do?"

"Like I said, if someone has rigged up my house I'll find the stuff and send their ass to jail. Or, if there really is a ghost, then honestly I don't know. Deal with it, I guess, because I love this house and I don't want to move."

"I hope you figure it out. I wouldn't want you to move either. You pay well." Mark smiled then took another long drink of his Ale8.

16

Leslie waited in baggage claim for Beth to appear on the escalator. The area was clean and brightly lit, and on every wall were large-scale photographs and artwork depicting something related to Thoroughbred horses and the racing industry. As far as airports go, it was average for a city its size, which was tiny by Chicago-O'Hare standards. But with Keeneland race course and Calumet Farm across the highway, Blue-grass Airport was a showy welcome to the area.

Leslie looked away from a photo of a mare and foal grazing in a green meadow to see Beth waving her arm with large sweeping motions as she glided down the escalator. Leslie met her friend and they hugged. "How was your flight?"

"Uneventful, which these days is good. We had a little turbulence over Indiana, so I just ordered up another cocktail and I was good to go."

"I've never been able to drink on planes, especially when it's bumpy. I'd get sick for sure."

"Must be an inner-ear thing because I know you can hold your liquor. Anyway let's get my bags and you can tell me everything that has happened since this morning." The two positioned themselves in front of the baggage carousel and waited for what Leslie knew would be enough luggage for the grand tour. "Here, this one is mine." Beth hoisted up a large rolling duffel that was bulging. Leslie was surprised the zippers hadn't split open. "And this one, too." Leslie grabbed the next bag which was almost as large as the first.

"I'm assuming you have at least one more."

"Smart ass. No, I don't, but only because I tried to pack light. Besides, I had my carry-on." Leslie looked down at the soft-sided rolling garment bag.

"How did you carry all this stuff?"

"I had Mom's driver take me to the airport, and he helped me get my bags to ticketing."

"I'm surprised they didn't want to search your bags."

"I think they were intimidated," Beth said with a giggle.

"Wait here; I'll get a luggage cart."

"Nonsense, what's the point in buying luggage with wheels if you are going to get a luggage cart?" Beth bent over and picked up the handles of the two smaller pieces, positioning them behind her like a horse pulling a cart. "See, piece of cake. You take the biggest one and I'll take these two."

Leslie had her doubts but agreed. "If you say so." The two women made their way through the airport with the oversize luggage trailing behind them. Every few steps they were either becoming entangled with each other or catching the corners of the bags on the luggage of other travelers. By the time they made it to the parking garage, both were in tears from laughter. "I don't think I've laughed this hard in a month."

"See, I'm a good influence on you. You never should have moved away. You could have found a perfectly good musty old mansion, complete with ghosts, right there in Chicago." Leslie frowned. The reality of why Beth had upped the date of her visit came rushing back.

"I know, but my family roots are here. And I just wanted to connect with that. Army brats never feel like they have roots. I just wanted to be here." Beth looked at her friend with sympathy. She understood Leslie's feelings and the need to belong somewhere. She had often times felt out of place with her own family, a Bohemian in a family of capitalists.

"Believe me, I understand better than you think. Now let's go meet the ghost, shall we?"

17

"Oh, Leslie. This is beautiful. You need furniture of course, but beautiful. How did you find this place?"

"I just told the agent what I wanted and then just lucked out. I think I told you the house had been vacant for almost two years. Now I know why."

Beth looked up at the crystal chandelier in the dining room. "Is this an original lighting fixture? It looks old enough to be."

"I'm not sure, I think it may be. I talked to some people from the county's historical society and they are trying to find some old photographs of the house and neighborhood. I thought I might join their group – it might be fun."

Beth made a face. "I don't see you as a member of a small town historical society. I would bet a pitcher of margaritas that you will be the only member who doesn't have blue hair."

Leslie smiled. "There are probably a few things you don't know about me."

"Name one!"

"Well, let's see, I love to watch the History Channel, and when I was in seventh grade I won an academic award in history and social studies."

Beth slapped her hand to her chest covering her heart. "Were you a closet nerd?"

"I guess that would be one way to put it."

"Please don't tell me any more, I'm in shock. Now let's pour a glass of wine for ourselves and you can give me the grand tour." Leslie walked Beth through each of the downstairs rooms, explaining her plans for each and asking for opinions. They walked through the living room, dining room, study, maid's room, butler's pantry and kitchen; then they headed for the second floor. Beth ran her fingers over the smooth dark wood of the stair rail. It felt massive under her hand and reminded her of her own grandparent's home near the lake. It was larger than this house, but it had been built in the same era and with striking similarities. She could see why Leslie fell in love with it.

The tour of the second floor was a quick walk-through of the empty bedrooms, with Beth giving short comments on what could be done with each. For the largest of the spare rooms, she recommended an exercise room, and for the next to largest, a media room complete with surround sound, a high definition TV and wet bar. Leslie wasn't sure she wanted anything that modern to detract from the beauty of the old house, but the idea was not without its merits.

After a quick look at the master bedroom suite, they walked to the narrow stairway which led to the third floor. "So is this where our friend the ghost lives?"

Leslie looked up the stairs. "Yes, or whatever it is that I saw up there." Leslie placed her hand on the railing then hesitated. Beth could see the apprehension on her face.

"Look on the bright side girlfriend, now you have back up."

Leslie looked at her friend. "I don't know what I'm more afraid of."

"What do you mean?"

"I'm not a religious person and I'm not superstitious either. I guess I've always felt there was something more than this physical life, but I just wasn't sure what that entailed. All those people you see on television, claiming to have been visited by spirits, is a bunch of bullshit in my opinion. But what if there really are souls that can't move on? I don't know if I buy into this heaven and hell stuff, but what if there is another level of existence. What if ghosts are nothing more than people who have somehow been trapped in between? But you know what scares me even more? What really scares me is the thought that maybe there's nothing there and I'm going crazy. I could be schizophrenic or have a brain tumor."

Beth could see the anxiety in Leslie's eyes. She moved closer to her friend and put her arm around her. "Honey, you are not going crazy! If it was just you, then the neighbor kid wouldn't have said he saw something too. And the last owners wouldn't have moved out and sold the place."

Leslie felt tears well up in her eyes. "I'm sorry; I was just so scared last night. I'm not used to being afraid, and I'm so tired."

"It's okay. We'll get to the bottom of this. Come on, let's get my bags up here, and you can tuck me in and then we'll get a good night's sleep. I'll even sleep in the room with you if you would feel better."

Leslie straightened up and wiped away the tear that was leaving a moist trail down her cheek. "You snore." The two women laughed. "No, I want to go up there first. It's my studio."

Beth turned and looked into Leslie's green eyes, which were now red-rimmed and on the verge of welling over again. "Okay then, let's go." Beth took Leslie's hand and together they climbed the stairs.

The two women paused at the top. "There is a small room over here. I don't know what it was used for. I'll probably use it to store art supplies." Beth leaned forward and looked inside. The room was square and small, with one equally small window. The walls were bead board, not plastered like the other rooms.

"My guess is this was the upstairs maid's bedroom. For a house this size, they probably had two. I would guess the room off the kitchen was for the downstairs maid and cook."

Leslie's eyes scanned the room. "I hadn't thought about it, but you're probably right. I guess it pays to have a friend who comes from old money."

Still holding Leslie's hand, Beth took a step backward. "Well, are you ready?"

Leslie sighed. "I guess." She paused. "And this is my studio, a.k.a. the ghost room." They walked in together.

"Ooh, I like this." Beth walked in a small circle in the center of the room. "This is a wonderful room – the molding along the ceilings, the big windows and these floors. Did they wax them before you moved in? I can see some serious art happening in here."

Leslie smiled. "This room is one of the main reasons I bought the house. Even on cloudy days, the light just pours in here."

"I can see that it does." Beth looked out the window and across the street. "Is that your neighbor's house, the one with the spooky kid?"

Leslie joined her at the window. "Yes, and Mark isn't spooky. They are the ones I told you had me over for dinner the first night I moved in. They're friendly enough. I think Barbara, the wife, is probably a little too much into the country club scene. I can't tell about the husband. Probably just your typical blah, blah, big-talking business man, but he was still nice enough."

"What about the kids? You said they have two boys."

"Yes, the youngest one, Thomas, is still basically just a kid. He seems a little immature for his age. I got the impression Barbara babies him a lot. Mark, the older one, tells me Thomas is just like their father, and judging from his tone of voice, I don't think that is a good thing."

"So then, Mark is like his mother?"

"I don't think so. He might be, but he seems a little out of place in that family."

"Some things never change do they?" Beth crossed her arms and leaned against the wall.

"What do you mean?" Leslie asked.

"Kids feeling out of place in their own families."

"Oh." Leslie didn't pursue that turn in the conversation; she knew that Beth had always felt like an outsider.

"Okay, so show me where the ghost was."

Leslie walked closer to the window. She was here by the window." Leslie pointed. "The first time I saw her, she was sitting on the floor with arms up on the windowsill. She looked up and out the window, then, when I yelled at her and asked what the hell she was doing in my house, she looked in my direction then just vanished."

"Was she looking at you?"

"I don't think so; it was more like she was looking past me. And she was crying."

"Crying? Are you sure?"

"I'm certain. The expression on her face was like sorrow or hopelessness."

"That's interesting. Did she do the same thing both times?"

"No, the second time she was standing and then she flinched and put her arm up like this." Leslie demonstrated by ducking downward and swinging her right arm upward, as if to shield her face and head from a blow from above or from a falling object.

"Then what happened?"

"Poof! She vanished."

"That's it?"

"Yes, just like that."

"Describe the flash of light you said you saw."

Leslie knitted her eyebrows and looked down at the floor. She had a habit of breaking eye contact when she was concentrating on details. She had been told once that it made her appear to be lying or lacking in self-confidence, but she couldn't help it. Breaking eye contact helped her form a clearer mental image and recall details. "When I called, I know I said I saw a flash, but I was pretty freaked out at the time. It wasn't really a flash. It wasn't blinding." Leslie squinted as she stared at the floor. "It was more like the intensity or brightness of the light in the room changed."

"Were the lights turned on?"

"No. The only light in the room was from the street lamps. It was like moving a dimmer switch up and down. If you had a photographer's light meter aimed at the room then you could register a very distinct change, but it wasn't blinding." Leslie looked up now and directly into Beth's eyes.

Beth shrugged her shoulders. "I have no idea what you could have seen. All I can say is you and I need to camp out and watch for your ghost to come back. We also need to go through the stuff in the attic and see if we can find a clue as to who she might be. That is assuming she is a real ghost or something like that, and not just some perv paying a joke on you."

"Going through that attic will be like going on a treasure hunt."

"So you said. I can't wait. I love poking through other people's things because you never know what secrets you're going to uncover."

"Technically it is my stuff now."

"It wasn't until you bought the house."

"I guess I have been so wound up the last few days I didn't think about that."

"I'm surprised at you. What has happened to my partner in crime?"

Leslie shook her head, and then swirled the red contents of her nearly empty wine glass. "I was just so scared. I didn't think of anything except being frightened out of my own home and calling you for moral support."

Beth threw back her head, and with a long sip emptied the remaining drops of burgundy from her glass. "Come on, let's go back downstairs and fill these up again and sit in front of the fire, and I'll catch you up on all the gossip back in Chicago. Then we'll turn in.

"Sounds like a plan."

Leslie had insisted Beth take her room and the bed rather than sleep on the futon, but Beth wanted no part of it. She simply stated that tomorrow they would go shopping and purchase a beautiful antique bedroom suite, then hit the mall and buy a mattress and box springs and the issue would be settled.

18

Whether it was the bottle and a half of wine they consumed or simply fatigue, both women slept soundly throughout the night. There were no noises other than old house sounds, no flashes of light and no ghostly apparitions. Beth awoke first and walked across the hall to check on her friend. She didn't want to walk into Leslie's bedroom, for fear of waking her suddenly and frightening her. She wanted to let her friend sleep as long as possible – she knew she needed it.

Beth looked at her watch, it was about eight; early for her on a day when she had nowhere she needed to be. She walked lightly back to her room, trying to prevent the wood floors from creaking under her step. There was a chill in the air, so Beth slid on her scuffs and bathrobe, and then went downstairs to make coffee. Leslie wasn't much for coffee but had stocked up for Beth. The aroma filled the kitchen as the dark liquid began to drip into the glass pot. Beth opened a bag of donuts and select-ed her favorite; she was happy to see Leslie remembered she liked cake with chocolate icing. She poured milk in her mug, turning the coffee a creamy light brown. Seated at the table, Beth took a visual survey of the kitchen. There was so much Leslie could do with the house. She wouldn't be able to go modern with her decor, but she could probably do Shaker or Scandinavian with a few antiques mixed in and get away with it. "Some retro appliances would look great in here, but so would stainless steel," Beth said aloud to herself.

Beth freshened her cup and grabbed a second donut, then after looking through all the downstairs rooms, she headed back to the second floor and her room. Leslie was still sleeping and had only slightly changed position. Beth smiled. She hated that her friend had moved away, but she understood. If she weren't so tied to her family's businesses and foun-dation, she might actually consider moving away from Chicago herself.

Beth looked at the stairway leading to the third floor, then without hesitation climbed the stairs to get a fresh look at everything. Stopping at the last step, she looked around. Nothing. Cautiously, she walked for-ward then stopped just outside the studio door. She took a sip of her coffee. The house was quiet, too quiet was how she would describe it: no movement, no sound, just silence. Other than an occasional noise from the servants, her grandparent's mansion was like this. Big, old and most of all, quiet. Her grandparents had a large hand-carved grandfather clock they had imported from Switzerland before the Second World War. As a child Beth hated the chimes from that clock; in the big silent house it sounded melancholy and lonely.

Leslie's studio was neat and tidy. Most of the artist studios she had seen were in shambles. It was like creativity had run a muck. But not her friend's, no; Leslie found comfort in order; her mind needed order around it to race and create and make beautiful things. Beth ran her fingers down the dark wood of the massive easel near the center of the room. Leslie had positioned it so the sunlight from the windows would shine on the oversized canvases as she painted. In an earthenware jar, Beth recognized the paintbrush she had given Leslie as a Christmas gift early in their friendship. She had noticed her admiring it when they had gone shopping together for paints. Leslie had wanted it, but at the time couldn't afford to spend one hundred dollars on a single paintbrush. So Beth had gone back the next day and bought the brush. Leslie had protested that it was too much, but she gratefully accepted the gift in the end. She later told Beth it had become her favorite brush.

Beth felt the soft bristles and smiled. What was a few dollars when you could see a friend's face light up? Glancing around the room one more time, Beth turned, and sipping her coffee, she walked through the doorway into the hall. Beth had only taken a couple steps down the hall when she felt a slight tingling sensation on the tops of her arms. It was like the static you feel in the air when scooting across carpet on a cold, dry winter's day. For reasons that weren't quite clear to herself, she turned to look back into the studio. What greeted Beth was a girl standing in the room facing her. Within a split second, the girl was charging straight for her. Beth screamed and threw the mug of hot coffee in the direction of the girl, only to see her vanish before her eyes, just as quickly as she appeared.

Leslie was in a light sleep when she heard the scream. It took her only a moment to realize it was Beth. She jumped out of bed and ran across the hall to the guestroom. Finding it empty, she yelled for Beth. "Beth! Beth, where are you?"

"Leslie!" Beth screamed.

Leslie bolted up the stairs, two at a time. She saw her friend standing in the hallway facing the studio doorway. Leslie grabbed Beth around the shoulders and Beth flung her arms around her. "Are you alright? What happened?"

"You're not crazy, and you don't have a brain tumor. I just saw it. I just saw a goddamn ghost!"

Leslie looked up. Other than a couple sheets of drawing paper lying on the floor, the studio was as they had left it the night before. "Are you sure you're okay?"

Beth ran her fingers through her hair, brushing it away from her face, then she straightened her back and lifted her head. "I'm sure; it just scared the hell out of me. Oh shit, I threw coffee all over your floor." In a release of tension, the two women began laughing at the sight of coffee splattered over the walls and floor.

"Do you want to go downstairs?"

"No, I'm fine, really. That is, as soon as my heart slows down. Wow. That was something else." Beth ran her fingers through her hair again. "I want to go in your studio. Nothing is going to scare me like that and get away with it."

"Why did you come up here?"

"I woke up early, and I wanted to let you sleep. I knew you needed it, so I just went down to the kitchen and made some coffee, ate a couple of donuts. And thank you by the way, for having my favorite."

"You're welcome."

"I looked in on you again and you know me, nosey, curious, so I just decided to have a look around myself." Beth pulled up the sleeves of her robe. "Look at this I still have goose bumps."

"Let's go downstairs."

"No, I'm okay; I want to walk through this."

"Okay then, let's start at the beginning. Were you in here when you saw her? It was a girl, wasn't it?"

"Yes, it was a girl. A young girl, I think. Early teens maybe, but I didn't get a good look, I was already in the hall. I had just walked out of the studio and turned around." Beth paused. "It was the oddest feeling. It was like a tingling sensation on my arms and the back of my neck. I'm not sure how to describe it. Just tingly, I guess. Then I turned around and saw her in your studio. When I looked at her, she just bolted and ran toward me."

"Did she come out in the hallway?"

"No, just as she reached the doorway she vanished. And that light you described, I saw it, too. Just as she vanished, I saw the light."

"So what do you think? Is it real?"

Beth looked Leslie square in the eyes. "I think the first thing we do is get someone in here who can do a sweep for electronic devices. My father's corporation has the offices of their top executives swept periodically. But my gut tells me this is the real thing."

Leslie closed her eyes. "I don't want to live in a haunted house."

19

Beth made phone calls to people she knew in her father's corporation; people who could arrange a sweep of Leslie's house on short notice. Beth swore them to secrecy. It wasn't an issue of cost, she just didn't want her parents to learn she was ghost hunting. In the last two years she had begun playing a minor role in the operation of the company, even though she often downplayed it to her friends.

While Beth made arrangements, Leslie looked up the address of the previous owners from her closing papers. When she called their house and found no one home, she went to work locating their places of employment. From Mark she knew Joel Anderson was a doctor in Lexington. It didn't take long to locate his practice, but he was with patients and couldn't come to the phone. Patricia Kincade-Anderson taught at the University, so she was a little harder to track down, but Leslie eventually got the number.

Leslie called and left a message, talking about items in the attic and was any of it hers, and did she want it back and to please call. Beth walked from the living room into the study, where Leslie, in the empty room, was seated in the floor near the fireplace. "Boy, don't you look cozy. I think the best way to take your mind off a haunted house is to go shopping for furniture."

Leslie looked around her. "It is a little Spartan isn't it?"

"That's an understatement. You don't even have a desk and chair."

"That's what you're here for, to help me pick out furniture."

"I thought I was here to help scare away ghosts?"

"That, too. What did you find out?"

"Tomorrow at noon a team from Information Security Consultants will arrive and do a complete and thorough sweep of your house, and if there is one bug, micro camera, anything, they will find it."

"Sounds expensive. What is that going to cost?"

Beth waved her hand in the air. "Nothing, we keep them on retainer and they just happen to have an office in Louisville."

"We?" Leslie was puzzled.

"Dad's company. I haven't really said much about it, but over the last couple years I've gotten a little more involved in the business side of things." Beth extended her hand and gave Leslie help up.

"I thought you hated big business and had devoted your life to playing?"

"In essence yes, but Mom and Dad aren't getting any younger, and I know Dad would like to retire and hand the business over to one of his offspring. Since my brother has turned into a worthless little shit – that leaves me."

"Your dad could still turn everything over to him anyway. After all, he is the male heir."

"No, he won't. It's already been taken care of, signed, sealed and notarized."

Leslie looked at her friend. "I'm impressed."

Beth rolled her eyes. "Don't be, this is out of necessity and family responsibility."

"Don't you just enjoy it even a little?"

"Hush, you are going to ruin my image. Besides, if I admitted that to you, then you would know too much and I'd have to kill you. And we don't want that. One ghost in the house is enough."

They walked into the living room and sat down on the sofa; Beth, with her legs stretched out down the length of the sofa, and Leslie, with one bent under her and the other hanging over the edge. "Okay, Beth. This is what I thought we could do. Stop off at Elsa Van Meter's and see if she has any historical information on the house or the former owners. She is part of Winchester's blue-blood set and is an active volunteer with the local historical group."

"How did you meet her?"

"On my second house-hunting trip, when I found this house and decided to put an offer on it. I stayed for a couple extra days, just to look around a little more and make certain I was comfortable with my decision. So in the process I got in touch with the historical society, and bribed them with a small donation in exchange for information on the house and original owners."

Beth interrupted, "Very sly of you. Amazing the cooperation money will buy, isn't it. Now, I would concentrate on maybe the twenties through the forties, or possibly as late as the fifties. But the fifties aren't likely. I don't know about you, but what little I can remember about the clothes the girl was wearing is that they seemed old. Sorry, I interrupted. Go ahead."

"Good idea. Anyway, then we could hit a couple of antique stores on the way out of town. Go into Lexington and maybe stop in a furniture store or two, or another antique store."

Beth interrupted again. "While you were in the shower, I looked through the paper and there is an estate auction next Saturday that I think we should hit. I'm going to try to stay for the entire week. Also, we should check out the antique stores in the small towns that circle Lexington. With all these old horse farms around here, I bet there is a treasure out there just waiting to be found."

This time Leslie interrupted, "I don't want to fill the house with antiques. I mean I really don't like them that well. I just want some key pieces mixed in with more contemporary things."

"We can do that. But you might be surprised. You may actually find them attractive once you start picking out pieces. And first thing on the list is going to be bedroom furniture, so you can get rid of that god-awful futon."

"I like that futon."

"It was fine for your apartment, but not this house. Put it in your studio if you have to keep it. Then, when you invite a guest over to see your etchings, they will have a place to lounge while you impress them with a demonstration of your talent."

The two friends finished mapping out their plans for the day. Visiting the individual offices of Joel and Patricia Anderson was number one on their list when they arrived in Lexington.

Their visit with Elsa Van Meter was short on information, but it made up for it with entertainment. They guessed Elsa to be in her late fifties, early sixties maybe, and from the slight rasp in her voice they could tell she once had a fondness for cigarettes and bourbon. Leslie guessed Elsa still had a taste for the bourbon. Elsa knew some of the history behind the house, as well as a few assorted stories about the activities of Major Nathan Weatherly. His reputation for having an eye for beautiful women and fast horses had apparently fueled much gossip during his day. She said it was rumored he had an illegitimate child by the housekeeper and was a regular patron of Madame Belle's. She had to explain that Madame Belle was the famous and infamous Belle Breezing, who had operated a "house of ill repute" out of a three-story mansion in Lexington. Belle Walling in *Gone With the Wind* was patterned after her, or so the stories say. Elsa added that Margaret Mitchell's husband was from Lexington, in order to give the legend extra credence.

Elsa knew nothing of the house or its occupants during the twenties but promised to locate some photographs for them. Beth was instantly drawn to Elsa and invited her out for drinks the next time she was in Chicago. Once outside and in the car, Beth's first comment was simply, "I want to be like her when I start getting older."

Next on their agenda for the day were the antique stores. Their first stop was a small shop on Main Street. They only had a few pieces of furniture, but Beth did convince Leslie to purchase an art deco lamp. The base was green marble with ornate metal legs. The stem was a woman in a flowing shear robe, holding a bulb topped with a Tiffany-style shade. She said it would look good with the two statuettes that had been found in the house. Leslie agreed and handed the owner a check for two hundred dollars. She, however, could not be persuaded to buy an 1880 Victorian walnut and burl armoire. Leslie did agree it would look good in the house, but she wasn't yet convinced that she wanted something that ornate. "It looks too antique," she contended.

"Leslie, you live in a big empty, and I want to emphasize empty, Victorian mansion. You need big Victorian furniture."

"But I don't like antiques."

"Then why did you buy an old house?"

"Because I like big old houses."

Beth closed her eyes and shook her head. "Next stop."

At the next store, on Paris Road outside town, Leslie did buy a four-poster bed and matching dresser with bevelled glass mirror, nightstand and armoire with no coercion, to Beth's amazement. "So what made this one catch your eye?"

"The lines were cleaner, and I liked the spiral carving on the four posts and the carved torches on top." Leslie put the key in the ignition and started the engine. "My grandmother had one similar to it, but she just had the matching dresser, not the other pieces. When I would come back to the states for a visit during the summer, we would lie in bed in her room and listen to the sounds of the farm through the open windows and she would tell me stories about herself when she was younger, and also, stories about the family. You know, just talk."

"Sounds like the two of you had some special times together. So the bedroom set reminds you of her?"

"We did. And yes."

"What happened to her things?"

"I don't know, my parents were in Belgium then, and I was in college. Everything was just divided up or sold off. It was always strange after she died."

"How so?"

"Without her and my grandfather, it was almost like we weren't full members of the family any longer. You know, because we didn't live close enough to visit on a regular basis."

"So, why come back?"

"I do have a few relatives here, some cousins I was close to, we have just lost touch. Really, this is the only home I've ever had. The rest were just apartments and army bases."

Beth put her hand on top of Leslie's. "You have a home in Chicago, too, with all of your friends. We love you. I love you. And if you ever want to come back we want you."

Leslie's voice faltered. "Thank you. I love you, too."

Beth turned away before a tear could form in her eye. "Okay, enough of this mushy shit; this reminds me of a Lifetime movie. What's next on our list?"

"I vote for lunch and then drop in on Patricia Anderson."

"Works for me." Leslie merged onto I-64 west and the two headed into Lexington. To save time, they ate at a little health food store off South Limestone, near the building where Mrs. Anderson worked. Beth had soup and a pieta sandwich, Leslie a baked potato and salad. Her appetite had returned now that she was away from the house and relaxed a little.

Beth paid the bill, and they gathered up their raincoats and umbrellas. The sky was threatening rain. As they walked across UK's campus, they made plans for how to best approach Patricia Anderson. With each step, Leslie was becoming angry. She could visualize herself bursting into Anderson's office, demanding to know what was going on in her house and why she and her husband hadn't been honest with her.

Beth's idea was to use the earlier ruse of the items left in the attic, then launch into something along the lines of, "So what's going on up on the third floor?" Then threaten to sue. Since becoming more active in the family business, she had come to both love and revile that simple three-letter word.

Once inside the building, the two rode the elevator in silence to the fourth floor. They exited to an empty center hallway. The building was designed with elevators in the center of the structure, and with offices and laboratories along the exterior wall and the inner hall. The soles of Leslie's sneakers were damp from the rain that had started to fall just before they had entered the building, and now they made a high pitched squeaking sound with each step she took on the brightly polished tile. "I feel like we're on a covert mission, and I'm blowing our cover because my shoes squeak."

Beth cast a sideways glance at her friend and smiled. "You were getting wound up to do battle a few minutes ago. Did your squeaky shoes take the wind out of your sails?"

"Yeah, it's like telling someone you are going to fight them, while you are wearing a clown nose and polka-dots." As Leslie and Beth rounded the corner, they entered a reception area. There was a young woman, probably in her mid-twenties, sitting at a dark metal desk and talking on the phone. The woman placed her hand over the mouthpiece of the receiver. "May I help you?"

"Yes, we're here to see Patricia Anderson," Leslie replied, looking in the direction of the offices at the end of the hall.

"Do you have an appointment?" The girl looked down at an appointment book lying open on the desk in front of her.

Before Leslie could respond Beth spoke, "No we don't, but we're friends of hers. She's expecting us."

The receptionist looked back at the two unfamiliar faces standing in front of her. "Oh, okay, well she is right down the hall in four fifteen."

"Yes, we know. Thank you," Beth replied and smiled, then quickly began to walk down the hall with Leslie in tow before the receptionist could reply.

20

Patricia Anderson's office door was ajar. Leslie knocked, then opened it. Patricia Anderson was setting with her back to the door, concentrating on the computer monitor in front of her. "I'll be with you in just a second."

"That's okay. I just want to know what's going on up on the third floor of the house you sold me."

Patricia stopped typing, her fingers motionless on the keyboard. She slowly pivoted her desk chair around to face Leslie and Beth. "Why did you move out of the house and let it sit for two years when you only moved twenty miles away?"

"So much for my plan," Beth mumbled under her breath.

"I'm sorry, but I'm very busy today and I don't have time…"

Leslie, taking Beth's cue, sat down in one of the two chairs in front of Patricia's desk. Beth straightened her back and crossed her legs. "I think you do have time."

"I think perhaps you should contact our lawyer and direct any questions you have to him," replied Patricia Anderson.

Beth reached into the pocket of her jacket and removed a brown leather business card case. She pulled one of her cards from inside and tossed it on the desk. "Don't threaten us with a lawyer. Leslie is one of my best friends; we're like sisters. And I really don't like it when things upset my best friend, so don't talk to us about lawyers. You see the company name on that card? My family owns this company; I'm one of the officers. I have corporate lawyers on staff and at my disposal, and I have very deep pockets."

Patricia read the card. "The sale was final. You signed the paperwork; you closed on the house. We won't take it back."

Now Leslie spoke. "I'm not trying to reverse the sale. I just want some information. I need to know why you sold the house. I need to know what you saw in there."

Patricia looked down at the card again. "I should talk to my husband first."

"Look, I love the house. I fell in love with it the first time I saw it, but there are some things that have scared the hell out of me and I need answers."

Beth interrupted, "I'm sure once my people do a sweep of the house tomorrow something could turn up that wasn't disclosed in the contract, which could reverse the sale."

"Please, we've been through enough already. My children have been through enough."

"Then talk to me."

"All right, but I'd rather have my husband present."

"Then when? I want a time!"

"Come to our house tonight." Patricia pulled one of her own business cards from a cardholder at the corner of her desk, and then hurriedly wrote down her address on the back. "Do you know where this is?"

Leslie looked at the card. "Not really. I'm not too familiar with Lexington."

"If you are coming from Winchester take Man-O-War Boulevard south, then exit at Harrodsburg Road." Patricia gave the remainder of the directions. They were straightforward and easy to follow. "You can come at seven. That will give me time to get my son out of the house."

"Maybe Chris would have something to contribute to our conservation."

Patricia' eyes widened. "How do you know my son's name?"

"The neighbors mentioned him." Leslie didn't want to be more specific and betray Mark's confidence.

"He is just now getting to where he will sleep at night. I don't want him brought into this."

"Our intention is not to upset your children. Just tell us what we want to know, and I'll leave you alone."

21

As Leslie and Beth left Patricia Anderson's office building, which was on the University of Kentucky campus, it began to rain in earnest. They walked at a brisk pace back to the car. Once inside, Leslie started the engine and turned on the heat and defogger. When she turned on the windshield wipers, she was surprised to see a white rectangular piece of paper swiped across the glass. "Shit!" Leslie opened the car door and reached outside twice, grabbing for the piece of paper before actually catching it.

Beth sat smiling. "You should have turned off your wipers first."

"Well now, if I had done that it wouldn't have been nearly as entertaining, would it." Leslie looked at the paper. "They gave me a damn fifteen-dollar ticket! That meter couldn't have expired more than two or three minutes ago. What do they do, sit and wait for it to tick down?"

"Don't you remember what it was like when you were in college? We had students on our campus who were part of the ticket patrol. They did nothing but walk around and write parking tickets for their work study. I always affectionately called them the Hitler Youth; they took their jobs way too seriously."

Leslie looked in her side mirror to check for on-coming cars. "I didn't have a car in college. I had a bicycle." Beth said nothing, she felt as though she had put her foot in her mouth. She knew she sometimes took too much for granted; things like a car to drive in college. Leslie pulled into traffic. "What do you want to do next?"

"What are our options?"

"More shopping, sight-seeing, or back to the house."

Beth thought for a moment. "Sight-seeing sounds attractive, but since it's raining and doesn't look like it's going to let up any time soon, I vote for shopping. You need bedding for that bedroom suite you just bought. Where is the best place around here to buy bedding?"

"Probably Fayette Mall."

"Where is Fayette Mall?"

"That way." Leslie pointed over her shoulder.

"I'm impressed. Here only a week and you already know where the mall is."

"That mall was here when I used to visit my grandparents. It's just a lot bigger now."

"Lexington looks like a nice little city. Why didn't you move here."

"The house I wanted was in Winchester, and honestly, there weren't any Victorians on the market in Lexington. We looked, but Cathy, my real-estate agent, said most of the ones that were left were converted into offices years ago."

"So you end up buying the house on haunted hill."

"Wasn't that a movie?"

"Probably. It sounds familiar. Let's hit the mall. Hi ho, hi ho, it's off to shop we go," Beth sang out. By the time Leslie and Beth found a parking space near a main entrance, the rain had stopped and a few rays of sunshine were piercing through the cloud cover. Leslie began to feel her situation was looking up when the bedding she selected was in stock at the warehouse. She paid an extra fee to get next day delivery. If all went as planned, the antique dealer would deliver her bedroom suite tomorrow morning, Beth's security people would do a sweep and find something, and then the bedding would be delivered in the afternoon. Her mood lifted enough that Beth was able to talk her into new sheets, comforters, and towel sets for all the bathrooms. On the way out of the store, table linens caught Beth's eye. She bought a table cloth, cloth napkins, place mats, and matching napkin rings, and a crystal decanter set. Beth then presented them to Leslie as a house-warming gift. Leslie protested, reminding Beth that she didn't even have dining room furniture. "These linens are for the kitchen; you need a nice looking kitchen as well. You know as well as I do that when you entertain most people end up in the kitchen."

"With what I'm going to put into decorating this place, people better not hang out in the kitchen."

Leslie and Beth decided to make the short trip back to Winchester and drop off their purchases before their meeting with the Andersons. Leslie placed all the linens in the maid's room off the kitchen. A previous owner had converted it into a laundry room. She filled the washer with sheets, guessing they had enough time to at least wash the bed linens if not begin to dry them. Beth put the art deco lamp in the empty study, and standing in the middle of the room with her hands on her hips, she did an estimation of how many books Leslie would need to fill her shelves. She based her best guess on the number of volumes she knew to be in the library at her parent's house. "You need some books in here," Beth called out.

Leslie walked into the room. "What'd you say?"

"I said you need some books in here."

Leslie looked at the empty shelves. "I didn't want to rush out and buy a bunch of books I'd never read just to fill shelves. I have a few hard backs, but most of my books are paperbacks and I didn't want to put those up there. I was afraid it would look chintzy."

"Nonsense. Books are books. I'd rather look smart and well-read than have no books at all."

"That's a good point I guess..." Leslie paused. She held up her hand to stop Beth from speaking. "Did you hear something?"

Beth shook her head no, then slowly she turned her head so that her ear was in the direction of the open study door. The two women listened to the stillness of the house. Leslie closed her eyes for a moment and shook her head. "Maybe I was hearing things. It was probably the house creaking and popping again. I'm getting jumpy; you should have seen me yesterday morning, I..."

Now it was Beth. She put her fingertips lightly against Leslie's lips to stop her from speaking; then frowned. They listened, this time more intently. "Do you hear that?" Beth whispered.

Leslie felt her pulse begin to race and a knot form in the pit of her stomach. She affirmed that she heard the noise by quickly nodding her head. In a whisper that was barely audible, she replied, "That was what I heard the other night." With her thumb she pointed upward and indicated to Beth she wanted to follow the sound upstairs. They cautiously left the study, walked through the drawing room and into the foyer. The sound was now more distinct. "It doesn't sound like crying this time. Last time, I heard crying and I saw tears on her face."

"Do you want to go up?" Beth asked.

"Safety in numbers, right?"

Beth took a deep breath and exhaled. "I've already had the shit scared out of me once today, I might as well make it two for two."

"At least this time you won't be caught off guard."

"Yeah, unless hands start coming out of the floor and grabbing our legs."

Leslie rubbed the tops of her arms. "Don't say things like that. Let's go before I lose my nerve." She then turned and began to climb the stairs. Half way up the first flight, she looked down at Beth's feet. "Where are your shoes?"

"In my hand," Beth said holding up her shoes.

"Why are you carrying your shoes? Are you going to do throw them at it?"

"No, smart ass, my shoes make too much noise."

"Then why are you carrying them?"

"In case we need to run."

Leslie rolled her eyes and then exhaled in a snort. "So if something is chasing us, you are going to stop long enough to put your shoes on?"

"Alright, I hadn't really planned all that out; now just keep moving." With the sole of one shoe, Beth smacked Leslie on the behind.

"Hey!" Leslie began to giggle. Beth covered her mouth and laughed too. For a moment they forgot they were frightened, but as quickly as the moment came it was gone. Without saying a word, they climbed the stairs and together stood in the middle of the second floor hall, looking down its length to the stairs leading to the third floor.

Beth leaned closer, her mouth near Leslie's ear. "Do you still hear it?"

"Yes. But it sounds almost like singing."

"You didn't leave your clock radio on did you?"

Leslie thought for a second then replied, "No, I haven't had it on since I moved in."

"Then let's go before it stops." With hurried steps, they quickly made their way to the end of the hall and the foot of the stairs. Beth, with shoes still in her left hand, squeezed Leslie's arm with her right.

"Thank you for being here," Leslie whispered, then took the lead climbing the stairs to the third floor. Before reaching the top, Leslie crouched down, her knee resting on one step her elbows on the last step at the top of the stairs. She then raised her body enough so that her head was above the floor, giving her a clear line of vision into her studio. At first she saw nothing and started to stand, and then she stopped, her body stiff and motionless. Beth joined her on the stairs, keeping her body only slightly lower.

They saw her; the young girl that had so frightened them. She was gliding through the room as if she were dancing. Her arms were extended as she swung them out from her body with large sweeping motions. She danced away from the door, out of their line of sight. Then she appeared again, this time with a doll in her hands. The girl lifted the doll into the air and softly sang a song that neither Leslie nor Beth recognized. The melody reminded Beth of old phonograph recordings from the twenties her grandmother had in their library.

"I'm not crazy am I?"

"If you are then it's contagious," Beth whispered. "What do you want to do?"

"I don't know. Just watch her for a few minutes and see what happens."

"Didn't you tell me she vanished when you tried to go into the room?"

"Yes, why?"

"I don't know; I was wondering if we should try to go in there, or make some noise and see if she hears us."

Leslie picked up one of Beth's shoes, which were sitting between them on the steps. "Let's see what happens." Leslie threw the shoe. It landed on the hardwood floor with a thud that echoed through the short empty hallway.

The girl stopped dancing and clutching the doll close to her chest, standing only on the tips of her toes as she rushed to the studio doorway.

"She heard it," Beth whispered. "I wonder if she can see us?"

"I don't know, give me your other shoe." Leslie took the shoe and tossed it into the hall. It landed near the other one. The girl clutched the doll tighter and backed away from the door. Leslie and Beth watched as she sat down on the floor in front of the windows, drawing her knees up to her chest and all the while holding the doll as if she were protecting it. She began to rock and hum the same tune she had just danced to, but now the expression on her face was different. It was no longer the face of a young girl happily playing with a doll and dancing in a make-believe ball. Now the face of the girl was frightened, as if the noise she had just heard was the signal of something terrible.

"What now?" Beth asked.

"We could sit here and watch her to see how long before she disappears."

Beth looked at her watch. "We are supposed to meet the Andersons in forty-five minutes. How long does it take to get there from here?"

"With traffic, thirty or forty-five minutes, but I'm guessing."

"Then if we're going to do something we'd better do it now." Leslie slowly stood. Beth was behind her. "What are you doing?"

"I'm going to walk to the doorway, but not go in my studio. I want to see if she can hear me, or if I can hear anything else."

"I'm right behind you."

"Good, then you can catch me when I pass out."

"What do you think she is doing?"

"I don't know." Leslie turned to Beth. "Can you see her face? She looks scared."

"I would agree with that assessment. Are you going to try to talk to her?"

"Got any other ideas?"

"Not yet, but I still have the technicians coming tomorrow. We might be doing all this for nothing." Leslie and Beth moved to within a foot of the door. They watched as the girl stopped rocking, but still she sat in the floor holding the doll. Her hand moved up to wipe her eyes.

"Hello. My name is Leslie. What's yours?"

"I don't think she heard you," Beth whispered in Leslie's ear.

"You mean the people with the video equipment didn't hear me?!" Leslie yelled up at the ceiling.

Beth grabbed Leslie's shoulder. "Look she's reacting to that. Maybe she can only hear louder noises. Or should I say their microphones can only pick up louder sounds." They watched now as the image of the girl stood and walked to the door. She was now directly in front of them and not more than two feet away.

The girl stood about five feet tall and had short dark hair, which was cut blunt at the ends and parted on the left side. Her eyes were light blue and had an almost transparent quality to them. Her dress was made from a light checked-patterned fabric and was a straight cut that hung just below her knees, with a narrow belt at the waist. The sleeves were short and the neck was rounded with a large lace collar. She wore ankle socks, but no shoes, and the socks had lace around the top, which had been folded down.

Leslie and Beth studied the girl, but she only seemed to look through them focusing her eyes somewhere in the hallway behind them. "Leslie, look at your studio."

Leslie was still staring at the apparition. "What about it?"

"I can't see your drawing table or your easel. We should be able to see it from here."

"Oh my god, you're right. It's gone. All my art stuff is gone! Someone has stolen my things."

"Wait," Beth whispered. "Look over there by the window." She pointed. "That chest, I don't remember it being in here earlier. Is that yours?"

Leslie's heart was pounding. "No, that's not mine; I don't know where it came from."

"I don't think we're seeing your studio."

"You've watched too many X-Files episodes. Someone has to be doing this. And I'm going to get to the bottom of it!" At that instant Leslie rushed into the room, her left arm extended and grabbed for the girl. But no sooner had she entered the room, than there was a flash of light and the girl was gone. Leslie spun around, looking in all directions. Her easel, drawing table, pads of paper, canvas, and paint brushes, everything was there just as it should be. And the chest she had seen from the hall was gone.

"Are you alright?" Beth asked, her voice a full octave higher than normal. Leslie was still standing in place, turning first one direction then another looking for any changes. "What the hell just happened here?"

Leslie didn't answer at first. She felt dizzy. She closed her eyes and rubbed them, then she readjusted her focus. "I don't know. I just don't know." She touched her drawing table and felt the soft bristles of the paintbrush Beth had given her for Christmas. "I feel sick."

Beth went to Leslie and took her arm to steady her friend. "What do you mean, sick? What's wrong?"

"I don't know. I just feel sort of nauseated, like my equilibrium is off."

"Here, sit down." Beth guided Leslie to a chair and helped her sit.

"The last time I felt like this was a couple years ago. Remember when I had an ear infection and didn't know it until I woke up one morning and almost fell out of bed when I tried to sit up? I had to crawl to the phone and call you to come and take me to the doctor."

"I remember."

"This feels the same, just not as bad." Leslie closed her eyes, then opened them wide and blinked. "Wow. This is weird."

"Do you think you can make it down the stairs to your room? Maybe you should lie down for a while."

Leslie blinked and focused on her wristwatch. "No, we need to get moving; we're going to be late for our meeting with the Andersons." Rising slowly from her chair, Leslie stood and took in a slow deep breath then exhaled. "There, see, I'm fine."

"You don't look fine. But we do need to go. I'll drive; you just sit there and give me directions."

Leslie raised one eyebrow. "So the tables are finally turned; I get to tell you how to drive."

"I didn't say tell me how to drive, just where to drive."

"You do that, too."

"Yes, and when I've helped you clear up dishes after dinner, you re-arrange the dishes in the dishwasher."

"But it was my dishwasher, and I know how to arrange things to fit more in."

Beth put her arm under Leslie's. "Oh hush, and just lean on me so we can get you down the stairs in one piece."

Leslie smiled. These arguments were typical between Beth and herself, and they were done more for one another's amusement than out of any seriousness. By the time they reached the car, Leslie was feeling almost normal again. Beth got behind the wheel and started the engine, then looked over at Leslie. "I have taken the helm and am preparing to leave orbit."

"Before you engage warp drive, why don't you hand me that plastic bag in the back seat. I want it up here just in case I feel sick while we drive."

"That is so not allowed. I flew down here to help you deal with a haunted house. Vomit was not in the fine print of that agreement. You know I have a weak stomach."

Leslie looked at her friend and frowned. "Is this the same person who last year said her clock was starting to tick and she needed a child, an heir to pass the family fortune to? How are you going to have a child if you can't even deal with throw-up? That and every other kind of mess is all they do for the first eighteen years of their lives."

Beth adjusted the rear view mirror, and then moved a strand of hair behind her ear that had fallen out of place. "Honey, that is what nannies are for." Beth shifted into reverse. "Reverse thrusters." Then she laughed and gunned the engine out of the driveway and into the street.

22

Only twice did Leslie slam her foot into the floorboard of the car in reaction to Beth's driving. Leslie, with concurrence from their circle of friends, often remarked that Beth only knew two speeds, fast and stop.

They shared an order of fries from a fast food restaurant, and by the time they reached the Andersons' home, Leslie's dizziness was completely gone. She hoped Patricia and Joel Anderson would cooperate and tell them what they wanted to know. She was tired, still hungry and ready for some answers.

"Four fifteen. This looks like the place." Beth pulled into the driveway and put the car in park.

Leslie looked at her directions. "Brick house with green shutters, four fifteen on the mailbox. Looks like it to me. Shall we?"

"How's your head?"

"It's fine. After I got a little something in my stomach I was okay. Actually, I'm getting pretty hungry now. I hope this doesn't take long."

"You always get grouchy when you're hungry."

"I resent that remark," Leslie replied as she opened the car door and stepped out. Leslie rang the doorbell. They only waited a few seconds before the silhouette of Patricia Anderson appeared behind the cut-glass door. "She must have been watching for us," Leslie whispered.

Beth cast a sideways glance at Leslie and raised her right eyebrow. The door opened. Patricia Anderson looked first at Leslie, and then at Beth, then smiled. It was a tenuous smile, like the one Leslie had observed in the lawyer's office the day she closed on the house. "I'm sorry we're late. I'm not familiar with Lexington yet; I underestimated the time it would take to get here," Leslie offered.

"That's quite alright. My husband Joel just got home a few minutes ago. He had an emergency at the hospital earlier today. Please come in." Patricia stepped aside, so Leslie and Beth could enter, and closed the door behind them. She led them from the foyer into a formal living room, where Joel Anderson was waiting. Joel was only slightly above average in height but was slender and appeared to have a somewhat muscular build. He was standing at the far end of the room with his right arm up, resting on the mantel above the fireplace. In his left hand he had a tumbler of something, which appeared to be scotch.

When the three women entered the room, he straightened his stance and shifted his right hand from the mantel to the front pocket of his trousers. Patricia offered them a seat on the sofa. Leslie and Beth sat down. There was an awkward silence for a moment, then Leslie spoke. "I understand there is a lot of tension here, but all I want is a little information, then we will leave you two alone."

"We are not taking back that house!" interrupted Joel Anderson. "And if you are here to get out of the sale, then you can just talk to our lawyer." Joel jingled some change that was in his pants pocket and took a step forward away from the fireplace.

Beth started to stand and square off with Dr. Anderson, but Leslie placed her hand on her friend's arm and stopped her. "Dr. Anderson, I don't want to get out of the house, and I don't want to sell it to someone else, at least not yet. I just want you and your wife to talk to me. I've seen some things, and I don't know what to think about them. Now we can all sit here and talk about this in a calm manner, or I can let my friend Beth here unleash her family's corporate attorneys. She has put them at my disposal for free, but it would be expensive for both of you. Don't make this harder than it has to be."

Patricia, who was seated in a loveseat opposite Leslie and Beth, looked at her husband and spoke. "Joel, let's just tell them what we know and move on." Joel Anderson looked at his wife then down at the glass still in his hand. With a circular motion he swirled the ice cubes. "What do you want to know?"

Leslie and Beth looked at each other. They each had a look of relief on their faces. Leslie looked back at Dr. Anderson, who was still staring at the ice cubes. "Just be very blunt and to the point and tell me why you sold the house."

Joel Anderson looked Leslie directly in the eye. "It's haunted. There, I've said it."

Leslie wasn't sure what to ask next. Beth broke her silence. "Why do you say the house is haunted?"

Joel blew air through his nose and made a snorting sound. "You've seen things, heard things in there. If you hadn't, then you wouldn't be here right now." Joel began to pace across the living room floor.

Now Leslie spoke, "You're right, I'm not going to sit here and tell you I haven't. I know you had paranormal investigators in the house. And

106

I'm just trying to understand what I've seen, because I work with computers and I deal with logic, and what I've seen is not logical."

Patricia stood and walked to her husband who was now standing in the middle of the room. "How do you know about the investigators?"

"Some neighbors mentioned it."

Joel swirled the ice in his now empty glass. "Anything you see in that house you better keep to yourself because you'll lose any friends you make in that neighborhood. We went from welcomed with open arms, to having people cross the street to get away from us."

"I'm sorry. It must have been hard on all of you."

Patricia rubbed her husband's arm. "We both have good jobs. Joel is a doctor, I'm an English professor at the University, and we have good salaries. But being stuck with that house for two years was still a strain on us financially. We had to get out; living in it was hard on our children. It was hurting our family. Our son wouldn't sleep upstairs in his room. He slept either in a sleeping bag on the floor of our room or downstairs on the sofa. Our daughter is in college here in Lexington, at Transylvania, and she stopped coming home. She wouldn't stay in the house, not even for one night. And frankly, we were scared, too. We had to sell."

Beth interrupted, "So you pass it off to my friend here who buys it, thinking that it was just more house than you could manage and that she had found her dream home."

"I'm sorry; we didn't know what else to do."

Leslie was angry because they had not been honest with her before she bought the house, but still she felt sorry for the couple; she could see the strain on faces. And admittedly, she knew had they told her the house was haunted she wouldn't have believed them. "Beth is bringing some people in tomorrow to check out the house for electronics that might be creating what we've seen and heard. And other than that, I just want to know what your experiences were to see if they match with mine. Please, just talk to me."

Patricia and Joel looked at each other. "Let me freshen my drink. Can I get anyone anything, mixed drink, wine or beer?" Both Leslie and Beth declined. Joel Anderson returned with a full glass of scotch and sat down with Patricia on the loveseat opposite the sofa. He looked at his wife. "You start; you probably remember how it all began better than I do."

23

Patricia Anderson asked that Leslie and Beth call her Pat. Most people who knew her did; she liked Pat, and it sounded less formal than Patricia. She liked things to be relaxed. This was how she started explaining what had happened in the house. With such a large house, each person could have his or her own space; a place that was theirs and theirs alone. The study was Joel's office; she had one of the bedrooms upstairs as hers, the kids each had their bedrooms. In addition, the third floor, the turret room, was to be a game room for the children, a place where they could take their friends and watch TV or listen to music and just hang out. This was where everything started, in that room.

They had moved into the house in February. There had been an ice storm and the power all over town was out. They had fun roasting marshmallows and hot dogs in the living room fireplace. The oven was gas but this was more fun, quality family time, huddled around the fireplace telling stories, lighting candles throughout the house. It had seemed like a good omen.

For the first few months there was nothing out of the ordinary. The Anderson family had settled in, unpacked, met the neighbors and started establishing a routine. Then in the early fall, sometime in September, they noticed the first changes. Pat described how the family pets, a small dog and a cat, both of which had the run of the house, began acting oddly. Just as she said this, a long slender Siamese with pale blue eyes strolled through the living room. She arched her back and rubbed against Joel Anderson's leg. She then sniffed the air near Leslie and Beth then turned, as if indicating the strangers weren't worth her attention, then exited the room.

Pat continued, "Our dog and cat wouldn't go up to the third floor. The kids would carry them upstairs, and as soon as they walked in the game room, they would fight to get down and run down the stairs."

"Were they in the habit of going to the third floor?"

"Oh yes. Shelly, our cat, loved to lie in the windows and watch the squirrels in the big sycamore. And Reba, our dog, loved to hang out with Chris when he watched TV."

Joel leaned back in the loveseat; he had begun to relax and let down his guard. "It was maybe about two weeks after that we started hearing noises up there. The first couple times we ignored it. We just thought it was one of the kids. We would ask them about it the next morning; they would both deny having been up during the night."

"I thought one of them was walking in their sleep," Pat added.

Joel continued, "I guess that went on for a couple weeks, then one night there was a lot of noise coming from the third floor. I remember it was a school night, and I had a surgery the next morning, so I got pretty mad that one of them was up making noise, waking up everyone in the house when we all needed to be in bed asleep."

"Joel got up and went up to the third floor; I stayed in bed. I was going to let him handle it."

"That was when I saw it for the first time. It was a girl sitting in the floor, leaning on the windowsill looking out the window. I was sleepy and the lights were out; I thought it was our daughter. I was mad. I yelled for her to get up and get back in bed. When she turned her head, I saw it wasn't Karen. I walked toward her and when I walked in the room she just vanished." Joel looked at his wife. Pat took his hand in hers.

"I saw her too, after that. So did both our children. They were scared. We were scared."

"What about the paranormal investigators? What did they tell you?" Leslie asked.

Pat shook her head. "They really didn't know what to tell us. They said there were some energy readings in the room, but I think those people just hook up a lot of gadgets and find what they want to find."

"What kind of energy?" Leslie asked.

Joel set his empty glass on a stone coaster on the coffee table in front of him. "I don't know. They said a bunch of crap about how spirits who stay in this world and don't move on have energy signals – I don't know. They didn't have any more of a clue about what was going on then we did."

"How much longer did you stay in the house?"

Joel looked at Pat. "Things calmed down for a while during the spring and summer, then they got worse again the next fall. I guess about a year and a half after we first started seeing the girl was when we put the house on the market."

"We were going to stay in it until it sold, but there weren't any offers, and Chris and Karen started having more problems," Pat added.

"How did you find the paranormal investigators?"

"We did some research on the internet and then, working at a university, especially one the size of UK, you meet a lot of people with various interests."

Leslie thought back to her own years in college, and the variety of people she came in contact with. "Yes, I know what you mean."

Beth, who had remained relatively silent, now asked, "Did you ever see this girl or spirit anywhere else in the house?"

"No." Joel answered, "Only on the third floor, in the kid's game room. I guess I should say the turret room. We never got around to finishing it off as a game room."

"Were any of you ever in the room with the spirit, or did she always vanish when you walked in."

Pat looked away and stared at the gas logs in the fireplace. "Once I was up there, when she appeared." Pat continued to watch the blue and yellow flames flicker and dance between the logs. "Our cleaning lady hadn't come that week, and I don't even remember why now, but I went upstairs to the third floor. I bent over and picked up something off the sofa, and when I rose and turned to leave, she was standing there between me and the door."

Beth felt the hairs of her arms stand on end. "What did she do? What did you do?"

"I don't remember exactly, but it was the strangest feeling. I know I screamed. I had seen her before, at night, but this was in the middle of the day. I think I threw what was in my hand, but I don't remember if I threw it at her or just threw it in the air out of reflex. Then I suddenly felt dizzy after that, like I was going to faint. The room was spinning, like when you've had too much to drink and you try to lie down and close your eyes. It was the same sensation."

"What did the girl do?" Leslie asked.

"I'm not sure about that either. I think she walked toward me but everything was spinning, my eyes were playing tricks with me. It felt like the room looked different, so I just ran toward the door. I don't remember much after that."

"I came home and found her lying in the floor of the downstairs bathroom; she had been throwing up and had passed out. It was right after that we closed off the entire third floor. We moved into this house as soon as they could get it ready."

The four had little more to say. The Andersons apologized for not

110

telling Leslie about the house, but as they put it, "Even if we had told you, would you have believed us?" Leslie and Beth bid them good night and then left for Winchester and home.

24

Leslie got behind the wheel of her Mercedes, glad to have control of the car again. Beth sat in the passenger seat and fastened her seatbelt. "So, do you think they are telling the truth?"

Leslie put the car in reverse and turned to look over her shoulder. "I believe they believe what they are saying."

"Well, I guess we'll know more tomorrow when the team arrives to do a sweep of the house."

The two friends stopped for dinner on their way out of town. Sitting in a booth in a dimly lit corner of the restaurant, they developed a plan "A" and a plan "B". In plan A they discover someone has actually wired the house, and they track down the person responsible and "sue their ass," as Beth very bluntly put it, and then have them put in jail. Plan B was more complicated. It involved tracking down some history on the house, its past owners, and discovering the identity of the ghostly girl. Beyond that they were both at a loss.

Beth suggested they start in the attic. While the team searched the house, they could look through the trunks and boxes. Perhaps the information they needed was right there under their noses.

25

When they arrived back at the house, Leslie pulled through the carriage entrance and parked in front of the old stable. "What are you going to do with this building?"

"It used to be the stable, there is still a stall in it and some tack hanging up in the rafters. I thought I might get the tack down and preserve it if it hasn't deteriorated too much, and keep the one half as is, so it looks like a horse stable. This side over here, I would like to take these doors off and put in an electric garage door opener, but I don't know if the building is sturdy enough to handle the torque of the motor."

"So you would have this beautifully preserved stable with a white metal door?"

"No, of course not. I would get one that looks like a real stable door."

Beth smiled, "Just checking." Leslie and Beth entered the house through the back door. Stepping inside the kitchen, Leslie flipped up the light switch. She then paused just inside the door. Beth looked scared. "What are you doing? Is something wrong?"

Leslie's eyes scanned the room. "No, I was just checking to make sure all my dishes were still in the cabinets."

Beth wrinkled her nose and squinted. "What are you talking about?"

"Remember that movie where the little boy sees ghosts and no one believes him, and there is a ghost of a woman who rearranges all the dishes in the kitchen when his mother's back is turned?"

"Yes."

"Well, I was just checking to make sure all my dishes were still in the cabinets."

Beth thought for a second. "You know, under normal circumstances I would say that you have a mental condition. But, given the last twenty-four hours or so, I'll refrain from making value judgments about anything having to do with your transparent houseguest."

"Wait!" Leslie turned quickly and faced Beth, who was still standing in the doorway.

"What? You startled me!"

"You said transparent."

"Yes. Ghosts are transparent aren't they?"

"On TV and movies sometimes, but this girl we saw, was she transparent?"

Beth thought for a moment. She tried to recall the image of the girl running toward her, and when they watched her dance through the studio and stand only a few feet from them. "No, I don't think she was. And remember, it looked like all your art supplies were missing. It looked like not much of anything was in the room."

"Beth, I didn't say anything earlier because I was so dizzy after running into my studio I wasn't quite sure, but I could have sworn I touched her. I know I felt something. What did it look like to you?"

"I can't be sure. As soon as you crossed into the room there was a flash of light, and I couldn't see exactly what happened, but it did look like you at least got close enough to touch her."

"What do you think we should do?"

Beth looked at her watch. It was almost midnight. They had stayed at the restaurant much longer then they realized. "My vote is for going to bed and getting a good night's sleep. It's almost eleven, Chicago time, and these days that is a late night for me."

Leslie put her to-go box in the refrigerator. "Getting responsible in your old age?"

"Preparing myself to take over daddy's companies requires that I get up earlier. And I don't want that shit of a brother of mine getting his hands into anything and ruining it."

"So I take it he hasn't changed."

"Not in the slightest. I think the heir-apparent crap went to his head when we were in our teens, and from there he just developed the attitude that he could do anything with no consequences.

"None of us ever had that issue. First there was nothing to inherit, and if there was, because we were usually living overseas, we were out-of-sight-out-of-mind for the rest of the family."

"Sounds like you had good memories with your grandparents?"

"With them I did, but everyone else always seemed to forget about us, at least the aunts and uncles did, but my cousins were okay." Leslie paused. They were now standing at the foot of the staircase. She looked at Beth then looked up the stairs, which seemed somehow steeper and to lead upward into a dark abyss. Leslie sighed.

"Nervous about going upstairs to bed?"

Leslie hated to admit she was afraid, but Beth was her best friend, and if there was one person with whom she could be open and honest, it was Beth. "A little, I guess. Well, maybe more than a little."

"Me too. How about we both sleep in your room?"

Leslie was relieved Beth had offered. She had thought about it herself but didn't want to appear helpless by asking. "That sounds good to me. So long as you don't hog the covers."

"I do not hog covers!"

"Yes, you do. Remember two years ago, when we all went skiing, and you and I ended up sharing a room in the chalet? All night long you kept jerking the comforter off me."

"Me! What about you? You snored all night long."

"I did not!"

"You most certainly did."

"Well, if I did it was because I was freezing to death and my head was stopped up and my nose was running because of the cold. Besides, we drank a lot of wine, and wine stops up my head a little."

"You snored."

"Not normally I don't."

"How would you know? When was the last time you had anyone sharing your bed long enough to tell you that you snore?"

Leslie made a snorting sound and put her hands on her hips like a gunslinger ready to draw. "It's been a while, but I don't normally snore."

"It's been a while because you snore." With that, Beth let out a playful laugh and bounded up the stairs. Leslie squealed and swung her open hand at Beth's behind in an attempt to slap it. She missed and raced up the stairs behind her friend.

26

Leslie awoke early. It was light out, but fog still blanketed the ground outside. She rolled over and looked at Beth who was still asleep. She let out a soft snore as she inhaled. "Snore my ass. You're the one who snores," Leslie whispered.

Her bedroom was slowly becoming brighter as light shone in through the windows. "I'll need to have custom interior shutters made for the windows," she thought to herself, "then some kind of drapery." Beth stirred and made a loud snorting sound, which caused her to wake herself. Leslie nestled her head down into her thick pillow, so she could look Beth eye-to-eye. "See, you're the one who snores."

Beth rolled over and covered her head. In a muffled voice she asked, "Did you hear anything during the night? Did the ghost show up again?"

"If she did, I slept through it."

Beth rolled over. "Me too. What time is it?"

"Early."

"How early is early?"

"Seven."

"Seven!" Beth replied with a moan. "What on earth possessed you to wake up at seven?"

"I don't know, I just couldn't sleep. My brain starting racing, and I just couldn't stop thinking. The bedroom furniture is coming this morning. The consultants are coming at noon and the mattress and box springs are coming – sometime. We are going to sort through things in the attic. Casper the Friendly Ghost is living in my art studio." Leslie rolled over on her back and stared up at the ceiling. "You know Beth, I've never really believed in ghosts and spirits and stuff like that. I'm not even a religious person. I mean, I'm not an atheist, I don't think, but I'm not sure I believe in God. I've always hoped there is a God. I hate to think that we go through this life with all its problems and hardships and there is nothing more than this."

To her regret, Beth was now more awake. "So what has made you so philosophical this morning? You usually don't talk about religion."

"I know. Like I said, I'm not a religious person, never have been really. The theory of a God or a Supreme Being doesn't seem logical to me. Science is logical; I understand science, not to say that I don't think it isn't a wonderful idea that there is a God watching over all of us. But with this ghost thing, it is really just throwing me for a loop."

Beth fluffed her pillows and propped them against the headboard, so she could sit up and lean against them. "I guess I'm more religious than you. I do believe in God or a Goddess, as some of our friends might prefer. In my opinion, and I'm going to get a little politically correct on you, I don't think we can assign gender to God. Something that powerful probably transcends gender as we understand it. Next, I disagree with the idea that God watches over us. I think that God watches over our soul, not our physical bodies. If I choose to do something risky that could get me killed or hurt then God isn't going to reach a big fat divine hand out and catch me. It's called free will. Just like I think blaming all the bad things in the world on the devil or Satan is a bunch of crap. It's just free will. Do you see where I'm coming from?"

"With the religion part, yes, but I'm not sure I follow where this is going."

"Actually, now that I started talking neither am I, because this is damn seven o'clock in the morning. I guess the point I'm trying to make is this: if this is a ghost, then maybe there is a way to explain it that is logical. People used to think a giant bird swallowed the sun each night, then spit it out in the morning. Then they thought the world was flat, and then they thought the world was round but the sun revolved around the earth. It took time for science to develop explanations."

"Okay, so you are saying that this thing we are calling a ghost might have a scientific, logical explanation, but our science just hasn't developed to the point that we can explain it?"

"Exactly. And now that I've made you feel better and your world isn't going to be shaken to its core, and I'm awake to the point that I won't be able to go back to sleep, you might as well cook breakfast for me."

"I feel like I should hang up a big poster that says, "The truth is out there.""

Beth raised an eyebrow. "You need to watch some newer TV shows and I'm not eating sunflower seeds for breakfast."

Leslie threw back the blankets. "Want to check on my studio? I'll cook eggs, hash-browns and bacon, if you go up there with me."

"Count me in." Beth rubbed the sleep from her eyes. "The things I'll do for a decent breakfast."

The house was cold, so Leslie and Beth put on bathrobes and slid their feet into bedroom slippers. They then, slowly and quietly, made their way up the stairs to the third floor. Leslie was the first to enter her studio. She looked around the room. Everything was as she had left it. Nothing was out of place. "What do you think?"

Beth, who was now looking out the window, replied, "What time did you tell the people at the antique store to deliver your bedroom suite?"

"I just said I'd like to get it before noon if possible. Why?"

"Looks like they just pulled up."

"What?" Leslie walked to the window. "Son-of-a-bitch, I'm not even dressed yet. Who delivers furniture at seven-thirty in the morning?"

"Obviously he does. And do you kiss your mother with that mouth?"

"Why don't you go to the door while I change."

"Hello, I'm in my pajamas, too."

"Yeah, but your hair looks better than mine." At that moment they heard the doorbell chime.

Beth rolled her eyes skyward and grabbed the sleeve of Leslie's robe. "Oh, take a pill. Now come on. This is going to be like Christmas morning and Santa is delivering furniture."

Leslie greeted the men from the antique store, while Beth looked around the kitchen for something for a quick breakfast. Seeing that Leslie was still in her robe and slippers, the oldest of the three men apologized for arriving so early. He explained that the store belonged to his wife, and that the young burly man with a day's growth of beard and a UK cap on his head was his son, and that he wouldn't be available to help later in the day. Leslie thanked them and said, "That's quite alright; early is always better than late." She led the men upstairs, and even though they offered to do the work for no charge, Leslie gave them a considerable tip to move the furniture currently occupying the master suite to the guest room that Beth had used the first night of her visit.

"It's an awfully pretty house you got here ma'am. I love these old ones. The new houses just don't have any personality."

"Oh, I agree. I fell in love with this house the first time I saw it."

"Looks like you're going to need a lot more furniture to fill it up."

"Yes, I have a long way to go."

"Well, my wife and I go to a lot of estate auctions, furniture auctions, and we work with other stores in the state. If you want to work with us and let us help you fill it up or just do a few rooms for you, then maybe we can work out something on the price, too."

Leslie smiled. "I'd like to take you up on that. I think the next thing

I would like to do is concentrate on the parlor and dining room, since anyone who visits will see those rooms before they see anything else."

"I'll tell you what, I'll tell my wife. You know her; you met her yesterday. She could come over here, if that's alright, and look at these rooms and talk to you about what you like. Then she can have a better idea of what to look for."

"That would be great. You have my phone number right?"

"Yep, got it right here." The older man patted the invoice that was sticking out of the pocket of his flannel shirt.

"Just tell her to call first because I'm in and out a lot getting things for the house, and I wouldn't want to miss her."

"I'll do that, and you have a nice day now. And sorry we got you up."

"No problem. Thanks." Leslie closed the door behind the men, and with a slight skip in her walk, she joined Beth in the kitchen. She leaned around Beth, who was standing at the stove, and grabbed a piece of bacon lying on a paper towel between two burners.

"Hey! Wait until it's ready!"

"I just had an attractive offer."

Beth, with a spatula in her right hand, turned around and faced Leslie. "Oh? And what would that be? Don't tell me you've got the hot's for the muscled delivery guy."

Leslie scowled. "Oh, please. The older guy's wife owns the shop, and he said if I furnish the house through them they'll cut me a deal on the prices."

"I think I'd still shop around if I were you. Their deal might not be that good."

"I will, but it would be nice to have them on the look out for things for me."

"True. Are you ready to eat?" Just as Leslie opened her mouth to reply, the otherwise silence of the house was shattered by a distant scream. It startled both women, Leslie dropped the tiny piece of bacon she was still holding between her fingertips, and Beth nearly sent the skillet flying across the stovetop. "Shit, what was that?"

Leslie stood motionless, listening for any other sound. Her voice was a barely audible whisper, "It sounded like it came from inside the house."

Beth nodded her head yes. "Did the Andersons say anything about screams?"

"I don't think so. Do you want to go upstairs?"

"No, but I think we should." Beth turned off the burner, then followed Leslie to the doorway leading into the butler's pantry. She placed her face close to Leslie's ear and in a soft voice asked, "Should we take anything up stairs with us?"

"Like what?"

"I don't know. Do you have a camera? We could take a picture of her as proof."

Leslie turned her head to look at Beth. "My camera is in my studio."

"Then use the camera on your phone." Leslie and Beth walked through the butler's pantry, into the dining room and then the foyer. They paused at the foot of the stairs and waited. There was nothing but silence; everything was still, as if death had settled over the house. They looked at one another, then, in unison, they climbed the stairs to the second floor. Their walk down the long hallway seemed longer than before. Each knew the dread the other felt. They paused only briefly, then ascended the short flight to the third floor.

There they saw her, the apparition of the girl, lying on the floor, her body a crumpled heap. The doll she had danced with the night before was beside her, its arms and legs askew. Leslie pulled her white cotton robe tightly around her body, while Beth stood motionless, neither of them wanting to move forward toward the studio. "Do you think she is dead?" Leslie asked.

"Under normal circumstances I would reply, 'That's a big duh!' But right now I'm too tense to be a smart ass or come back with any quips."

"You know what I mean. Do you think the scream we heard was her dying or being murdered?"

"You mean like she relives the event over and over – forever."

"Something like that, although it sounds too Hollywood; but yeah, I guess so."

"I have no idea." Beth replied. "Wait, she's moving."

"Are you sure?" Leslie asked, as she and Beth literally held their breath, watching for any movement and listening for any sound.

Slowly, the image of the girl stirred. She lifted her torso up off the wood floor; her head still hung down, her bobbed hair covering her face. Leslie and Beth heard a moan. The ghost of the girl was sitting now but appeared dazed. Together they moved closer to the studio doorway. Their ghost raised a hand to her face and pushed her hair away from it, then she lifted her head. "Oh my god!" Leslie exclaimed. "She looks like someone just beat the crap out of her."

The ghost had what appeared to be blood coming from her nose, and a trickle of blood in the left corner of her mouth. Her left cheek was swollen, and she had a black eye. The girl reached for the doll, and picking it up, she held it tightly to her chest. Leslie could now plainly see tears running down the girl's cheeks. "This is terrible. No wonder she is haunting this house."

"I wonder if whoever was beating her eventually killed her here," Beth commented. They continued to watch as the ghostly girl wiped the blood from her mouth and nose, then, still on her knees, she crawled across the floor of the room to pick up a hand mirror lying in the seat of a wooden rocking chair. A rocking chair Leslie had never seen before. "You see that rocking chair?"

"You don't have a rocking chair. And look, we can't see your easel and drawing table."

"I know. Do you think when she appears we see the room the way it looked then?"

"That's the only explanation I can think of. Remember, Pat Anderson said the time the ghost appeared in the room with her, everything looked different."

"I know, I thought about that. Also, if we can see and hear her, I wonder if she can see or hear us. The other day when I yelled at her it seemed like she could."

"Why don't you try it again?"

"What you mean yelling at the top of my lungs?"

"Just call out to her."

"I feel stupid." Leslie paused, took in a deep breath then glanced at Beth. "Here goes." Leslie projected her voice, so that it would carry throughout the third floor. "Hello, little girl, can you hear me? Little girl, I'm here in the hallway. We want to help you." They waited. There was no reaction from the girl. "She can't hear me." Leslie took another step toward the doorway of her studio. A floorboard creaked and popped under her foot. The girl turned and looked directly at them.

"Who's there?" She clutched the doll and the mirror tighter. "Is anyone there?"

"She heard you!" Beth exclaimed. "She heard you when the floor popped! Make the floor creak again." Leslie shifted her weight from one foot to another, trying to make the floor broads sound again but to no avail. "I think she can hear sounds from the house, but she can't hear us."

Leslie, still shifting her weight from one floorboard to another agreed, "You may be right. If I could just get this floor to make some more noise."

Beth watched her friend. "You look like a damn jack rabbit bouncing

121

around. If she could suddenly see us you'd scare her into another dimension."

"Well, that could be one way to get her to 'rest in peace'." Just then Leslie found the right spot in the floor; it made a loud crackle. Leslie and Beth froze in place, waiting for a reaction from the apparition.

"Please, if someone is there..." The ghost asked in a voice that echoed with fear and dread.

"We've made contact!" Beth exclaimed.

"Okay, now what?" Leslie asked her friend. Before she could comment further the door chime rang. "Shit, I wonder who that is?"

"I don't know, but she didn't hear the chime." The door chimed again. "No reaction. See?"

Leslie crossed her arms across her chest. "I have a theory. Maybe this particular door chime isn't original to the house, and she can only hear or react to things that were part of the house when she died."

"Good point, but I think we better get the door; it could be your mattress and box springs." Beth looked at her watch. "Or the security consultants could be early."

"Okay, go ahead; I just want to watch her for another minute."

"Don't try to go in that room without me here."

"After last night, don't worry." Beth turned and walked down the stairs. Leslie lingered for another moment. She watched as the young girl leaned back against the wall in a corner of the room. She also watched as the girl held her doll close to her as if it were the only thing in the world she had to love. Then, as the girl buried her face in her hands and began to sob, there was a flash of light and she was gone.

27

When Leslie reached the foyer, she was surprised to find Barbara Rogers standing in the middle of the room talking to Beth. "Good morning, Leslie. I was just telling your friend Beth that normally I wouldn't call on someone this early in the morning, but I saw the delivery truck and thought I would stop by."

Beth had turned slightly so that Barbara could not see her face. She raised her eyebrows, cocked her head slightly and smiled in a mocking gesture. Leslie saw the expression and tried to suppress a smile of her own. "How have you been Barbara? I'm sorry I haven't been very sociable the last few days, but I've been so busy working on the house."

"Oh, that's quite alright. I just wanted to invite you and Beth here, if she is going to be in town, to a cookout at our house this Saturday. UK is having a big game and we always have at least one cookout during the football season. We invite everyone on the block and a few friends."

"Yes, that would be great. I think Beth will still be here won't you?" Leslie turned to her friend.

Beth smiled. "I wouldn't miss it."

"Is there anything we can bring?"

"I think I have almost everything covered. Jim and I always do the meat and bread, and we're getting a keg of beer." Leslie was surprised Barbara was furnishing beer. She hadn't seemed like the beer type. Jim must have insisted on that for his friends. "Let me think, the Stewarts are bringing a dessert, and so are the Longs. I think everyone else is bringing a covered dish with a vegetable."

"How about some kind of hors d'oeuvre? Something everyone can snack on?"

"That would be great. Now don't go to a lot of trouble, because I know you are still getting settled in and everything."

Beth interrupted, "Don't worry, it won't be any trouble. Leslie here is a great cook when she wants to be."

"Oh really. You certainly are talented aren't you," bubbled Barbara. Leslie narrowed her eyes and looked back at Beth as Barbara continued relaying her plans for the cookout. Then she shifted her attention to the still empty dining room that was visible from the foyer. Barbara craned her neck. "Did you have furniture delivered? I bet you picked out something beautiful."

"I bought a bedroom suite for the master bedroom; bed, dresser, mirror, armoire, night stands. The new mattress and springs should be delivered sometime today. Then I have a security company coming to check out the alarm system."

"My, you do have a busy day today; I'll not hold you up any longer."

"You aren't holding us up Barbara," Beth smiled again and placed her hand lightly on Barbara's shoulder. "Leslie has the antique dealer looking for a dining room suite for her. Hopefully, they will find something before I have to go back to Chicago, and then we can all have dinner together over here."

"Jim and I would love that." Barbara turned to leave, then stopped. "Oh, I just wanted to mention that I appreciate you letting Mark help you around the yard the other day. It isn't necessary to pay him, but he really appreciated it. It is just so refreshing to finally have a pleasant neighbor in this house."

"Thank you Barbara. I appreciate how your family has gone out of their way to make me feel welcome in the neighborhood." With that, Barbara gave both Leslie and Beth broad smiles, then left and headed across the street to her own house.

After closing the front door, Beth turned to see Leslie seated on the bottom step of the staircase, with her head down and her face resting in her hands.

"What's wrong?"

Leslie lifted her head. Beth could see that her eyes were rimmed in red and she looked as if she might cry. "I just feel so bad for that young girl."

"You mean the ghost?"

"Yes. I stood there and watched her after you left. She just sat there with her doll and started crying. I just feel so sorry for her; I want to do something to help her."

Beth sat down beside her friend. "I'm afraid we may be about eighty years too late."

"I know, but it's just so sad to think that this girl was beaten and abused in this house and most likely died right here. She probably had no one to turn to for help. I just wish there was some way we could help, so she could find some peace."

Beth was quiet for a moment and sat staring at the floor. "If all this took place seventy or eighty years ago as we suspect, then whoever was beating her is long dead, so there is no bringing them to justice. I don't know what there is we could do"

"We could find out who she is. Try to find out who did this to her." Leslie's left eye was beginning to tear, and she wiped the moisture away with her fingertip. "I know I can't help her now, at least not physically help her – she's dead. I just really want to know who she was and find out anything we can about her. I'm not really afraid anymore, just sad."

"Where do you want to start?"

"I think we should stick with our original plan, only change the objective. Instead of running off the ghost, we try to help her move on to whatever ghosts move on to."

"You know that might not be possible. That may just be one of those things we see in the movies."

"I know, but I want to try something – anything. I think the plan for today should be to shower, and then I say we hit the attic."

"How about breakfast first, then a shower, then the attic? Actually we should probably pay a visit to the courthouse and identify all the past owners. That way, if we find something significant in any of those old trunks, we won't overlook it."

"We can't do that until after the mattress is delivered and the security team leaves."

"Then breakfast it is." Beth stood up, and extending her hand, with a tug, she pulled Leslie up from the step.

"You really are full of yourself you know. I saw the face you made when Barbara Rogers was talking," Leslie remarked to her friend as they walked down the hallway to the kitchen.

With a mockingly shocked expression Beth replied, "I can't believe you would say that. I was just being friendly to your neighbor."

28

The truck from the department store arrived, and two deliverymen hauled the mattress up the two flights to the master bedroom. It was a perfect fit, and the linens complemented the antique bed perfectly. Still, the large room looked too empty. Beth recommended area rugs and drapery, and then two small chairs and a table to form a sitting area in the rounded turret section of the room. Something in an art deco design was Leslie's preference.

The security consultants arrived on schedule. They did an electronic sweep of the entire house, including the cellar and the old carriage house in the back. They then did a closer examination of the second and third floors. As Leslie and Beth had expected, the team found nothing. As they were leaving, Brad, the supervisor of the group, spoke briefly with Beth. He promised a complete written report of their findings to be on her desk by Monday of the next week. His only additional comment was that, while on the third floor, the studio in particular, they sporadically detected high levels of static electricity. He found no obvious cause for it but made the recommendation that Leslie not hook up sensitive electronics in that room, unless they were well grounded.

29

"I guess that settles it. Your house is clean."

Leslie winced. "Don't say that. A scene from Poltergeist just flashed through my head. And we know how that ended."

"Just don't go watching any snowy TV sets. So, what now? Attic or courthouse?"

Leslie looked at her watch. "We don't have much time, but we might make the courthouse if we hurry. I really want to know who we are looking for."

"Do you know where it is?"

"Not exactly, but it's not like Winchester is that big. Come on, grab your coat and let's go."

At the court house, an elderly woman who worked in the Clerk's office helped them find the books they were looking for. After about forty-five minutes of searching back through the records, they were able to determine the house had four, maybe five, owners after it was sold by the original family. A Mrs. William Miller sold the house in 1952, then, it sold again in 1980 to a Mr. and Mrs. Clarence O'Neil, then again in 1996 to a family named Tharpe, then finally to the Andersons.

Leslie nudged Beth. "I think she wants to go home."

"Who?"

"The old lady that helped us."

Beth looked at her watch. "I guess so. This was just starting to get interesting. I still don't see a record of anyone with the last name Miller buying the house."

"Maybe we just haven't gone back far enough. The original family could have sold it in the 30s or 40s. We're only back to 1950."

"Maybe we need to start with the original owner and work forward," Beth suggested.

"That might be the best way to go." Leslie again looked up at the old woman who now, had her A-frame shaped black leather purse setting on top of her small desk. "Come on, I'll thank her then we can come back tomorrow – maybe." Leslie slipped a small piece of paper from her pocket into the old ledger book to mark her place, then closed the volume. "Thank you ma'am, for helping us. We'll probably be back next week if we can't make it tomorrow."

"That's alright honey, I'm here all the time," the old woman replied. "What is it that you're looking for exactly?"

"I bought an old house on Elm Street, and I've been told it has an interesting history. I'm just trying to find out what I can about the house and who lived there." Leslie paused. "I've always been a history buff."

"You know I used to live near Elm Street years ago. Now we didn't live in one of those big fancy houses, but we had a nice little home. Daddy had a good job with the railroad. We did alright when most other people were having trouble just getting by."

"Really, where did you live?"

The old lady bent slightly, her stiff limbs struggled to pull her wool coat over her shoulders. Seeing her difficulty, Beth quickly moved to help her with the garment. "Thank you, honey," the old woman said as she smiled and patted Beth's hand. "We lived on Birch Street."

"That's just a couple streets over from me."

"Is your house a new one or one of the old ones?"

"It was built in 1887 by, if they told me correctly, Major Nathan Weatherly."

"You bought the old Weatherly place? Oh, I loved that house. I was only in it once when I was a girl. I remember it looked like a castle to me."

"You were in it. Did you know the owners?"

"No, honey. I was just a little girl, but my oldest sister was sweet on one of the Todd boys. Todd? Yes, Todd, I believe that was their last name."

"Todd? I didn't see a record of any Todd's owning the house."

The old woman hung her purse on her forearm and began walking to the door. "Talk to me while I walk up here to the front door. I need to watch for my daughter. She picks me up in the afternoon, you know. Traffic is so busy now; it makes me nervous to drive."

"Yes ma'am. Now you were saying a family named Todd owned the house?"

"That's right. Our mother and daddy would have had themselves a fit if they knew we had gone inside that house. Mr. Todd was a drinker you know. I remember daddy wouldn't let my sister Gracie see the Todd boy anymore. He said no daughter of his was going to associate with a drunk's son. And that they liked to act like they had a lot of money, living in that big house and all, but they didn't have no more than we did."

"Did Mr. Todd have a daughter?"

"I don't think so. I don't remember one anyway. Of course, sometimes these days just because I can't remember something doesn't mean it wasn't so. She could have been older I guess, maybe already married and gone."

"What happened to the Todd family?" Beth asked.

"I don't rightly recall. We moved over to Mount Sterling for a few years, and I lost track of them."

"Would your sister know? I mean, is she still living?"

"Oh, Lord, no; she was a bit older than me. She died a few years ago. Had a stroke and died in her sleep."

"I'm sorry to hear that," Beth interjected.

"That's alright. She had a good life, stayed active right up until the end. I hope that's how I go, so I'm not a burden to anyone."

"Yes ma'am, I think we all want that. Is there anyone else who would know the Todd family, or any of the other past owners for that matter?"

"Well, I'm not real sure. Not too many of us left who remember those days. But you stop by again, and I'll give you my Cousin Jane's phone number. You can call her. She doesn't get around too well any more, but her mind is good and she'd love the company." The old woman leaned closer to Leslie and Beth, as if she were going to share a secret. "Jane always did like to keep up with everyone else's business. Still does." Leslie and Beth smiled when they saw the sparkle in the old woman's eyes. There was something about her that reminded Leslie of her grandmother. Maybe it was just that she was old and friendly.

The two helped her into her daughter's car and promised to pay another visit to the courthouse.

30

Leslie put her car in reverse and backed out of the parking space. "What do you think?"

"About what?"

"About what the old lady told us. You know, I didn't even get her name. Shit!"

Beth smiled, "We can go see her tomorrow. It sounds like she enjoys talking."

"Tomorrow is Wednesday. We really need to spend some time going through those papers in the attic. I wonder if Elsa Van Meter came up with anything for us."

"Give her a call when we get home. And speaking of home, I'm starved. What do you have to eat?"

"Not much. Would you like to eat somewhere or get carry-out?"

"What about that restaurant, Hall's, that you told me about? Is it far from here?"

"No, it's very close actually. We could go to happy hour for a drink and have their famous beer cheese, then order dinner."

"Sounds like a plan. I know you want to get home and start going through the attic, but all those trunks and boxes have been up there this long; they aren't going anywhere in a couple hours."

31

It was almost eight when Leslie and Beth arrived home. The house was dark. They had left in such a rush that Leslie had forgotten to leave on a light. Beth got out of the car and opened the doors to the old stable, so that Leslie could park inside. "I think you should tear this down and build a regular garage."

"I couldn't do that, I hate tearing down old things like this, especially when they are in good condition."

"You need a regular garage." Squinting in the darkness, Beth scanned the back yard as they walked through freshly fallen leaves to the house. "You may have enough yard to build one here on the back of the property."

"I'll figure something out. Right now I'm only worried about finding out who is haunting my house and why."

"I think we know why."

Leslie opened the back door and flipped on the light in the kitchen, then laid her car keys on the counter-top. "I'm going to change into some sweats and get more comfortable. I want to get this bra off. I hate wearing these things."

"You barely need one."

"I'd talk if I were you!"

"I'm not complaining, just commenting. Angie complains that hers get in the way of her golf swing."

Leslie knitted her eyebrows. "I'd never thought about that, but I guess that could happen."

Beth followed Leslie into the foyer. "Here, take my coat and drop it in the bedroom. I'll get us a bottle of wine and a couple of glasses, then meet you upstairs. I want to change, too. Wine is in the butler's panty, right?"

"Yes, it's on the bottom shelf. I'll get some flashlights. We might need them to go through some of those trunks; there is not a lot of light in the attic."

Beth met Leslie on the second floor, bottle and glasses in hand. Leslie took the wine bottle and one glass, leaving Beth with the second flashlight and her own wineglass, which Beth had already filled for herself. Leslie climbed the stairs to the third floor but passed by the attic entrance, walking into her studio instead. She looked around the room, trying to recreate a mental image of it as it had appeared when she and Beth saw the ghost. There had been a chest here, by the window, a rocking chair over here. What else? She couldn't be sure. Leslie had been so caught up in the obvious suffering of the girl. She turned when she heard Beth coming up the stairs.

"I feel better." Beth was wearing sweatpants and an oversized olive-green cardigan.

"You certainly look more comfortable. But I'm surprised Angie hasn't thrown out that sweater."

"This is my favorite sweater. She knows I would never forgive her if she got rid of it." Beth took a sip of her wine. "Was she back?"

"No. I just came in here to look around. Ready to get started?"

"You bet. I feel like I'm being so bad," Beth said with a giggle. "Like I'm sneaking around and going through other people's things."

"I guess, in a way, we are. When I first called you, I just thought of how much fun it would be to rummage through everything. Like you said, it's like we are nosy and sneaking around and going through someone else's things. And it still feels like that, but now it's like I have a mission. Am I making any sense? I feel like I'm babbling."

"You are babbling, but I understand exactly what you mean." As the two women entered the attic, Beth cautioned, "Make sure you prop the door open; I don't want to accidentally get locked in here.

"I will, but I do have my cell phone and the cordless." Leslie pointed to the bulging pockets of her sweatpants.

"You think of everything. Where do you want to start?"

"I was thinking about that a minute ago. When I was up here the other day, I noticed that the boxes and trunks seem to be of varying ages. Like they go from trunks with leather strapping and brass hardware, to an old steamer, to cardboard boxes and so on. And then you have my additions." Leslie pointed to the plastic containers in the corner.

"Ah, Rubbermaid."

"At the courthouse you suggested looking for records of the original owner and working our way forward. Why don't we start with what looks like the oldest trunks and work forward from there."

"Sounds like a good idea to me. So which is the oldest?"

Leslie looked around, both to examine the trunks and determine their approximate age, and for a table to set the wine bottle and glasses. "I don't know. Let's open these two over here." Leslie selected the trunk, which had first caught her eye earlier in the week. Beth shined her flashlight down on the top of the trunk and rubbed the brass plate with her thumb. "Can you read it?" Leslie asked.

"Not very well. Do you have any cleaning rags?"

"Yes, I put some in the hall closet on the second floor and some cleaning supplies, so I wouldn't have to go up and down the stairs all the time to get things." Beth watched as Leslie struggled with the lock. "I think there may also be a screwdriver on one of the shelves in the closet."

"Is it locked or just rusted shut?"

"I don't know. I can't tell."

"Have you looked for a key?"

"You actually think I would find a key after all these years?"

"You never know. Look and see if there are any hooks on the walls, or check the drawers of that old dresser. I'll get some stuff to clean off this nameplate."

Leslie checked the dresser first. She was surprised to find the drawers full of linens. Some were beautifully embroidered, most likely by hand. She knew that girls from wealthy families were often taught embroidery and sometimes drawing. Everything was in good condition. Good enough to use in her own dining room, once she had furniture. Next, she looked around the walls for hooks or nails with keys and spotted a curio sitting in a far corner with its shelves full of glassware and trinkets. She hadn't noticed it the other day.

On the top shelf were two vases made of carnival glass. They looked remarkably like the two her grandmother had kept in her own small china cabinet for years. They had been so beautiful; they always mesmerized Leslie as a child, but she had never dared touch them for fear they might break. The vases were just another one of the little treasures she remembered from her grandparent's house.

"Hello. Earth to Leslie. You look like you were somewhere else."

"I was. My grandmother had two just like these."

"Carnival glass. I love those. You can't buy them any more; too many reproductions on the market. Did you find a key?"

"Not yet. I was just going to look through everything in this curio."

"There was a screwdriver." Beth held it up for Leslie to see. "Why don't we just see if it was stuck before we go on a scavenger hunt?"

Beth slid the tip of the screwdriver blade under the flat plate of the lock and pushed. The locked popped opened. She looked up at Leslie:

133

"Did I ever tell you I was mechanical?"

"Yeah, like a monkey with a hammer."

"I can fix things. When I was a child, I hung out with the gardener and watched him repair things. What about you?"

"I know my way around Lowe's." Leslie was impatient. "Okay, so let's open it."

"Don't you want to see the name on the faceplate first?"

"Sure." Beth scrubbed the brass plate with the damp cleaning rag.

"All I did was wet this with soap and water. I didn't want to use any of the cleaners you had down there. I was afraid they might damage either the plate or the trunk itself."

Leslie leaned over to better see the engraved name. "Elijah Weatherly." Leslie said aloud. "Major Nathan Weatherly built the house. Elijah must be a son or grandson."

"Our first clue – maybe." Beth carefully raised the lid. Lying on top was a uniform or some type. Leslie carefully picked up the plumed hat. "Wow! I think this is from West Point. I remember one of the colonels my father worked for on a base in Germany had a hat a lot like this in his office. He graduated from West Point."

"It would make sense. Major Weatherly builds the house and has a son or grandson named Elijah, who goes off to West Point." Beth gently held up the jacket. "I bet you are right. Look at it."

Leslie touched the buttons and braided cord. "It is in such good condition." They carefully placed the items on the closed truck behind them. "Let's see what else we have." There were several letters tied together in a bundle with a faded red ribbon.

Beth carefully pulled them apart, trying to see the names and addresses. "This handwriting is beautiful. I love the way people used to write." Leslie held the flashlight so Beth could see. "Looks like all of these are addressed to Elijah Weatherly from a Sarah Jane Breathitt."

"There is a Breathitt County in Kentucky, and I believe a hundred years ago or more there may have been a governor by that name."

"If this Elizabeth is from that family, it looks like Major Weatherly was well-connected."

Leslie reached inside the trunk and pulled out more articles of clothing. There was a baby's dress and shoes, child's cap, what looked like a man's tuxedo from the latter part of the nineteenth century, and a walking stick and white gloves. In the bottom of the trunk was a leather portfolio full of photographs, and beside it a second stuffed with papers which appeared to be legal documents.

"Do you want to go through these now or wait until we see what's in the second trunk?" Leslie asked.

Beth thought for a moment. "Let's wait. I want to see what's in this one." She pointed over her shoulder to the trunk behind them.

"Me too. Here, hand me the screwdriver." It took two tries, but Leslie was able to open the latch that sealed the trunk. She looked at Beth and smiled. "Here goes!" The lid was heavy from their seated position, and it took both of them to raise it. "Oh shit, would you look at this!" Leslie's eyes widened as she reached inside the truck and took, by the handle, a long curved saber in a sheath. It was heavy, but perfectly balanced, and the grip was a perfect fit for her hand.

"It's a cavalry sword." Beth spoke up.

Leslie slowly slid the blade from the sheath and turned it in her hand, watching the lights from the dim overhead bulbs reflect off the steel.

"How do you know?"

"The blade is curved. Infantry officers didn't use their swords for battle, just for giving directions and signals to troops. Cavalry soldiers needed curved blades, so that when they hit someone at full gallop the force of the impact wouldn't knock them off their horses."

Leslie narrowed her eyes and looked at her friend. "How do you know this? I'm the army brat and the one who likes history."

Beth shrugged. "It's one of those rich-kid things. My parents sent me to fencing lessons, and the instructor had a fetish for swords. He was always talking about the different types, sizes, what they were used for, you name it. Looking back on it now, I think his sword stories were somehow veiled references to his penis."

"Interesting. The stuff in the trunk, I mean, not the penis stories. Well, I guess that is interesting, too, but in a perverse kind of way. Anyway, I bet this belonged to the Major. Look at this hat. It is a grayish brown color and has C-S-A on the front." Leslie set the hat on top of her own head, then with the sword still in hand, she reached for a confederate officer's jacket that had been neatly folded and was resting under the hat. "Here, hold this." She handed the sword to Beth.

"You are like a kid going through a new toy box."

"This sword is going on the mantel over the fireplace."

"And I suppose you are going to wear the uniform?"

"Only on dates." Leslie laughed and took the jacket from the trunk without unfolding it for fear of damaging the garment. Then, looking deeper into the trunk, she remarked, "Pay dirt – look at this, Beth."

Beth read aloud the words which were written with gold embossed letters. "Isaac Weatherly, Holy Bible. I would say we have a family bible. This could be the key to everything."

In addition to the family Bible, there were a few photographs wrapped in what looked like butcher paper, along with a long roll of papers and a leather portfolio similar to the one found in the first trunk. "Let's start going through this stuff before we start in on anything else."

"I think that would be the best use of our time. We probably have enough here to keep us busy for a day or two." Beth stood up and stretched her arms into the air, making a grunting sound. "We weren't on the floor long, but god I'm stiff." Beth placed her hands in the small of her back and arched her spine. "I think it's time for a snack and another glass of wine."

"Sounds good. Here, you take the bottle and glasses and I'll take the Bible and this stack. I don't want to get the papers and photographs from the two trunks mixed together. There might be something significant there." Leslie secured the sword under her arm. "I'm taking this downstairs, too. We'll probably need to make a second trip."

"I thought you had a dumbwaiter?"

"I do, but I'm not certain how well it works, and I'd freak out if this stuff got stuck between floors."

Beth smiled at her friend and put the portfolio of photographs from the first trunk under her arm, then gathered up their glasses and the nearly empty bottle of Merlot. "Lead the way."

32

"Did you know your house has a name?"

"What?"

"Right here." Beth held the brittle yellow paper out for Leslie to see. "Major Weatherly named the house Wood Hurst. There are several references to it in these papers. And here is his original deed to the land."

Leslie took the papers from Beth. "This is amazing. We're putting together the entire history of this family. I wish I knew as much about my own." Leslie picked up her note pad and recorded the dates from the deed. "Okay, so we know Isaac was the Major's father. We also know the Major bought the land in 1880, but didn't build the house until 1887. In the meantime, his son Elijah goes off to West Point. After he graduates, he comes back to Winchester and marries Sarah Jane Breathitt; he does a stint in the army and they have three children. A son, Clay is the eldest, then two daughters, Rebecca and Constance."

"Do you think the ghost could be either Rebecca or Constance?" Beth asked.

"From what you said, the clothes on the ghost look like the 1920s. Rebecca and Constance would be too old." Leslie picked up the family Bible and turned to the center, where she had found a beautifully printed page, adorned in gold leaf. "Here it says Constance, who was the youngest, died in October 1918 and Clay died in September of that same year."

Beth leaned over Leslie's shoulder. "Does it say what they died from?"

"Not here, but I bet there is something in some of these papers. We still have that other stack to sort through."

"Why don't we save it for tomorrow morning. My eyes are starting to cross." Beth looked at her watch. "No wonder, it's almost midnight! I didn't realize it was so late."

"Me either, but I want to look at some of the old photographs again."

Beth lay backward and stretched her body across the floor, crossing her arms over her face to shield her eyes from the light of the chandelier overhead. "That's it. I'm on strike. You're going to have to carry me up the stairs. I can't get off the floor."

"That's why I'm not going to lie down, because I know, physically, I'll just crash." Leslie pulled a bundle of photographs from a leather pouch. "Here, look at these. See this man in the uniform. I bet that is Clay Weatherly in his World War I uniform. And this one is definitely the same man, only younger. He is in a West Point cadet's uniform."

Grudgingly, Beth uncovered her eyes and sat up. "It would appear that all the men in the family went to the Point and had military careers before doing whatever it is they did. Have we figured out how they made their money?"

"No, I want you to figure that one out from these." Leslie tossed a stack of papers in Beth's lap.

"No. No more tonight. I'm too tired to think."

"Alright. We'll work on this more tomorrow, but I'm so hyped up right now I don't know if I can sleep."

"Trust me, you'll sleep, even if I have to knock you in the head with a mallet."

33

Sleep came quickly for Leslie, but it was restless. Dark dreams full of foreboding filled her subconscious. She saw herself struggling against shadowy figures whose faces could not be seen. She saw men in uniform and herself on horseback with the long saber in her hand, but the shadowy figures clawed at her and pulled her from the back of her mount. Leslie awoke in a sweat; she was cold and her limbs trembled. She thought about going into the guest bedroom and climbing in bed with Beth, but she decided against the idea. Beth could probably only stay a few more days. Then what would she do, alone at night with terrifying nightmares? Leslie looked at the clock radio on the nightstand. It was almost half past six. It would be light soon. She closed her eyes and drifted off to sleep.

34

For the next two days Leslie and Beth sorted through old letters, photographs and a variety of documents, all from her attic. They began to construct a family tree of the Weatherly family. Through one letter, they were even able to identify the Major's grandparents. They now had a wealth of information, but felt they were no closer to learning the identity of the ghost in Leslie's studio. Several times they heard her, but by the time they reached the third floor, all they saw was the same flash of light that occurred each time she vanished.

On Friday, they both decided they needed a break and spent the day sightseeing around Lexington. Leslie knew Beth had already been away too long. Beth's calls to the office were becoming more and more frequent. Leslie wanted a breakthrough in their search for answers before her friend returned to Chicago, when she would be left to deal with this alone.

* * *

Leslie awoke to the sound of the door chime. She grabbed her bathrobe from the foot of the bed, slid her feet into her slippers, and headed down the stairs as quickly as possible. She looked through the glass side panels of the front door and was surprised to see Mark Rogers.

She opened to door to great him. "Mark, good morning. What are you doing here?"

Mark looked at Leslie's robe. "Did I get you up?"

"Sort of, but I was almost awake anyway. I haven't slept well the last few nights." Leslie opened the door wider and stepped aside so Mark could enter.

"Did it keep you up last night?"

"It?" For a moment Leslie was confused; she didn't understand what Mark was asking. "Oh. The ghost."

"So you believe it's a ghost?" Mark asked.

"I never thought I would say this, but I don't see any other logical explanation."

"I saw Chris last night. Chris, the Andersons' son." Leslie nodded in acknowledgment. "He said you stopped by the other day to see his parents. And that you were going to try to figure out who the ghost is."

"His parents must have told him about my conversation with them because he wasn't home when I was there," Leslie said.

"He said they did. They hadn't wanted him there because they didn't know what talking to you was going to be like."

"I see." Leslie rubbed her eyes and yawned. "So, that doesn't answer my original question. Not that I'm trying to be rude, or that I'm not glad to see you, but what brings you over here this early?"

"You know that cookout is today?"

"Oh shit! I forgot about that. Today is Saturday; I've lost track of what day it is."

"I've got to help Dad make sure the yard is ready. You know, get the grill set up, set up lawn chairs, that kind of stuff. But I just wanted to tell you I'd like to help you find out who the ghost is."

"Not that I don't appreciate it, but why the interest in helping?"

Mark lowered his head and stared down at his scuffed and worn sneakers. "You know the other day when we were talking about the ghost?"

"Yes."

Mark looked up and at Leslie. "The times I saw her, it scared the crap out of me. I told Mom and Dad about it, and they went ballistic. They didn't believe me; they still don't." Mark paused. "There was another time, too, that I didn't tell you about. This one time, she was real close to the door and I could see her face. I could see how sad and alone she was. It was like I could feel it." Mark rubbed his arms, and Leslie noticed the goose bumps that had popped up. "I guess it's like I feel sorry for her, you know."

"Yes, I know. So do I, and I want to find a way to help her if that's possible. But maybe those kinds of things only happen in the movies."

"Hello there." Leslie turned to the sound of Beth's voice. "I would bet money you are Mark."

"Yes, I live across the street."

"Leslie has told me about you."

"Mark, this is Beth. She is from Chicago and probably my dearest friend. The other day I had the crap scared out of me too, so when I called Beth, she took the first available flight and came down to baby-sit me."

"Are you trying to help figure out who the ghost is?"

141

"Yes, and we're making a little progress." Beth looked at Leslie. Aren't we?"

"Would you like to see what we are doing?" Leslie offered. "Maybe you would know some people we could talk with about the families who lived here before the Andersons."

"I don't know, but yeah, sure." Leslie and Beth led Mark into the study where they had spread out the stacks of papers from three of the trunks they had opened. "Wow. What's all of this?"

Leslie walked around the papers. "Here we have deeds, letters, bank drafts, business correspondence and some other miscellaneous documents, all belonging to Major Nathan Weatherly. He was the man who built the house in 1887." Beth walked to the next pile of documents. "These belonged to his son Elijah." She pointed to the last stack. "These we haven't gone through yet, but they belonged to Elijah's son Clay." Mark listened intently.

"Do you have any ideas?" Leslie asked.

"I don't know. I would have to read through everything. Maybe the girl was a servant that they beat and didn't feed."

Leslie and Beth looked at each other. "Actually, that is a good idea. We hadn't thought about that. We just assumed it would be a member of the family," Leslie said. "But from what we've seen, that might make sense."

"Why, what else have you seen?" Mark asked.

"The other day, when she appeared, I could see blood coming from the girl's nose and mouth, and she had a black eye."

Mark winced.

"And she sat in the floor with a doll and cried." Beth added.

"That was what I saw the first time. That, and then it looked like someone hit her, but I couldn't see another ghost in the room."

"Perhaps only the abused girl is haunting the room, acting out the events that led up to her death. Maybe the person who did the abusing isn't haunting the house. That would explain why we can't see their spirit."

"My girlfriend Jamie works at *The Winchester Sun* a couple afternoons a week. She could look back through the archives and see if there were reports of any murders of young girls."

"Since this was a wealthy family, then the death of the girl may not have been reported as a murder." Beth reminded them. "It may have been accepted as some sort of accident or sudden illness. And if she were a servant girl, then they could have dumped the body somewhere and explained the disappearance as a runaway."

Mark knitted his brow. "During what time period do you think all this happened?"

"We are guessing the 1920s, because of the clothes the girl is wearing, but we might be off there. You still want to help?" Leslie asked.

"Yeah. I'll talk to Jamie. She'll help me look through the archives at the newspaper."

"You may not need to do that. We still have several stacks of papers and letters to sort through."

"Can I come over tomorrow and help?"

"Sure. Just give me time to wake up."

"Sorry about that. I just didn't think I'd get a chance to talk to you at the cookout, without someone listening in." Leslie showed Mark to the door and then locked it behind him.

"Hopefully, we won't get any more visitors this morning. I need to put an intercom system in, so that I don't have to rush down the stairs every time the doorbell rings."

"I think that would be an excellent idea. I have a suggestion. Why don't you take a shower while I sort through some more of these papers, then I'll take one."

While Leslie showered, Beth found what she considered a gold mine of information. Constance, the youngest of Elijah's three children, died of influenza. There was an obituary clipped from a newspaper, and a lock of soft auburn hair; its strands were held together with ribbon, then wrapped in a tiny silk handkerchief and tucked neatly into a small cedar box.

Beth began remembering some of the history she had learned as a child. There had been a large outbreak of influenza all across Europe and the United States near the end of World War I. It had killed hundreds of thousands. She remembered her grandmother had talked about an aunt and two cousins who had died of influenza before she was born, and that Beth's great-grandmother had nearly died herself.

Then she found a letter from the War Department, addressed to Mrs. Elizabeth Weatherly. Carefully, she opened the yellowed, fragile envelope. In it she read:

Mrs. Weatherly,

It is with great sadness that we inform you of the death of your husband Captain Clay Weatherly, U.S. Army Company A 132d Infantry, 33d Division. Bois de-Forges, France, 26 September, 1918. Your husband showed conspicuous gallantry in action by rushing across fifty yards of open ground, directly into the face of hostile machine-gun fire, and with a grenade he killed the crew of a machine-gun nest before being killed himself. Captain Weatherly enabled his line to advance and saved the lives of many of his men and fellow officers. It was an honor to have served with him.

Sincerely,
Colonel Henry Ryffel

"So now we know what happened to Clay." She said aloud to the empty room. "But that still doesn't tell us who you are, our little ghost."

Beth's hand jerked, and she nearly tore a corner from the letter, when she heard Leslie cry out.

"Beth hurry! Help!" Beth sent a stack of papers sliding across the slick wood floor, as she scrambled to her feet. She grabbed the heavy oak banister and took the stairs two at a time. As she reached the second floor, her left ankle twisted and she fell hard on her knee. Through the pain, half crawling, she fought to regain her footing. Again she broke into full stride as she raced down the hallway of the second floor.

"Beth!" She heard Leslie cry out again. Beth bounded up the last flight of stairs to the third floor falling as she reached the top step, her ankle failing her again. Beth lay in the floor of the short hallway, her arm outstretched reaching for her best friend.

"Leslie!" She screamed out. "Get out of there!"

Beth felt helpless as she watched Leslie's studio change before her eyes. One moment she could see her friend's easels, canvases and drawing table. Then, in an instant she could see the room as it appeared a few days before, nearly empty, with the only furnishings visible from the door — an old rocking chair, a small trunk and a doll lying in the floor. Then she saw the girl. The apparition moved toward Leslie with an outstretched hand.

"Leslie, my ankle, I can't... Hurry, get out!"

Inside the room, Leslie's head was spinning. No matter what direction she turned, the room appeared to swirl within itself. She held to the corner of her drawing table to steady herself. She could feel the table under her hand, see her knuckles turn white from the pressure of her grip, but in the same instant it would vanish from her view.

"Beth, help me! What's happening?!"

"Are you an angel?" a small voice asked. Leslie backed away from the voice and stumbled, and she fell to her knees. "Did you come to help me? Did Mama send you?" Leslie felt a small hand touch her arm. Leslie looked up and into the clear blue eyes of a young girl, the same girl she and Beth had watched cry and cradle a little doll.

"I want to help you." Leslie said as she extended her hand. "I want to help you get free of whoever is hurting you." She saw the corner of the girl's lip turn upward slightly as if a smile was beginning to form. Suddenly Leslie gasped. She felt the warm, soft palm of the girl's hand in her own. The flesh wasn't transparent, it wasn't cold – it was as warm and real as her own. "How can I help you?" Leslie asked, just as the girl vanished in a flash of light.

Leslie collapsed on the floor beside her drawing table. Beth, limping from the pain in her ankle, was at her side. She knelt down and pulled Leslie to her, cradling her in her arms. "Are you alright? Talk to me! Are you alright?"

Leslie began to cough. "I feel sick." Leslie breathed in gulps up air, then gagged.

"Come on. Can you make it to the bathroom?" Leslie tried to stand, but she was still too disoriented.

"Air. Fresh air."

Beth, half dragging not only Leslie but herself as well, helped her friend to the window. Unlatching one of the windows, she opened it wide and pulled Leslie to it.

"Did you see? Did you see?" Leslie asked in between taking in large breaths of air and coughing.

"I saw it. I saw both of you in here together. What happened?"

"I got dressed and was going to come downstairs, but I came up here instead to get another note pad and some highlighters." Leslie coughed and gagged again, then she took another deep breath. "I picked up my pencil off the drawing table, and I started feeling lightheaded and a little dizzy. I looked up and the room was changing, it was flashing back and forth. One second it looked like my studio, the next it had a few pieces of old bedroom furniture in it."

"Was the girl in here when that started happening?"

"I don't know; I'm not sure. She was appearing in flashes, too. It reminded me of a TV screen, when a satellite dish is losing the signal and picking it up again. She wasn't in here when I walked into the room. Of that much I'm certain." Leslie paused for a moment. "Beth, she could hear me and see me. She touched me; I could feel her hand. Her skin was warm. Beth, she was real. And the weirdest thing is, when she first saw me, I think I scared her."

"What do you mean?"

"Well, she jumped like she had been startled and stood behind a rocker that was sitting over there." Leslie pointed in the direction of where she saw the rocking chair materialize along with the apparition of the girl. "That was when I yelled for you. Then she spoke to me. She asked who I was and where I came from, and was I an angel sent by her mother. Did you see her touch me?"

"I did. I saw it. It scared the hell out of me, too. I thought I was going to have to start yelling for you to come away from the light. I thought she was going to take you with her." Beth laughed, but the sound was mixed with tears of both worry and relief. "Let's get out of here before she comes back."

"Beth, I know we can help her. We have to be able to help her; she was so real."

"I know. We'll figure it out. Now come on, let's go." As Beth stood, she winced with pain.

"What happened?"

"I twisted my ankle and banged my knee when I was running up the stairs."

"How bad is it?"

"I don't think I did any major damage. It should loosen up in a few minutes. I sprained it in college playing field hockey, and it has been weak ever since."

"You never told me you were a jock."

"I wasn't much of a jock. Now let's get out of here." Leslie and Beth both struggled to get to their feet. Leslie's head still spun when she made any quick movements, and Beth's ankle ached with each step. Once downstairs, they wrapped Beth's ankle in a cold pack, and Leslie took a Dramamine and chased it with diet ginger ale. Leslie described her experiences in detail, while Beth sat on the sofa with her foot elevated.

After a while, Leslie's head began to clear and the pain in Beth's ankle subsided. Beth instructed Leslie to bring the letter, news clipping and cedar box. Leslie read the letter from the Army, which had been addressed to Clay's wife, the obituary and then checked the family Bible again. There were no entries for children belonging to Clay and Elizabeth. "You know this doesn't mean they didn't have children. It just means there are no entries for them," Beth reminded her. "In many cases there is one person in the family who is rather diligent about keeping track of those things. Then, when they die, the family information is never recorded again."

"Do you know anything about your family?" Leslie asked.

"A little. My grandmother traced our family to Ireland about seven generations back, and I know the family stories she told me from when she was young. I know who came from Ireland and when, but not much more than that. Oh, and there were some shady dealings during Prohibition that helped establish the family fortune, but if there is anyone still alive who knows that story they aren't talking. What about you?"

"Not much about the Newkirk side of the family. I do know I had a great-great-great-grandmother who smoked a clay pipe. Everyone called her Granny Pop."

Beth smiled. "How did she get the name Granny Pop?"

"I have no idea. All I know about her is what my grandmother told me. She said Granny Pop worked as a housekeeper. She had three children, one of which was my great-great-grandfather."

"Granny Pop. That's a neat name for an old lady."

"Yeah. Come on, let's get back to work on these papers. We don't have a lot of time left before that cookout."

"Actually, dear, we need to get busy in the kitchen so we will have something to take to the party."

Leslie groaned. "I forgot all about that. What did I tell her we would cook?"

"I don't think you gave her any specifics. I believe we just said finger food."

"I think I have all the ingredients for spinach and artichoke dip. And that won't take long to prepare."

"Good idea. I'll help."

"No, just sit here and keep your foot up. I feel bad enough about you spraining your ankle."

"Like I said, it is no big deal. And on the bright side, it keeps me out of the kitchen. Now go get me a stack of papers, woman, and get your butt in that kitchen and start cooking."

Leslie raised her left eyebrow. "Do you talk to Angie like this?"

"Are you kidding? Now go get busy. I'll sit here and read these, and then when you finish in the kitchen, you can help me limp up the stairs so I can shower."

"Do you want me to help you up there now?"

"No. To be completely honest with you, I'm as eager to find out who Casper the Friendly Ghost is as you are."

"Then I have an idea. Let me help you move into the kitchen and you can read through some of this stuff while I make the dip."

"Most excellent idea!"

35

Beth read aloud from letters Elizabeth and Clay had written to one another while he was in France. He wrote of the terrible conditions in the trenches, and how his men were cold and fatigued from battle, and he wrote of his longing for home and Elizabeth. In one letter, Elizabeth spoke of their unborn child, and that she hoped that if it were a son, he would be brave and strong like his father.

Leslie turned away from the counter-top, where she had been busy slicing artichoke hearts into small pieces. "Those letters are so loving. It just makes it that much more sad knowing he was going to die just a couple months after most of those were written."

"I know. Wars are like little boys fighting on the playground, but on a larger, more deadly and tragic scale. I honestly believe that if this world were controlled by women, there would be no more wars and we could turn this planet into the paradise it was meant to be."

Leslie looked at Beth, a bit dismissive. "We now know Clay and Elizabeth had a child, and Elizabeth would have given birth in 1918, based on the dates on the letters. Now we can look for birth records from 1918."

"If the ghost was their child," Beth reminded her. "It could be the child of Clay's other sister or a servant girl. We still have two more boxes of things to sort through. We may not need to look up birth records."

"True. But at this point, my money is on her being the child of Clay and Elizabeth."

"Okay. Let's say it is their daughter, assuming they had a daughter, so who is beating her up? We know it can't be Clay. He was long dead by the time she would have been as old as we think."

"Maybe it was the grandfather or some other relative."

"Maybe it was the mother."

"I doubt it. I know women slap children around, too, but I doubt it was the mother. You saw the bruises on her face and the blood. Whoever hit her had some strength behind their punch, and when she shielded herself from one of the blows, she was looking up like this." Leslie demonstrated by holding her arm above her head as if shielding her face and head from a blow being delivered from far above.

"The ghost is a child; of course, Elizabeth would have been taller."

"I would bet not that much taller," Leslie said as she stirred the dip.

"Elizabeth could have been a big ol' Amazon."

"Then we need to find a photo of Elizabeth. The other thing that makes me think it wasn't the mother – and again I'm making assumptions that the parents were Clay and Elizabeth – is because the girl asked me if I was an angel sent by her mother."

Beth thought for a moment. "How many cemeteries does Winchester have?"

"I have no idea, probably several. And I'm sure there are small family cemeteries outside town. Why?"

"I wonder if the Weatherly family has a family plot somewhere."

Leslie's eyes widened. "I never thought of that. There could be a headstone for every one of these people. You're a genius."

Beth arched her back and sat straighter in her chair, then elevated her chin slightly. "That, darling, is why you called me. Now, help me hobble up the stairs. I don't want to overdo it on this ankle just yet, and I need to take a shower so we can go meet all your lovely neighbors."

Leslie looked at her wristwatch and frowned. "We only have about thirty minutes. But we don't need to be exactly on time."

"That's right. Always better to make a fabulous entrance."

Leslie, who was now standing beside Beth and providing support, cast a sideways glance at her friend. "Oh yeah, I can see it now. We'll walk in together, and Barbara Rogers will introduce me as the artist across the street and you as my friend from Chicago. Then I'll shake hands with people and someone will ask what I do besides art and I'll say, 'I'm Leslie, and I see dead people.'"

"We see dead people, and it could be worse. I might not have flown down right away, and then you would have to go to the party alone."

"If you hadn't flown down right away, I might have the house on the market and be living in an apartment by now."

Beth smiled as she limped out of the kitchen. "No, you wouldn't; you're too tough for that. And as much as I miss you, had I been in your shoes, I would have moved back here, too."

"You don't think I made a mistake?"

"Only you can make that determination. Do you feel like you have made a mistake?"

"I don't know. I didn't grow up here. I didn't grow up anywhere, but I also grew up everywhere. Chicago didn't feel like home and I don't know if Winchester will either."

"After we get through all of this you should call your cousins. Just based on my personal experience, brothers and sisters can be great if you're lucky. Yours are okay. My brother happens to be a lazy jerk. Cousins, on the other hand, can be a perfect blend of friend and family."

"What do you mean?"

Beth explained, as she carefully negotiated the stairs, "You don't have the conflicts with cousins that you have with siblings, but you can still have the closeness. You can have a friendship and the bond of being connected by family."

Leslie helped Beth into her room. "Do you need some help getting in the shower?"

"No, it's feeling better already. I think the ice helped. Now the hot shower will probably do wonders."

"I feel so bad about that."

"Leslie, it wasn't your fault. I was the clumsy one who fell up the stairs."

"Yeah, you fell running to my rescue."

"Just don't go getting sucked into the spirit world again, okay. If you disappeared and we were the only two people in the house, I don't know how I would explain that one. It might take all of Dad's lawyers to get me out of it."

Leslie made certain Beth could manage without her help, then went to her own room. The heavy wood furniture she had purchased two days earlier still looked foreign to her, even though a couple of the pieces closely resembled those that had belonged to her grandmother. She ran her fingers across the top of the dresser. There were small dents and nicks in the surface from years of use. "I need a mix," she said aloud to herself. "I need a mix of antiques and modern pieces." She knew she wouldn't be happy with a home filled with only antiques.

Leslie stepped out of her room and into the long, wide hallway. She could hear water from the shower. Beth had left her bedroom door open. Leslie looked inside the room then stepped back into the hallway. "Hello," she said to herself. Her voice echoed back. With swift strides, she walked the few steps to the third story staircase, then with her hand gripping the stair rail, she quickly climbed the stairs.

She paused outside her studio for only a moment, then went inside. "Beth was right. I am too tough." Leslie walked around the room. "I'm here. I came back to help you. Please come back so I can. I know someone is hurting you, and I want to make them stop. I want you to find some peace after all these years." Leslie waited – nothing. She exhaled in a sigh, then sat down at her drawing table and began to sketch what she could remember about the room as it had appeared earlier. She began to sketch the girl's face. It had an oval shape, of that much she was certain. The cheekbones had been high, or had they? The chin, she couldn't remember the chin.

"Who are you?" The voice asked. Leslie jumped back, nearly knocking over her chair. It was the girl! She had returned.

"Did my mama send you to look after me?" Leslie said nothing. She tried to speak, but the words wouldn't form in her mouth.

"What's this?" The girl looked at the drawing table. "Sometimes I can see it, sometimes I can't. Mr. Todd says I'm crazy, and he's going to send me to the crazy house in Lexington and lock me up forever."

Leslie stuttered, "You...you aren't crazy. I'm real and, and I...I want to help you." The girl approached Leslie, and Leslie took one step backward. She remembered Beth's caution about being sucked into the spirit world. She didn't know if that could happen, but a week ago had anyone told her that she would be standing in her own home chatting with a ghost, she would have thought them completely insane.

"Who is Mr. Todd?"

"He married my mama after Daddy died in the war." Leslie watched as the girl picked up her drawing and examined it. "Is this going to be me?" The girl looked up and smiled. The blue in her eyes reminded Leslie of the sparking clear water of the Caribbean.

"What's your name?"

The girl quickly turned and ran to the door of the studio to listen. "It's Mr. Todd! He's been out drinking, and he's coming up the stairs." The girl looked panicked. She raced around the room, as if looking for a place to hide. She appeared to no longer be aware of Leslie's presence. Leslie then turned and watched as the girl fumbled with a ceramic tile on the front of the fireplace. The girl's back was now toward Leslie, so she couldn't see what she was doing. The girl then ran for the studio door and vanished.

Leslie saw light flash, and for a moment, she lost her balance and nearly fell. She felt nauseated, but it was not like before. Sitting down in the chair, she closed her eyes and took long slow breaths until the nausea passed.

36

When she opened her eyes, everything about the room was as it should be. Her easels, her brushes, the few odd canvases she had stacked against the wall were all in place. Leslie's first impulse was to run to Beth, but instead, she grabbed her sketchpad and began writing down, word-for-word, what the girl had told her. "Mr. Todd married mama after Daddy was killed in the war," Leslie repeated to herself as she wrote. "There, I think that's everything. Beth, I've got to tell Beth." Leslie quickly walked to the door. She turned to survey the room one last time, then went down to the second floor.

Leslie burst into Beth's room. "Beth! It happened again!"

"Shit! You scared me. What happened?"

"I was in my studio and she came back. I was sitting at the drawing table sketching and poof! She was there, just standing there and she asked me my name."

"You shouldn't have gone in there alone. What if something had happened? I wouldn't have known until it was too late."

"I know, you're right, but I had only intended to be in there a second. Then I started sketching. I couldn't have been in the studio more than five minutes, tops."

"It didn't make you sick this time?"

"A little at first. Right now my head feels a little swimmy, like I had maybe one too many glasses of wine, but other than that I'm fine. Here, read this." Leslie handed Beth the page she had torn from her sketchpad.

"What's this?"

"I wrote down what she said while it was still fresh in my head. I didn't want to forget anything."

"So it was a stepfather that was beating her up."

"That's what it sounds like to me. In the papers we brought down from the attic did you see any reference to a man named Todd?"

"No, nothing, and there were no records of a Todd on any of the deeds for the sale of the house. The last one we found was that Mrs. Miller."

"Let's go to the cemetery!"

"What about your neighbor's cookout?" Leslie, with her arms crossed, stood silent in front of Beth. "Well?" Beth asked again.

"I'm thinking. We could not go and blame it on your ankle."

"I also have a nice little knot on my knee. I'm not going to run any marathons anytime soon, but otherwise my ankle is fine." Beth narrowed her eyes. "I think we should go. It might be fun. And the tombstones aren't going anywhere."

"You just want to get the neighbors going."

Beth looked at her watch. "Honestly, I think we would make better use of our time if we called ahead and had the caretaker locate the family plot for us, then we could enjoy ourselves at the party, and this evening drink wine in front of the fire while we sort through more documents. Then, tomorrow, we'll have all day to walk around the cemetery if needed."

"You're probably right. But I am just so psyched. I feel like we are a step closer to finding out who this girl is and helping her."

"Leslie, let's be realistic. I think it would be safe to say that the world, as you and I had always understood it to be, has changed in the last few days. Or our perceptions of it have changed. Now, we suddenly discover that haunted houses really do exist and you are the proud new owner of a one-hundred-plus year-old house with a resident benevolent spirit. We are both trying to get a mental grip on this, and we both have been affected by seeing the suffering this girl endured, but logically, what can we do? She is dead."

"She obviously doesn't know she is dead."

"Maybe we should just tell her. You know it could be just as simple as: 'Excuse me Miss, but did you know you died about seventy years ago?'"

"Okay, and what if that just pisses her off, and then she turns into a poltergeist or something?" Leslie sat down on the edge of the bed beside Beth. "There has to be an answer. We could figure out how to help other spirits who are trapped between worlds and can't move on."

"You mean start a franchise?"

"No, smart-ass. Publish our information on the internet for other people to use."

Beth bent her head down slightly and rubbed her eyes. "Why do I suddenly feel like I'm acting out a B-movie, and I'm a twisted cross between Miss Cleo and the pet psychic." Beth lifted her head. "Give me a minute to mentally digest all this. But for now, promise me you will not go back into that room alone!"

"I promise. I guess we'd better get going," Leslie said, resigning herself to attending the cookout.

37

The cookout was uneventful. As predicted, Barbara Rogers introduced Leslie as her artist neighbor who bought the big Victorian mansion across the street. And just as Barbara Rogers had been surprised, so was everyone else when they learned there was no Mr. Newkirk and Leslie had made her money herself. Several of the men at the party asked for stock tips. Leslie deferred them to Beth, explaining she was the real business person. They were even more impressed, and some obviously a little intimidated to find that Beth was set to take over leadership one of the largest privately held companies in the Midwest.

Leslie enjoyed watching Beth. Beth had always known how to work a crowd. Leslie was slightly introverted in social settings, and she always assumed the ease with which Beth operated in group settings must be one of those skills automatically acquired from old money. While Beth captivated the other guests, Leslie managed to slip away from the crowd for a minute to speak with Mark. She told him that she had spoken with the ghost of the girl, and if he wanted, he could stop by the house tomorrow and she would tell him more.

Mark was shocked and a little unnerved. He told Leslie that the Andersons had never spoken with the ghost. "Perhaps they didn't try," was Leslie's reply. Leslie also asked Mark if he knew anyone in Winchester with the last name Todd. He told her Todd was a common last name in the area. "Mary Todd Lincoln and her family were from Lexington, Kentucky," Mark answered. It was obvious he was of proud of himself for knowing that bit of history.

Leslie and Beth bade their hosts and the other guests adieu after the Wildcats scored a last minute touchdown and clinched a victory. All the men and boys were giving each over high fives and telling each other the tide had turned. This would be the year.

Once across the street and locked inside her home, Leslie moved many of the papers and photographs into the parlor, then started a fire in the fireplace while Beth opened a bottle of her favorite Merlot and poured two glasses.

Only a handful of the photographs had names and dates recorded on their backs. But from those they were able to construct a crude family tree. They carefully examined the faces in each photograph, and they were confident they had accurately identified photographs of most of the Weatherly family members from childhood through old age, at least for those who lived into old age. Identifying the Major was easy. He had been photographed more than once in his Confederate uniform, and then again with his wife Harrietta.

Likewise, they were quickly able to determine which photographs were of Clay Weatherly. There were several of him as a child and of him as a young boy in knickers. They also found photos of him as a West Point Cadet and then in his World War I officer's uniform. He had been a handsome young man, and the girl specter haunting Leslie's studio bore a striking resemblance. There was also a large photograph that had been tinted with splashes of color, of Clay and Elizabeth, on what was probably their wedding day. In one of the trunks, they found a small silver baby's spoon, dated 1918, a photo of an infant, and a baby's dress and tiny bonnet. "I bet this belonged to Clay and Elizabeth's daughter," Leslie commented.

"Probably. We seem to have made some significant progress identifying everyone else and some of their belongings."

"I was just thinking about something."

"What's that?"

"The old lady at the Courthouse. She said Mr. Todd was a drinker and apparently her parents had very little respect for him."

"Correct. She also said he had two sons. I wonder if either of them is still alive."

"I would bet there is a good chance that at least one of them is."

"Do you think Elsa Van Meter would know?"

"She might. After all, she is probably the unofficial historian of Clark County."

"Did you get the caretaker of the cemetery on the phone?" Beth asked.

"Yes, I did. He said he knew the Weatherly family had their own plot because it was one of the older ones, and naturally, it was in the oldest section. He promised to meet us tomorrow around noon."

"He didn't mind going in on a Sunday?"

"No, he said he had to be there anyway for a graveside service at two."

Beth watched the flames dance around the logs like a dervish in a fiery robe. "I have been piecing a scenario together in my head about what could have happened in this family."

"So have I."

Beth continued to watch the flames. "You go first."

"I think Clay and Elizabeth married, and Elizabeth was pregnant when he was shipped off to Europe to fight in the war."

"I'll agree with that. And I think it is pretty safe to say that he was probably killed just before their child, whom we think is the girl upstairs, was born. Either that, or she was born just prior to his death."

"Elizabeth continues to live here in this house and marries this guy with the last name Todd, who drinks too much. Your turn again."

"This Todd guy beats the daughter to death, or causes her death some other way, and she has been haunting that third floor room ever since."

Leslie nodded. "I'll agree with all that, but we still need to confirm who she was and why the mother or some other relative didn't step in and stop it."

"You have to remember the time period we are talking about," Beth reminded Leslie. "Women just didn't have options then. They were at the mercy of their husbands or some other male relative. When this girl died, women had only been voting for about ten years. We've come a long way, but we still have a long way to go."

Leslie watched the flames from the fireplace reflect off her wineglass. "When do you have to go back to Chicago?"

"Probably I should go back on Wednesday. We have a board meeting on Friday, and Angie and I have some things we need to do."

"Could she come down for the last couple days you are here?"

"I don't know. I think she has a lot on her plate right now."

"It's late. The wine and the heat from the fireplace are making me sleepy."

Beth yawned. "Maybe we should call it a night and get a fresh start tomorrow morning."

"That's probably a good idea, but I want to look through the attic one more time to see if we missed anything. Are you up for that?" Leslie asked.

Beth drank the last sip of wine in her glass and set it on the coffee table. "Sure, why not. We need to get as much accomplished as possible before I fly back."

38

Leslie and Beth looked inside the third floor studio. All was quiet. If their ghost had materialized again, then she had left no evidence. Leslie quietly wished the girl had appeared to them. This time she would think fast, and remember to ask her name. She knew Beth was worried, and admittedly, she was, too. Beth had expressed her fear that somehow Leslie could be trapped with the ghost in whatever realm she existed. But neither of them knew, with any level of certainty, what was possible. To the best of their knowledge, there were no known credible sources of reference. At this point, all they could depend upon were their own instincts and logic.

Finding the studio vacant, they then set their sights on the attic. Together, they searched drawers of old chests, curio cabinets, cardboard boxes, inside vases and decorative bowls, but found nothing they felt would help them confirm the identity of the girl or how she died.

Leslie sneezed. "All this dust is getting to me." She sniffed and blew her nose on a tissue she had stuffed into the pocket of her sweatpants.

"We have combed every inch of this attic," Beth remarked.

"I just think it's strange that there is nothing that obviously belonged to that girl stored in this attic. It seems like everything else is up here."

"We did find the baby spoon, dress and photograph that were probably hers. And it is possible that her stepfather may not have allowed the mother to keep anything of her daughter's."

Leslie exhaled a heavy sigh. "I'm tired, but there is one more stack of things to look through." She pointed to a stack of what appeared to be old blankets.

"After this, I'm going on strike," Beth said as she pulled a cobweb from her sleeve.

"No problem. I'll be right behind you. I'm so tired now, I feel like I'm going to crash."

"You know we never did ask the Andersons why they left all this stuff up here in the attic. Of course, I'd also like to ask the other past owners why they left it here."

"We could call Pat and Joel tomorrow." Leslie pulled the top blanket off the stack and discovered that what they were looking at was actually a big stack of draperies. "Wow, would you look at this." Together, Leslie and Beth stretched out the dark green velvet fabric.

Beth ran her hand across the surface of the drapes. They felt soft and smooth. "I bet these are from the windows in the downstairs parlor or the dining room." Beth ran her hand across them again, then turned one over to look at the backside. "They look like they are in perfect condition. We'll have to inspect them for damage from mice and moths, but I bet you could hang these."

"They are beautiful." Leslie agreed as she reached into the stack to inspect another of the drapes. Just as she did this, the entire stack fell over in the floor. "Oh shit! Catch them."

Beth grabbed for them, but it was too late, they all lay toppled over in the floor. "Oh well, no harm done," Beth reassured Leslie. "Here, let's just get them up off the dusty floor." Beth bent over to pick them up. "I think they fell over because they were sitting on this little chest, and it was probably too small to provide support after we started moving them."

Leslie leaned over to get a better view of the chest. In their earlier searches of the attic, they had missed this one because it had been covered with the draperies. The wood chest was small in size, probably not more than three feet long and a little more than a foot deep, and it was supported by short study legs. The chest itself had been painted white, but the paint had yellowed and cracked with age. There were intricately carved flowers and vines and leaves on the sides and top, all of which had been painted over with pinks and greens, blues and yellows. It bore no resemblance to any of the steamers and luggage stored in the opposite end of the attic, nor did it look like a piece of furniture. It looked to Leslie more like a toy chest for a child.

"Beth?"

Beth was still busying herself with the unfolding, inspection, and refolding of the draperies. "What?"

"Does this chest look familiar to you?"

Beth turned and looked at the small, yellowed chest. "I don't know. Should it?"

"It may just be that I'm overly tired, but this looks like the little chest that was sitting against the wall, under one of the windows, when the girl appeared the other day."

Beth picked up her flashlight and shined it on the chest. "I don't know.

It might be. I'm not observant when it comes to those types of things, which is probably one of the reasons why you are the artist and I'm not."

The two women looked at each other. "I think it is," Leslie said confidently.

"Well then, shall we see what's inside?"

"Do you want to do the honors?" Leslie asked her friend.

"Let's open it together." Beth grasped one corner of the lid, Leslie the other, and together they slowly raised it and viewed the contents of the chest.

On the very top was a doll. It had a little turned up nose, tiny pursed lips, and long blond hair sewn into its scalp. It wore a white lace dress and knitted boots and sweater, both of which appeared slightly dirty, probably the result of having been played with by a child. Leslie and Beth began to speak at the same time. "You go first," offered Leslie.

"Do you think this is the doll? Her doll?"

"I think so." Leslie replied in a voice that was barely audible.

Not knowing how fragile it might be, Leslie carefully lifted it from the chest and cradled it, almost as if it were a child. This was the first tangible link either of them had to the girl haunting Leslie's studio. "What do you think we should do?" Beth asked.

Leslie, still holding the doll in her arms, thought for a moment as she looked into the chest at the rest of its contents. "The light isn't that good, and I don't want to disturb anything here. Do you think we could carry it downstairs?"

Beth lifted one corner. "I think we can manage. It's solid, but it doesn't feel that heavy."

"What about your ankle and your knee? I don't want you to re-injure them."

"Other than the knot, I'm as good as new. As long as I take it slow going down the stairs, I should be fine. Do you want to move it now?"

"Do you mind?" Leslie asked. She knew the thought was unfounded, but just the same, she was afraid if she didn't move the chest now and take control of it, that somehow it would vanish just as the girl did.

"Let's put the doll back inside and take everything at once."

Gently, Leslie returned the doll to its resting place. They closed the lid, and together, taking opposite ends, they lifted the chest. "Oh," Beth grunted. "This is heavier than it looks. I can tell I need to get back in the gym. I haven't been in two weeks."

"Me either." Leslie said, as she turned her head to see behind her so she could safely walk backwards toward the attic door. "I'll go backwards down the stairs." Leslie started lifting her end of the chest in the air as high as she could manage, so Beth wouldn't need to bend over. "Are you doing okay?"

"Yes, just keep moving. I don't want to lose the momentum."

"Are you down?" Leslie asked.

"Yes, I just cleared the last step. Now where do you want to go with this?"

"Let's take it to my room." Walking backward, Leslie entered her room and maneuvered closer to the bed. "Are you ready to set it down?"

"Oh, more than ready. I had no idea looking for a ghost would be so strenuous, but it could be worse."

They carefully lowered the chest to the floor, as much to prevent straining their own backs as to avoid damaging the antique toy box. "How do you figure it could be worse?"

"The ghost isn't popping up all over the house when we least expect it and trying to scare the crap out of us. She is confining her activities to that one room, and we aren't getting slimed."

"No, we aren't getting slimed; we must not lose sight of that." Beth, standing upright, put both hands in the small of her back and leaned backward, then from side to side. "Ooh, I have definitely got to get back in the gym when I go back to Chicago. I'm thinking about putting one in at the office. Did I tell you that?"

"No, you didn't. When did you decide to do that?"

"I've thought about it since I started taking an active role in the company. I guess I never really noticed before, but a lot of Dad's staff is very out of shape. Most of the women put in long hours then go home to housework, spouses and children. They don't have time to use a gym after work."

Leslie was now stretching out the muscles in her back. "I predict that in a couple of years *Industry Week* will write an article about you and the positive impact you have had."

Beth smiled. Leslie had no idea how much the complement meant to her. "Dad was always very concerned about the well-being of his employees, but employee needs have changed over the years. I want to be progressive in meeting some of those needs as well as grow the business."

"You'll do well. I know you will. Now, do we want to go through this chest now or wait until morning? It is after midnight."

Beth looked at the small white chest sitting before them. She could feel the fatigue overtaking her body and the need for sleep increasing.

She thought for a moment. "I'll put it to you like this: I'm so tired that I think I could curl up in a ball on the floor and go to sleep, and I'm guessing that you could, too. But I know you, and you won't get a wink of sleep until you know everything that is in that chest, and honestly, I probably won't either."

"You're right, and I'll probably get up in the middle of the night and start sorting through it."

"It is the middle of the night," Beth reminded Leslie.

"I want us to go through it together."

"And I don't want to miss out."

"I have an idea," Leslie offered. "Let's just take everything out and see what we have, and if there's anything useful, then we'll examine it more closely tomorrow."

"I can live with that."

39

Leslie felt as though she were holding her breath as they opened the lid to the toy chest for the second time. Beth removed the doll, and holding it carefully, she examined it for any identifying labels. There were none. "I wonder if this could be the same doll our ghost was playing with when we saw her dancing around the room?"

"Possibly, but I couldn't see it that well. Could you?"

"Not really." Leslie set the doll aside and they began removing one item at a time from the toy chest. Under the doll was a layer of baby clothes: tiny bonnets, knitted boots, a couple dresses and a small blanket. Under the layer of baby clothes, they found a stuffed teddy bear. Leslie picked it up, careful not to damage its frail cloth body. The front and hind legs moved at the joint, where they were attached to the body. It showed signs of wear but appeared to be in good condition considering its age. "Let me look at that for a second," Beth asked.

Beth examined it carefully. "I'm certainly no expert on antiques, but I would bet this is a Steiff."

"A Steiff?" Leslie asked.

"The Margarete Steiff Company manufactured stuffed animals in Germany during the teens and twenties."

Leslie looked at Beth with bewilderment. "How do you know this stuff?"

"Why are you always so surprised when I know something historical?"

"I don't know. You just never seemed to be interested in that kind of stuff."

Beth, still examining the stuffed bear replied, "I think you and our friends have stereotyped me. Because you are the artist and a computer systems analyst everyone naturally assumes you are the brainy one in the group. They also assume, because my family is wealthy and I didn't always work that I'm not very bright."

"That's not true; I have always known you were intelligent."

"I know. You thought I was smart, but just not very academic. It's okay; I'm not offended. I never gave anyone a reason to assume otherwise. All our friends know me as the free spirit, but I'll tell you a secret. I was actually a very good student."

Beth set the bear on the floor beside the doll. "I'm making an educated guess about the stuffed bear because my grandmother had a collection of them when she was a young girl. She kept almost all of them and displayed them in a glass case in her drawing room. Occasionally, she would open the case and let me look at them. They were so old and valuable. I could hold them but never play with them."

"Do you still have any of them?"

"She gave me her three favorites, which were naturally my favorites also. The rest were donated to a museum in her name."

In addition to the bear, they found two photographs they knew to be Clay and Elizabeth. There were three more photographs of a smiling child, which bore a striking resemblance to their ghost. "Look at these. I think these pictures are of the girl when she was little," said Leslie.

"She looks like a very happy child. I wonder when things changed for her?"

"I'll bet it was after her mother remarried." Leslie set the photos aside and looked back inside the chest with Beth. There was a stack of a half dozen letters tied together with a pink silk ribbon and then wrapped again in a lace handkerchief. The top letter was postmarked 1918 and addressed to Mrs. Elizabeth Bradshaw Weatherly. Leslie held them in front of her with both hands. "I'm dying to know what they say, but if I start reading them now I won't stop until I've finished all of them."

"Then my vote is to put them aside, because I don't think either of us will be able to last much longer."

Leslie followed Beth's advice and set them on the floor beside the Steiff bear. She reached inside the chest and removed two children's books: a first edition of *Billy Whisker's Treasure Hunt* and a hardcover picture book entitled *Talks About Animals*. Both were in excellent condition, with only a few bumps and dents around the edges. "These must have been her favorites." Leslie fanned through the pages, then set them aside. The remainder of the chest's contents consisted of a rubber ball, another doll, a girl's sailor dress, a silver brush, comb and mirror, a ring box with a child-size pearl ring, and a photograph of an older Elizabeth Weatherly sitting on porch steps with a little girl beside her, who happened to be the spitting image of their ghost. Leslie held the photo closer and squinted to better focus her eyes. "This looks like my house, what do you think?"

"Let me see." Beth took the photo and examined it closely. "Not much of the house is showing in the photo, but it appears to be." Beth set the photo aside with the two others from the chest then leaned over to peer inside again. "Is that everything?"

"Just this one leather pouch," Leslie replied. Beth reached inside and removed it from the bottom of the chest. It was small, the shape of a contemporary legal size envelope, just large enough to hold several sheets of folded paper. It closely resembled the pouches containing legal documents that they had found in the large steamers.

"Do you want to open it now or wait until morning?"

Leslie's eyes narrowed, not from any measure of concentration or contemplation but from fatigue. "I don't know if I can focus well enough to read, even if there is anything in it worth reading."

Beth rubbed her red-rimmed eyes. "Let's at least open it. The suspense is killing me, although I don't think anything could keep me awake at this point."

Leslie lay back on the floor and covered her eyes with her arm to shield them from the chandelier overhead. "You can read it to me. My second wind just blew itself out."

"You shouldn't have lain down." Beth set the document pouch beside the stack of letters and, making a groaning sound, she pulled herself up from the floor. She then leaned over Leslie and extended her hand. "Here, I'll help you up."

Leslie flung her arm into the air, allowing her right hand to hang limp. Then she began to laugh. It started first as a light chuckle, then seeing her arm still extended into the air, she began to laugh harder. She rolled over on her side and held her stomach; her entire body was now shaking from laughter.

"What's so funny?"

"I don't know," Leslie replied, and then rolled back onto her back and continued with more laughter. "I can't help it. I can't stop."

Beth also began to laugh. She leaned against Leslie's bed to watch her friend convulse with deep guffaws, which racked her entire body and made tears stream from her eyes. "Why are you crying?"

"I'm not; I'm just laughing so hard that I can't help it." Again, Leslie made a cackling sound that was akin to a cross between a chimpanzee's chuckle and a rooster's crow. After a few minutes, Leslie's laughter subsided.

"I don't think I've ever seen you laugh that hard."

"I don't think you have ever seen me this tired. I don't know why I started laughing so hard. When I flung my arm into the air, for some reason, that seemed funny and from there I just couldn't stop."

"When you look at what the last few weeks have been like for you – buying a house, packing up, moving, unpacking, and now all of this – you probably just needed a release from all of the stress you've been under."

Leslie wiped more tears from her eyes then sat upright. "You are probably right. I've been wound up so tight the last few days that if I had squeezed a lump of coal I could have turned it into a diamond."

Beth frowned. "That's pretty damn uptight." She then extended her hand for a second time. This time Leslie took it, and Beth helped her up from the floor. "Do you want to see what's in the leather pouch?"

"Not tonight. It has probably been here for seventy or eighty years; one more night isn't going to make a difference."

40

Leslie slept soundly most of the night; however, as the morning wore on her sleep became more restless and filled with troubling dreams. Images from the photographs she and Beth had found leapt out at her. Several times, she became aware of her surroundings and tried to wake herself. But each time, it was as if the dreams had hold of her and dragged her back into a netherworld of a lost childhood and shadowy figures from a past that was not her own.

In her dreams, it was as if the small toy chest, with its yellowed and cracked white paint, symbolized Pandora's Box; after all of the ills that plague mankind are released, the only thing that remains is hope.

Slowly, Leslie opened her eyes and then closed them again. She rolled over on her side. Light was streaming in through the bedroom windows. She opened her eyes again and blinked. She felt a need to close them and drift off into sleep, but instead, she fought to become fully awake. Leslie looked at the clock on her nightstand. It was nearly eleven, and they were to meet the caretaker at the cemetery at twelve. "Shit. Got to get up and get moving." She listened for Beth but heard no other sounds in the house. She assumed Beth was still in bed.

Leslie sat up, the room was cold and she rubbed her arms. Suddenly, she remembered the white chest. She chastised herself; how could she not remember the chest? Leslie grabbed her robe from the end of her bed and threw it around her shoulders. She walked over to the chest, which was still sitting in the middle of her bedroom with its contents scattered around it. The hardwood floor was cold under her feet as she stood there contemplating the objects. Leslie curled her toes and arched her feet so that only her heals and toes made contact with the cold floor. She bent down and picked up the small stack of letters and the leather document folder then she quickly walked the few steps back to her bed.

Promising herself she would only read one, Leslie pulled the heavy comforter over her legs and tucked it tightly around her feet to warm them. Leaning back against the pillows, which she stacked against the headboard, Leslie settled back to examine the letters. She carefully untied the ribbon that bound the stack, and gently opened the first envelope. It was postmarked 10 September 1918, and it was addressed with beautifully scripted lettering to Mrs. Elizabeth Bradshaw Weatherly. Leslie thought about how everyone is so rushed now, and how society is moving at the speed of email. Last year, of the few Christmas cards she received, most had been addressed with a printer. Letter writing and penmanship were things of the past. Leslie pulled the comforter up under her arms and began to read.

My Dearest Lizzy,

Over two weeks had passed since I last received one of your letters. Even though I knew it not to be true, I had begun to feel rather melancholy for fear that you had forgotten me. You should scold me for such ridiculous thoughts, as I have scolded myself. Yesterday, I received four of your letters. Our mail here is sporadic at best, but at least I have you and soon our child. I gave your letter, telling of the morning doves in the garden, to Sergeant Rowlett to read. I believe the poor man has yet to receive a letter, and I fear he has no one. Sometimes I wonder how many other fellows are here in this God-forsaken place with no one at home to pray for their safe return. How terrible to be cast such a lot in life.

My men and I rousted out a squad of the Kaiser's men in a little village near our current position. The army forbids me to tell you where, for fear that our mail will be intercepted by the Germans and used against us. But I can tell you that when the scars from this war have healed, I would think this a quaint and beautiful place to take a holiday. By chance, I entered a shop that had once sold all manner of items, and on the shelf I saw a lone little stuffed bear. I took the bear and left a silver dollar in its place as payment to the shopkeeper, should he ever return.

Now I should tell you to watch for a package to arrive, which contains the little bear. I took all manner of precautions to prevent it from becoming soiled by the muck in the trenches, so please give it to our child as a gift from its father, who wants so desperately to come home.

Your most devoted husband,
Clay

Leslie looked again at the date Clay had recorded at the top of the letter. She felt tears well up in her eyes. It was such a tender letter. In a few days from its date, Clay would be killed. She pulled a tissue from a box on the nightstand and wiped her eyes. "I don't think I can read any more of these," she said as she set the stack of letters aside.

Leslie looked at the little bear lying on the floor. "He never knew he had a daughter." Wiping another tear from her cheek, she now turned her attention to the narrow leather document case. It had an accordion fold in the bottom and a large flap that closed over the side and then a string to tie it shut. The first piece of paper Leslie removed was stained and yellowed but still legible. As she read it, her eyes widened. "This is hers," she whispered. "I know your name." Leslie held in her hand the birth certificate for Cordelia Elizabeth Weatherly, daughter of Elizabeth and Clay Weatherly. Leslie smiled and pulled from the case another set of documents, and she hurriedly began to read them. "Oh my God! Elijah left everything to Cordelia. Her stepfather must have killed her to get the house and money!"

Leslie jumped from her bed, with the birth certificate in her right hand and the last will and testament of Elijah Weatherly in her left. She rushed out the door and across the hall, the tail of her bathrobe flowing behind her like a cloak. "Beth! Beth, wake up!"

Beth slowly opened her eyes and squinted and blinked, trying to force them to focus. "What?" Beth replied in a voice weak and scratchy from sleep.

"I have the answer. I know for certain who she is." Beth pushed herself up in bed, and Leslie sat down beside her. "Look at this. It was in that pouch we found in the chest."

Still trying to focus, Beth rubbed her eyes then read the names and dates on the birth certificate. "I think you have it. I think this is our girl."

Leslie's face beamed with accomplishment. "And look at this." She handed Beth the will.

Beth carefully read through the first page then skimmed the remaining pages, "Elijah's will! He left everything to his grand-daughter Cordelia to be held in trust and administered by the executor of his estate, which looks like it was a partner in the law firm that drew up the will. It says here she would receive full control of the house and entire estate on her twenty-fifth birthday."

"I think he killed her in an effort to get her money," stated Leslie.

Beth looked at her friend. "I wonder how much there was?"

"I would like to know if this law firm is still in existence."

Beth looked at the will again. "All these years in a small town like this, I doubt it, but we could check it out. What time is it anyway?"

Leslie looked at her watch, she had forgotten to take it off when she went to bed. "Damn it! We have thirty minutes to get to the cemetery and meet the caretaker."

Beth ran her fingers through her hair and scratched her scalp. Several strands on the top of her head were standing straight up, and at the back there was a severe cowlick. Beth felt it and tried to push it down. "Oh," she groaned, "I have bad hair."

Leslie smiled, "You have eighties hair. You look like a cross between The Bay City Rollers and a Flock of Seagulls."

"Ah!" Beth shouted as she fell back in the bed. "I can't let anyone see me like this."

"Put a hat on your head."

Beth opened her eyes and looked squarely at Leslie. "I don't do hats. Hats give you hat hair. Unless I'm skiing of course, then I'll wear a hat, but that's different."

"If we hurry, you can wet and blow-dry your hair."

Beth, still lying back on the bed, looked again at Leslie. "Do you have a hat I can borrow?"

"Yes, now come on."

41

Beth grudgingly pulled the cap's bill down over her head and climbed into Leslie's Mercedes. It was ten minutes to twelve; they had to hurry to the cemetery. "You should let me drive," Beth commented. "I'll get us there with time to spare."

Leslie backed out of the driveway and shot down the deserted street. "Then I would have to give directions, and since I'm relearning my way around, it is easier for me if I drive. Besides, I'm not ready to join our ghost in the afterlife."

"What? What do you mean?"

"Your driving scares the hell out of me."

"I am assertive, and I go fast, but I'm very safe."

Leslie cast her eyes at Beth in a sideways glance, then she returned her attention to the road in front of her. "The caretaker said about twelve, so we don't have to be exactly on time. It's Sunday, he'll probably be running late himself."

It was a short trip to Winchester's main cemetery. Leslie pulled up in front of the office and parked. Then, as predicted, they waited another ten minutes for the caretaker to arrive and open the office.

Ted Williams was a friendly man in his early seventies. He walked with stooped shoulders and short measured steps. Leslie noticed the joints in his fingers bent very little as he turned pages of a large book, which listed names, dates and locations of graves. He must have arthritis, she thought to herself.

"Let me see here. Now these are in the old section, up closer to the front; there are lots of nice trees up there. Not too many trees in the newer sections." The two friends watched as he slowly turned more pages. With each turn, he would tilt his head upward to better align his eyes with his bifocals, then he moved his head down again as he scanned to the bottom of the page.

"I'm surprised all of this isn't on the computer," Leslie remarked.

"Well, the ladies that work here in the office tell me it is, but I'm too old to learn how to use those things. It's easier for me to keep up with these books. And you know, I read that if the big one ever gets dropped, then computers won't be worth diddly squat."

"Big one?" Beth inquired.

"Atomic bomb." Ted Williams replied in a tone that indicated his exasperation at her not knowing what the big one was.

"Why do you say that?"

Mr. Williams tilted his head upward again and began scanning the next page. Leslie felt herself growing impatient and wishing Beth had not asked the old man a question.

"If the big one goes off, then the insides of them things gets melted. You can't eat 'em. You can't burn 'em to keep warm. Can't do nothin' with 'em." Mr. Williams paused. "Here it is. Looks like there are several of 'em, all in the same family plot. Are you relatives of theirs?"

"Not really." Leslie offered. "I bought the house one of their ancestors built back in the eighteen hundreds, and I just wanted to find out more about the family."

Mr. Williams looked up from his book at Leslie, and then at Beth, in a way that made them both feel as if he were sizing them up and weighing their sincerity. "You can follow me; I'll take you over there."

The two followed Mr. Williams to his pick-up truck. They followed behind him down the narrow winding drive that snaked between sections of graves. Near the front of the cemetery, under a group of maple trees whose red and yellow leaves had been stripped from them by wind and rain earlier in the week, Leslie and Beth saw, chiseled into the base of a twelve-foot high stone obelisk, the name Weatherly. "We found them," was all Leslie said as she exited her car.

Leslie stood in front of the obelisk and gazed at it for a long moment, then walked to the opposite side. There she saw the names of Major Nathan Weatherly and his wife, Harrietta Scott Weatherly. Elijah and his wife, Sarah Jane Breathitt, were to the right of the Major, resting under a stone Leslie guessed to be approximately three feet thick and about six feet wide and five feet high. It was less ostentatious than his forebear's but still a massive piece of stone. Surprisingly, they found both Clay and Elizabeth to the left of the Major. They both had assumed that Clay would be buried somewhere in Europe in a military cemetery. Leslie was even more surprised to see fresh flowers on the graves. Since the house, Wood Hurst, had been sold years ago and they found no Weatherlys in the phone book, they had assumed there were no more surviving family members. But there was obviously still someone who cared or remembered.

"I guess they had enough money and influence to have him shipped home," Beth said as she read the inscription on the stone.

Leslie pulled from the pocket of her jacket the page of notepaper, on which she had fashioned a family tree for the Weatherly family. There were stones for all of them. All the names listed in the family bible. There was Judith and Lily, the Major's daughters, both of whom lived into old age, and the graves of their husbands, which sat in the shadow of the obelisk. There was a small stone for Rupert, Nathan and Harrietta's second son, who died just before his second birthday. Another row of graves contained stones for Elijah and Sarah Jane's two daughters – Constance, who died of influenza in 1918, and Rebecca, who lived to the ripe old age of eighty-seven and married a man with the last name Turner.

Leslie walked around the plot again and even looked at the names on stones in neighboring plots. "I don't see Cordelia anywhere."

Ted Williams was still standing beside the Major's grave. "Cordelia who?"

"Cordelia Weatherly; she was the daughter of Clay and Elizabeth. I think she may have died when she was about thirteen or fourteen, give or take a year or so."

Ted Williams surveyed the names on the stones. "You sure she died around here?"

"No, actually we aren't," added Beth. "Do you know anything about the family? Like for example are any of them still living around here? I noticed the flowers on some of the graves are fresh."

The old man thought for a minute. "Nope, don't know anybody with that last name. Of course people get married and last names change. But I'd say it's a fair guess that the Weatherly's still have people around here. If I'm not mistaken, and my memory ain't what it used to be, this is one of the plots where all the graves have flowers on them at Decoration."

"Decoration?" Beth inquired.

"Memorial Day," Leslie responded. "My grandmother always used the term Decoration, rather than Memorial Day."

"Interesting. I had never heard that term used."

Leslie walked to one of the far stones. "What about this one, Rebecca Weatherly Turner? She died in 1980. Do you know anyone who might be related to her?"

"We got some Turners in town, but I wouldn't know if they were any kin to her or not."

Leslie frowned. She was frustrated. They had found the Weatherly family plot, but they were still no closer to discovering the fate of young Cordelia. They were relatively confidant that Elizabeth had remarried not long after Clay was killed. Likewise, they were certain the man's last name was Todd, and of course by now, he was also deceased. He obviously did not rate burial in the Weatherly plot, and Leslie could guess why. He had most likely murdered one of their own.

"Are any Todds buried here?"

"Todd?" Ted Williams scratched his stubble-covered chin as he thought. "I think we have a good many Todds. Which one are you looking for?"

"I don't know."

"Well, then I can't help you much."

"Thank you for meeting us out here. We appreciate it," Beth shook the old man's hand. Ted Williams climbed into his pick-up truck and drove back through the cemetery toward the office.

Beth looked up at the sky. It was overcast and dark clouds were beginning to roll in. "What do you want to do now?" She asked Leslie.

"I want to find out who Elizabeth married, and I want to find the law firm that handled Elijah's will. Somewhere there is someone who knows what happened to that little girl."

The two women turned and walked through the wet grass back to Leslie's car. "Let's call your friend Elsa Van Meter when we get back and see if she found anything, and then tomorrow we'll go back to the courthouse and visit our old lady friend. She at least knew something about the Todd family who lived in your house." Beth tried to sound encouraging.

"It's a starting point. Maybe we can find a marriage license with his name on it." Leslie said, as she pressed the button on the key fob to unlock the doors. Beth was standing beside the passenger side, waiting for the sound of the lock to click. Leslie looked up at Beth, then beyond her friend to a man who was standing several yards away beside a red BMW convertible.

"What?" Beth asked, then turned to look in the direction of Leslie's gaze. She saw the man, and then she turned to Leslie and asked, "Do you know him?"

"No, but he looks like he's watching us."

"Maybe he is just looking for a grave."

"Maybe." Leslie looked at the man again. He was wearing a black calf-length topcoat and black slacks that reminded her of the styles worn by men in Europe. His dark brown hair was short, but still with just

174

enough length that it moved in the slight breeze. He wore small nonde-script glasses, and from his stance, he seemed to have a casual manner. Leslie wasn't sure, but from that distance he appeared to be in his early thirties.

"Leslie, you're staring."

"I think he was staring first."

Beth turned and looked again. "He looks attractive; at least from a distance. Why don't you introduce yourself?"

"And do what? Say 'Hi, I'm Leslie and why are you staring at me?'"

"Well, that would be an option."

"He is dressed in black and probably here for the graveside service Mr. Williams mentioned. And I'm sure I would make a good impression, hitting on him at a funeral."

"Stranger things have happened." Beth winked.

Leslie lifted her hand so that it was visible above the roof of her car, then with a hesitant motion, she waved to the man. The man returned the gesture, then got inside his car and drove off down the lane.

"Now that was weird," Beth said, as she noticed rain drops beginning to collect on the windshield of Leslie's car. "Come on, let's go. I need a shower, and you need to call Elsa."

"Okay," was Leslie's only reply, as she watched the red BMW disappear from view.

42

Beth, wearing a heavy bathrobe and drying her hair with a towel, walked across the hall to Leslie's bedroom. "Any luck?"

"Elsa Van Meter is coming over for dinner."

"Oh really!" Beth arched her left eyebrow. "Did you invite her over?"

"She sort of invited herself. When I told her about all the things we found in the attic, she got pretty excited." Leslie paused. "I think 'giddy' would be a good word to describe her reaction."

"I like Elsa. I bet she knew how to have a good time when she was younger."

"I would bet she still knows how to have a good time. She does have that air about her. Anyway, she said she would bring some information she was able to put together on the family and the house. Apparently the Weatherlys were a very prominent Clark County family during the eighteen hundreds and the early part of the nineteen hundreds."

"What happened to them?"

"She didn't go into any detail; she just commented that most of them either died off or moved away. I told her about the flowers on the graves, and she said there were probably still some descendants in the area, but she didn't think anyone was left who still carried the last name Weatherly."

"So, in other words, the men either died off or had daughters and didn't pass down the family name, or they just moved away."

"Just looking at the family Bible we found, and the headstones in the cemetery, it appears the family, at least the direct line of descent from the Major, just died off."

"Rebecca, Clay's youngest sister, died in 1980, and she had been married to...what was his last name?"

"Turner, James Turner."

"Right, so surely they had offspring. She was buried in the family plot, and there were flowers on her grave."

"I know. Hopefully, this won't be another dead end. This is really frustrating. Every time we think we have hit the jackpot it turns out to be a dead end."

Beth sat down on the edge of the bed beside Leslie. "We know more than we did three days ago. And we haven't seen or heard from the ghost in a day or so. Maybe that is a good sign."

No sooner had Beth spoken the words, than they heard a scream come from the third floor of the house. It was loud and shrill, the type of scream that one could imagine would emanate from someone who feared their life would be taken from them that very instant. Leslie, startled, dropped the phone. It hit the floor, and the sound echoed through the room. Both women jumped to their feet. Beth, holding her bath robe to keep it securely wrapped around her body, rushed for the bedroom door, with Leslie not more than a half a step behind.

"Beth wait!" Leslie called out, as Beth hit the top of the stairs in full stride. Beth skidded to a stop just outside the studio door, and Leslie plowed into her back. The two friends watched as the girl appeared to fend off blows from an invisible assailant. The girl's head jerked violently to one side as they saw bright red blood squirt from her nose. "The son-of-a-bitch just broke her nose!" Leslie yelled. They saw the girl look in their direction and extend her hand, as if reaching for them, before falling under the weight of another blow. "She sees us! I'm going to stop this!"

"No, don't go in there!"

"I have to!" Leslie yelled.

Beth could see the desperation in her best friend's eyes. "Then I'm going with you." Without a second's hesitation, Leslie grabbed Beth's hand and together they flung their bodies into the room. Both were instantly overcome with a feeling of vertigo. It was almost as if they were outside themselves. The walls seemed to flow, like batter being folded by the rotation of a mixer. "Cordelia!" Leslie called out. "Cordelia Weatherly, where are you?"

Beth still clung tightly to Leslie's hand. She was afraid to loosen her grip, afraid that they would be flung apart in the swirling room. "Leslie, I think I'm going to be sick." Leslie put her arm around Beth as she gagged and coughed.

"Beth, look! Over there!"

Beth blinked and squinted, trying to focus her eyes, but her head was swimming. She had lost all equilibrium. "What? I can't tell what's going on."

"There they are." For the first time, Leslie and Beth could see the girl's attacker. He was a stocky man, with a thick mustache and graying hair. "It's like they are in a strobe; one minute I can see them, the next they're gone. Come on, let's get to them and stop him."

Beth, leaning heavily on Leslie's shoulder, followed her friend to the center of the room. "Leave her alone!" Leslie shouted. The apparition of a man turned to face them. His eyes were wide and crazed, as if he were the one who had just seen a ghost, not the other way around. The man put his hand up, as if trying to protect himself from them and then began backing away from Cordelia. "No! Who are you? Get away from me!" He shouted.

"Leave her alone!" Leslie yelled again. Beth, still holding tightly to Leslie's hand, turned to look at the girl who was slumped on the floor like a discarded doll. Beth bent down and gently stroked her hair then whispered, "It'll be okay. We're here now."

It was no sooner than the words left Beth's lips that she felt Leslie pull away from her. She looked up to see her friend lunge toward the man. At the exact instant that Leslie's fists made contact with him, there was a dull flash of light and everything from the past was gone. The room was once again Leslie's studio.

With the man gone and nothing to stop her charge, Leslie stumbled forward, catching herself against the wall. Beth slumped down to the floor, then rolled over onto her back, coughing. It took a moment, but Leslie regained her footing then made her way to Beth's side. Leslie, on her knees, pulled Beth up from the floor, cradling her against her own body. "Are you okay?"

Beth was still gagging, "I don't know. What just happened?"

"I think we just stopped him from attacking her."

"Who was he?" Again she coughed and gagged. "I feel like I'm going to throw up."

"Hang on; let me get a trash can."

"No!" Another gagging cough, "I just want to get out of this room before they come back." With Leslie's help, Beth tried to get to her feet. "God, this is worse than an ear infection."

"I know, but it'll wear off." Leslie put Beth's arm around her shoulder, and then she lifted her up from the floor. "Come on, let's get you downstairs."

When they reached the stairs, Leslie looked back over her shoulder. The room, her studio, was calm and still. Everything was in its place, just as they had left it. Everything except a small piece of ceramic tile, which had fallen from the fireplace.

43

It was a little after six and Beth was lying on the sofa in the parlor. She felt almost normal again but didn't want to push her luck by moving around. Nor did she want to be upstairs alone. From the kitchen, Leslie walked down the hall into the foyer, a glass of Cabernet in each hand. She sat down on the edge of the sofa and placed the glasses on the coffee table. "Here. Do you think a glass of wine might help?"

Beth opened her eyes and looked at the half-filled glasses. "I don't know if I should."

"Now I know you're sick. I've never seen you turn down a good Cabernet."

"First time for everything, I suppose."

"How was your nap?"

"Just what the doctor ordered. It was like having a migraine but without the pain. Sleeping it off helped as much as anything. But don't expect me to go running up any stairs just yet."

Leslie smiled. "I'm sorry I dragged you into this."

"You didn't drag me. I volunteered – remember? Other than scaring the hell out of me, it was exhilarating to actually make contact with her like that. I could actually feel her hair when I touched her head. I could see the blue in her eyes."

"I know. It was like that for me the other day in the studio when she spoke to me. I felt such a connection to her."

"What was it like when you punched Harry Scary?"

Leslie knitted her eyebrows. "What?"

"Harry Scary from the old Casper cartoons."

"Oh. I don't remember him. We must have been overseas when that was on."

"You may have seen the world, but you missed out on far too many pop-culture references."

"I'll say. That's why I never did well when I drew those questions in Trivial Pursuit."

Leslie closed her eyes for a second and shook her head slightly, as if the gesture would help get her mind back on track. "I could feel him, too. I could feel my fist make contact with his face." Leslie looked down at her hand. "The redness is gone now, but my knuckle was actually red from hitting him."

"This is amazing." Beth pushed herself up on the sofa. Leslie helped by adjusting the pillows behind her back and head. "I would never have imagined being able to touch a ghost."

"Me either. I watched movies and read stories about ghosts, but once I got to a certain age I didn't believe they were real, just like I stopped believing in the Easter Bunny and Santa Claus. But still, there was always just a little doubt in the back of my mind."

"About the Easter Bunny and Santa Claus?"

"There you go, being a smart-ass again. No, about ghosts! Anyway, as I was saying, you still have a little doubt. You think you know what a ghost would look like and how it would behave but..." Leslie's voice trailed off.

Beth could see an expression in Leslie's eyes, an expression that said her thoughts were suddenly somewhere else. "What are you thinking about? Your mind went somewhere?"

Leslie looked at Beth. "I don't know. I was thinking about everything, about nothing. I don't know; my thoughts were just racing."

"I know. I've been thinking a lot, too. I wonder what will happen to me when I die. Will I repeat an event in my past over and over for eternity, or will my soul float off to some other place. And for that matter, what is a soul anyway?"

Leslie rubbed her eyes. "I can't think any more; I'm on overload." She picked up the glass of wine and took a small sip. "Sure you don't want some?"

"I'll wait until dinner. Since I still feel a little lightheaded, I want to get something in my stomach first. So, how about a fire in the fireplace?"

"Your wish is my command." Leslie took another sip from her glass, then stood up.

Beth looked up at her friend. "You are going to be a good catch for someone one of these days."

44

At six-thirty the doorbell chimed. Elsa Van Meter was right on time. Leslie rushed out of the kitchen and through the foyer to greet her. "Stay put," she told Beth, who ignored Leslie's command and rose from the sofa to welcome their guest.

Elsa had a large smile that stretched almost from ear-to-ear. Her lips were full and she accented them with bright red lipstick. Her gray hair hung loosely about her shoulders and face, framing it like a fine porcelain sculpture. She wore low-heeled sensible shoes, tweed slacks and a long wrap-around cloak which caught in the breeze and flew out from her body as she glided with the movements of a dancer into the foyer.

Even Beth, for a moment, was left speechless by the image of the older woman. "Hello, loves. I am so excited to be over here." Elsa tilted her gaze upward and turned a complete three-hundred-and-sixty-degree circle, like a ballet dancer performing a pirouette. "I haven't been in this house for years. I was so afraid it hadn't been maintained, but it's beautiful."

"You've been in the house before? You didn't tell me that."

"Didn't I? I'm sorry, dear. Oh, it was years ago. The O'Neil family owned it, Ken and Peggy O'Neil. That was in the early 80s. Hard to believe it has been that long, and I'm that much older."

Beth stood, smiling at the woman. "I don't think old is a word I would ever use to describe you."

Elsa reached out and squeezed Beth's arm. "I like you. We're going to be good friends."

"Show me what you've done with it. I must have a tour."

"Actually, I'm still looking for furniture, so I haven't really done much."

Elsa looked into the empty dining room and then the parlor, which contained only the few furnishings from Leslie's apartment in Chicago. "I can help you find just the right pieces. I know all the antique dealers." Elsa turned to look at Beth. "Beth, have you been ill? You don't look well."

Leslie and Beth looked at one another, not knowing how much they should tell their new acquaintance. "I'm fine. I was just feeling a little under the weather today."

"I hope you haven't caught something. There's always some virus going around this time of year." Elsa turned and breezed into parlor. "I love this room. There are so many things you could do with it."

"I'm planning to put a baby grand piano in the rounded section of the room," Leslie offered.

"That would look fabulous. Do you play?"

"A little. I had lessons for several years when I was a child. I hated it then, but I would like to start playing again, now that I have time."

"I know someone who deals in antique pianos. I'll give you his number." Beth returned to her seat on the sofa and took a long sip from her wine. "Are you sure you are feeling alright? Your face is so pale; you look as if you've seen a ghost," Elsa remarked, just as Beth began to swallow.

The wine caught halfway down Beth's throat. She choked and coughed. Leslie's eyes widened. If Elsa thought their reaction strange, she gave no hint of it. She merely set her Louis Vuitton handbag down beside the coffee table and seated herself in the chair opposite Beth.

"I'm sorry, I'm being rude; let me take your coat." Leslie took her cloak and headed back toward the kitchen. She stood there for a second in the butler's pantry not knowing what to do with the garment. If she were in her apartment she would just throw it across the bed in her room. The counter tops in the pantry were clean, so she deposited it there, then rejoined Beth and Elsa.

"Elsa, can I get you a glass of wine? I have several reds, whites, or I can mix a cocktail for you if you would prefer that."

"Wine is good, just whatever you have opened. Dinner smells wonderful. Can I help you with anything?"

"No. It is almost finished. I'll just get your wine and then start taking things off the stove."

"That would be wonderful, love."

Leslie had set the table in the kitchen, but Elsa insisted on eating in the parlor beside the fireplace. Both women were surprised when their guest picked up her wine glass, set it on the hearth, and then crossing her legs, sat in the floor with her back to the flames. Elsa came from old money; just how much Leslie wasn't sure, but there was nothing pretentious about her. Leslie smiled as she watched the older woman use her fingernail to remove a stubborn piece of meat from between her teeth.

When asked if she would like more wine, Elsa's reply was simply, "Of course."

After dinner when the dishes had been returned to the kitchen, Elsa was ready to get to business. She pulled from her handbag the few documents and anecdotes she was able to find on the Weatherly family. "Margaret O'Neil was a friend of mine. I think I mentioned they owned this house in the 80s. I called her, and she told me they bought the house in 1980 from a couple with the last name Sloan. She didn't remember their first names."

"That gets us back a little further than before," Beth commented. "We started looking up records in the court house, but didn't get too far. We got there late and it was closing."

"You two sound like you are on a mission. Other than the obvious, why are you digging into the history of this house?"

Leslie looked up from the papers she was reading. "No reason, other than I fell in love with the house the first time I saw it. I just want to know more of its history."

Elsa stared directly into Leslie's eyes, as if trying to will some unspoken truth from them. "Why do I detect such a sense of urgency from you? There is more to this story than the two of you are telling me."

Leslie avoided the question and hoping to distract Elsa, she answered, "I would like to see what else you have on the family, then I would like you to see what we found in the attic."

Elsa, at least for the moment, seemed to accept Leslie's response. "Oh yes, the attic, I must see that," she smiled, the expression on her face taking on a playful quality. "I'll warn you dear, I always get what I want." She then smiled at Beth.

Leslie made notes in her notepad, filling in some of the gaps in their information. Still, they had no information on the fate of young Cordelia Weatherly.

"Do you have any information on who Elizabeth Weatherly married after her husband Clay was killed in World War I?"

"You said his last name was Todd, didn't you?"

"Yes, as far as I know."

"I asked around, and this is what I came up with. Of course, the courthouse was closed this weekend so I couldn't verify this information, but I do have names for you." Elsa opened her notebook. "The name I came up with was Edward Todd Senior, and they had two sons named Edward Junior, the oldest, and Robert."

"That's great. When were they born?"

"I don't have the exact dates, but sometime in the early to mid nineteen twenties."

"Is either of them still alive?" Beth asked.

"I think one of them; Robert, I believe. Seems from what I was told, Edward Junior turned out to be a drunk, just like his father, and died rather young."

"Edward Todd Senior drank a lot?" Beth looked at Leslie. "That would match up with what the old lady at the courthouse told us."

"Old lady?" Elsa inquired.

"Yes," Leslie replied. "We met this elderly woman who works at the courthouse, and she lived near here as a child. She mentioned that her older sister had briefly dated one of Mr. Todd's sons. She also told us Mr. Todd was a drinker, and her parents didn't approve of the family."

"Interesting. From what I could learn, Edward Todd lost what money he had left when the stock market collapsed in 1929. He lived off his wife Elizabeth after that." Elsa pulled two old photographs from her notebook. "Here, this is a copy of a photograph of Edward and his wife Elizabeth, and this one is just Edward. A cousin of theirs let me borrow these."

Leslie took the photographs and held them side by side in front of her. When she looked at them she felt as if her heart missed a beat. Adrenaline rushed through her veins and she felt her face flush. She looked up at Beth and then again at Elsa. "Are you sure this is the same Edward Todd that owned this house with his wife Elizabeth."

"I don't think he ever held the title to the house, but yes, he did live here. I'm positive of that. Actually, the cousin told me Edward had lived in the house for years, until it was sold out from under him and he was kicked out. He lived like a pauper after that, with first one relative then the next, until he virtually died on the street."

Leslie looked back down at the copies of the old sepia-toned photographs. "At least in the end he got some of what he deserved." Leslie gave the photographs to Beth.

Beth looked at them and instantly uttered, "Oh my God!" She looked up, her eyes wide and bright, the flames from the fireplace reflecting in them. "It's him!"

"Sounds like your puzzle pieces have just fallen into place. So, when are you two going to tell me why you are really interested in the history of this house?" Elsa asked.

Leslie looked back at Beth. "Are you ready?"

"Hey, this is your party. I'm just the chaperone," replied Beth.

Leslie thought for a minute, not really certain how to begin, or if she should even tell Elsa the house was haunted. "I'm not really sure how to start. There really is a lot to tell."

"Start anywhere. I'm sitting here, dying of suspense."

"When I first toured the house, I knew there were still some things stored in the attic, but I thought the previous owners would have taken them out after I put a contract on the house. Anyway, they didn't. And what I realized, after we started going through the old trunks and boxes, was that everything in the attic had belonged to the original owners, the Weatherly family."

Elsa sat back in her chair. "That is amazing. As many hands as this house has passed through, I'm surprised no one pilfered through everything."

"I didn't understand that one either." Leslie turned now to Beth. "I didn't have a chance to tell you. I called Pat while you were napping." Leslie turned back to Elsa. "Pat Anderson. I bought the house from her and her husband. I asked her about the attic. She told me that they didn't know about the attic. She said it had been boarded up. A false wall ran the entire length of the third floor hall. They didn't discover the attic door until a few months after they moved in." Leslie added, "Pat said their children were afraid to go in the attic, and she and Joel never went in there other than when they initially took down the facade covering the actual wall and door.

Beth began to silently wonder if opening the attic could have been the event that triggered the appearance of Cordelia's ghost.

"Anyway," Leslie continued. "Beth flew down, and we were going to turn sorting through the attic into a little party for us. That's when we found things that led us to believe Edward Todd may have murdered his step-daughter to keep control of the house and her money."

"Oh my God! Seriously?"

"Yes. We brought a lot of things down from the attic and started researching the family. There are still more personal effects up there; we just concentrated on the photos and documents."

"Can I see them?"

"Of course. Everything we brought down is in my study. And I'll warn you, I don't have furniture for that room either, so everything is scattered around the floor."

"We did keep everything grouped together, based on the trunk or box we pulled it from," Beth added.

Elsa's eyes were wide with excitement. "Lead the way. I can't wait to see this." She followed Leslie into the study with Beth, wine glass in hand. Elsa stopped just inside the door, her eyes scanning the stacks of papers, photographs, clothes, uniforms, and the Weatherly family bible.

Leslie drew her attention to the mantel above the fireplace and the long curved sword. "That sword belonged to Major Nathan Weatherly. His sword and Confederate uniform were in one of the trunks. I need to get a nice display stand for it."

Elsa reached for the sword. "May I?"

"Sure, be my guest."

Elsa carefully lifted it from the mantle and held it in both hands, before she gripped it by the hilt and slowly pulled the blade from the scabbard. "This is magnificent. I can't believe all these things were in the attic. What are you going to do with them?"

"At this point, I haven't really decided. If I can find any direct descendants, I'll probably give them the family bible, photos, those sorts of things. Most of it, I'll keep."

"You should consider donating them to the Clark County Historical Society." Elsa returned the sword to the mantle.

"I might at some point."

"Now, tell me about this murder."

"This is what we know so far. Clay Weatherly was killed in World War I. His daughter Cordelia was born a couple months after his death. His wife Elizabeth remarried Edward Todd, and they had two sons, which you have helped us confirm. From what we can determine, just based on anecdotal evidence at this point, Edward Todd lost what money he had of his own when the stock market crashed. We know Elizabeth died in 1931, probably leaving Cordelia in the care of her step-father. At this point, Clay's parents and one of his sisters were dead."

"We also have a copy of Elijah Weatherly's will. He was Clay's father and the Major's son," Beth added. "In it, he leaves everything – this house, land, his estate – to Cordelia, his only grandchild at the time. Everything was to be held in trust and administered by a local law firm until she turned twenty-five. At that point, she would have gained full control of everything."

"Okay, I'm following you so far because we can establish a document trail to confirm those facts. Where does the murder part of the story come into play?"

Leslie looked again at Beth then took in deep breath. "What do you think?"

"It's your decision."

"I know, but I want your opinion."

"Hell, I'd go for it. What do you have to lose?"

Leslie rolled her eyes upward. She knew exactly what she could lose in a small town like Winchester. Leslie exhaled with a heavy sigh. "Elsa, do you believe in ghosts?"

A broad smile stretched across Elsa's face. "Don't tell me you've seen a ghost."

"Actually we have," Beth replied. "Leslie called me, scared to death, a few days ago. She thought either someone was playing a sick joke on her, she had developed schizophrenia, or had a brain tumor and was hallucinating. I naturally jumped on the first plane down here, and I'll be damned, I saw the thing, too."

Elsa narrowed her eyes into a skeptical gaze. "How do I know the two of you aren't playing some sort of joke on me?"

"You don't. But I stood there and watched as the ghost of a twelve- or thirteen- year-old Cordelia Weatherly fought off blows from an invisible assailant. I saw her with black eyes, sitting in a room crying. I saw her playing with a doll. And then this afternoon, we saw Edward Todd, the man in the photographs you showed us, beating her, and we saw blood squirt from her nose when he punched her."

"Can I have another glass of wine?" The three women returned to the parlor. Elsa sat down as Beth refilled her glass. "Where has all of this taken place?"

"In my studio. The turret room, on the third floor."

"Elsa, when you arrived this evening, you commented that I didn't look well."

"Yes, I'm sorry about that, love. Sometimes I'm far too blunt for my own good."

"No, that's fine. I didn't look well because I was sleeping off what felt like the equivalent of a bad hangover. The same thing happened to Leslie the other day. We were in the room when Cordelia's ghost appeared. It was a strange sensation. The air felt like it was statically charged. As a matter of fact, I had a security firm that my family's company uses, do a sweep of the entire house. They picked up static charges with their instruments. They had no explanation for it."

Elsa took a long sip of her wine. "Has this happened more than once?"

"Oh, yes. I've been in there three or four times now when the ghosts have appeared. It seems that the first time it happened my equilibrium got screwed up and I was dizzy, light-headed and nauseated. Each time after that, the side effects become less and less. We have actually been able to interact with her and today…" Leslie trailed off.

Beth continued, "…today, when we saw this man," she held up the photograph of Edward, "we both ran into the studio. Leslie had been in there before with Cordelia. This was my first time in the room, when the ghost of the girl appeared, so I was almost instantly overcome by a feeling of vertigo. Leslie, on the other hand, is becoming accustomed to it, and she was able to intervene and stop what appeared to be Edward's ghost."

"What do you mean 'stop'?"

"Edward Todd was beating Cordelia. Leslie lunged at him and hit him, and she almost knocked him off his feet," Beth explained.

"I think he killed her in that room," Leslie interrupted. "And I believe that if I can stop it from being acted out again, then Cordelia's spirit can move on."

"Any chance I can see this ghost?"

"We can take you up there, but her appearances are so sporadic, there is no way of knowing if you'll see her or not."

Elsa's mouth turned up at the left corner as she looked across the parlor at Beth who was now standing in front of the fireplace warming her hands. "How about you get me a vodka martini and we check out the third floor?"

Beth returned the smile. She would have sworn Elsa Van Meter, the grand dame of Winchester society, was flirting with her. "Coming right up, and I think I'll join you – Leslie?"

"Oh, why not. If you are making two, you might as well make a third."

45

Leslie gave Elsa a tour of the house, and she explained her plans for each room as they made their way to the stairs leading to the third floor. Elsa approved of the bedroom suite Leslie had purchased, and squeezed Beth's arm when she said she was happy to see the guestroom had inherited the old bedroom furniture and Beth wasn't sleeping on the futon. Beth was now more convinced than ever that Elsa was flirting. Perhaps she could manage to stay an extra day or two. She enjoyed the attention, and Elsa was easy on the eyes.

Once they reached the third floor, Leslie cautioned Elsa not to go in the studio if the ghost appeared. She didn't want her guest to suffer the same side effects from a first contact she and Beth had experienced.

"Let me see this ghost of yours."

"She doesn't appear on command. One minute we might be in the studio alone, and the next second she is standing beside us."

"Now, let me get this straight. The first time you tried to make contact with her, she couldn't see or hear you, and she disappeared when you tried to walk into the room."

"That's correct, but when the floor boards of the house creaked and popped under our feet she could hear the sound," Leslie explained.

"You should have seen Leslie jumping around on the floor like a jackrabbit, trying to make the floor creek," Beth added with a laugh.

"We assume she can hear and see things that were original to the house," Leslie explained.

Elsa walked into the studio and casually strolled around the perimeter of the room, taking in every detail. "If she can perceive sights and sounds from things that were original to the house, then how do you explain your ability to interact with her?"

Beth and Leslie were silent, then Beth offered, "We haven't gotten that far."

"Why do you think she was murdered?"

"First, there is the obvious fact that she is a ghost. Secondly, we can't find any records of her as an adult."

"You can't find any yet," Elsa corrected.

Leslie frowned, "Yes, that's right; we haven't found any yet. But we watched while Edward Todd beat the shit out of her. And we know he lived in this house for years after she was to have inherited it."

"I'm not trying to be difficult dear, and I'm not implying that I don't believe you." Elsa, now standing in front of the fireplace again, smiled at Beth. "I'm just playing devil's advocate and throwing out questions. Believe me; I'd love to find some proof of an after life other than Reverend Stone's dry sermons."

"That's fine, I understand. We just need to know when and where Cordelia died. But unless Edward Todd's youngest son is still alive and knows something, then we will probably never know the truth."

As Elsa began to walk toward Leslie and Beth, the toe of her shoe kicked a ceramic tile lying on the fireplace hearth. "Oops, you've lost a tile out of your fireplace, love." She bent down and picked it up. Turning it over in her hand, she examined it. "It doesn't appear to be broken. You should be able to attach it with a little mortar."

Leslie walked over and took the tile from Elsa, then bent down to fit it into the face of the fireplace from where it had fallen. Suddenly she stopped; something inside the opening caught her eye. The only light in the room came from the hall. She squinted in the semi-darkness. "Beth, flip on the overhead light; there's something inside here."

"Something inside? Probably a dead rat."

"Or worse, a live spider." Carefully, Leslie slid her fingers inside the opening and pulled from it a four-inch by six-inch book, with a paisley binding that was covered in dust. "Would you look at this!"

Elsa leaned over Leslie's shoulder. "It looks very old, love. You could have one of your puzzle pieces."

Leslie looked up at Beth. "I'm almost afraid to open it."

"Well, if you're not going to open it, then I will."

Slowly Leslie opened the small book, careful not to damage its pages or binding. Elsa and Beth huddled around her. "It's hers! This belonged to Cordelia."

"Are you sure, love?"

"See, her name and a date are written here inside the cover."

"What else does it say? There's something else written there," Beth was impatient to know the book's contents.

"It reads: 'To my darling daughter Cordelia, on her twelfth birthday. As you begin to grow into a young lady let this diary be your friend with which to share all your most personal secrets. Happy birthday, love

Mamma.' And it's dated November 13th, 1930."

"Are there any entries?" Beth asked.

"A few; not many." Leslie paused.

"What's wrong?"

Leslie looked up at Beth, and then at Elsa. "Remember when... was it yesterday or was it the day before? God, the last few days are running together. Anyway, remember when you had just gotten out of the shower, and I came in and told you I had been here in the studio sketching and Cordelia appeared and spoke to me. That was when she mentioned a Mr. Todd. Then she suddenly acted frightened, like she heard something or someone I couldn't see or hear." Leslie walked to her drawing table. "She was standing right here, talking to me. Then she started moving around the room." Leslie retraced Cordelia's steps as best she could remember. "She came over here to the fireplace and knelt down. I saw her put her hand in the pocket of her sweater."

Elsa's eyes widened. She wasn't sure if the story was an elaborate joke, or if her new friends were just insane. "Did you see her put the diary in the fireplace, behind the tile?"

Leslie thought for a moment. "No. She had her back to me. I couldn't see exactly what she was doing."

"This is fascinating. Let's read what she has in there. It might just be the answer you are looking for."

"Do you want me to read all of them?"

"Read the first one, a couple in the middle, and then the last," Beth directed.

"Okay." The three women sat down together on the floor, beside the fireplace. Elsa leaned close to Beth, her gray hair brushing Beth's shoulder. Leslie began to read:

"Today is my birthday. Mamma gave me this diary to write down all my secrets. I overheard her talking to Aunt Rebecca. She said she was afraid she might not live to see my next birthday. Aunt Rebecca told her to hush, that she didn't want to hear that kind of talk. I saw Mamma cry and ask Aunt Rebecca to watch over me."

"Oh my, that poor little girl, and that poor woman. They had already lost so much." As Elsa spoke, Beth watched the older woman's face. In her eyes she saw a tenderness she hadn't noticed before. Beth touched Elsa's hand and smiled.

Leslie turned a few pages, cleared her throat and again began to read.:

191

"March 3rd, 1931:

Mamma was feeling very poorly today. She got a letter in the mail from Aunt Rebecca. She didn't tell me what was in it. She just said that if she got worse that we would go live with her in Cincinnati. But I over-heard the doctor tell Mamma if she was going to go, she best go now, otherwise she might not survive the trip."

Leslie stopped reading. Tears had welled up in her eyes, preventing her from focusing on the pages in the little diary. "Here, allow me," Elsa offered. She took the diary from Leslie who, not having a tissue near, wiped the tears away with her finger tips as one left a wet trail down her cheek.

Advancing a few pages, Elsa cleared her throat and then, in a voice that was so fluid and clear it seemed to have a lyrical quality, began to read. "It is dated May 6th, 1931:

"I dropped a tray today. Mr. Todd said Mamma would have to go hungry now because I spilled all her food. He hit me in the head with his fist when I bent over to clean up everything. When no one is around he pushes me sometimes and makes me fall. He said if I told anyone that he would put Mamma and me out on the street. I don't believe he can do that. Mamma said Grandpa left this house and everything in it to me. She says there are papers that prove it, but I haven't seen them. I waited until Mr. Todd started with his liquor, then I took some food from the pantry up to Mamma. She doesn't eat much anymore."

"Sounds as though he was mentally and physically abusive to the girl," was Beth's only comment.

"Shall I read more?" Elsa asked.

"Sure." Leslie replied and then was silent again.

Elsa shifted her weight and leaned back against the mantle. She flipped a few pages ahead and began again.

"July 4th, 1931:

Today we took an automobile ride to Boonesborough. Mr. Todd made me watch after Edward and Robert while they played in the water. While I watched them, I pretended I was like the girl in the book that Aunt Re-becca sent me. But instead of a blue roadster, I would have a blue boat, and I would hit Mr. Todd in the head with my oar. Then Mamma and I would paddle off, all the way down the Kentucky River, and I would save us both when our boat went over the falls. When we reached the Ohio we would stow away on the Belle of Louisville, then sail up to Cincinnati and live with my Aunt. Mamma has some color in her cheeks today. I just know she is going to get better."

Elsa looked up from the passage. Beth's eyes locked on hers as she said, "Looks like she had quite an imagination."

"An abusive step-father, two small half brothers to care for, and a mother who was terminally ill. I'm sure she needed a good imagination."

Leslie watched the exchange between Beth and Elsa. For Elsa to find Beth attractive was not unusual. Everyone found Beth attractive. But for her to return the flirtation; this was unusual. She wondered if Beth and Angie were having problems at home. Beth had spoken of Angie very little the last few days. She had been so busy with their search for clues, she hadn't noticed until now.

"August 7th," Elsa began.

"Jenny, our house keeper, left today. She cried and told me she needed the money real bad, and she loved Mamma and me, but she just couldn't work for Mr. Todd anymore. She said her husband didn't want her to have to take that kind of treatment from some no-account drunkard, who was no better than anybody else. She told me to come see her if I ever needed her."

Elsa took the last sip from her martini glass. "Apparently, Edward Todd was a real bastard."

"The evidence seems to point to that assumption. Would you like another drink or some more wine?" Leslie asked.

Elsa examined her empty glass. "Of course. The night is still young, and we have several more pages to skim through."

"I'll get it," Beth offered.

"No. Sit still," Leslie said. "I need to stretch my legs. I'll run downstairs and get everyone a fresh drink." Leslie stood. "Do either of you have any preferences?"

"No love, just more of the same. Once I've switched to liquor I don't like to switch back again in mid-stream. If you don't mind, would you bring my reading glasses with you? They're in my handbag."

"Sure. Beth do you need anything?" Leslie looked directly into her friend's eyes, hoping Beth would somehow receive her signal of caution.

If Beth understood the look of concern, she gave no indication. As Leslie exited her studio, she turned to see Elsa lean forward and straighten a strand of Beth's hair.

46

"Anything new?" Leslie asked, as she refilled Beth's and Elsa's glasses, then her own, from the pitcher of martinis she had brought upstairs.

"No. We waited for you," Beth answered. Leslie gave Elsa her reading glasses, then returned to her seat beside the fireplace.

Elsa began to read again.

"September 10th, 1931:
Dear diary, I haven't written in three weeks because it has been so hard, what with Mamma gone and all. Mr. Todd is harder on me now. Aunt Rebecca tried to come see me, but he sent her away. Aunt Rebecca said she would get the Sheriff, but Mr. Todd told her to go ahead and try because Sheriff Rogers was a friend of his. He hits me all the time now, and except when I'm cleaning or washing, I have to stay up here on the third floor."

Leslie, with her knees drawn up under her chin and her arms wrapped around her legs, sat silently, staring at the floor.

Elsa's voice was soft and sympathetic. "It looks as if there are only a half dozen more entries. Why don't we stop?"

"No, just read the last one. I would like to know what was happening to her just before she died. I'll read all the others another time."

Elsa saw a tear forming in Leslie's eye. "If you're sure."

"Yes, please."

Elsa took a long sip of her martini, then began. "October 19th, 1931." Elsa paused. "October 19th, that's today's date. What a coincidence." She adjusted her reading glasses then continued.

"Mr. Todd hurt me really bad today. He said he was going to kill me if I ever messed up one of his shirts again. I think he might have done it today, but the woman stopped him."

Leslie looked up, her green eyes wide, her mouth slightly agape.

"What? What did you say?"

"She said, 'The woman stopped him.'"

Leslie looked at Beth, whose face had the same shocked expression. "Would you like to read it?" Elsa asked.

"No, you read it, please. I'm too tense."

"Do you think this is you?"

"I don't know, just read."

"...but the woman stopped him. She hit Mr. Todd and told him to leave me alone. He was real drunk, but it scared him. The first time I saw the woman she scared me, too, but Mamma said that if God was willing, she would send an angel to watch after me. Today she sent two angels. One of them spoke to me, while the one I had seen before saved me. I know she is an angel because she just appears from nowhere and she is real pretty."

Elsa looked first at Beth, then at Leslie. "I've always considered myself very open-minded and open to, for lack of a better term, extraordinary possibilities, but this is pushing the limit for me." Elsa studied the faces of both women for any indication that somehow this entire evening had been a setup. "I'm beginning to feel that I'm being conned for some unknown reason."

Leslie was oblivious to Elsa's words. "Let me see the diary." She took the diary from Elsa's hand and began quickly reading and rereading the last few entries. While her friend read, Beth tried to reassure the woman, with whom she had become so intrigued, that everything they told her had been in earnest.

"I swear to you Elsa, we have not staged any of this. When we left this room earlier today, everything was intact, including the fireplace tile. I don't know if we are seeing a ghost, but we are seeing something, and we have interacted with it. I promise you." Beth looked into Elsa's eyes. "Elsa?"

"Beth, love, I think I would prefer to remain skeptical. I'm comfortable with skeptical. Skeptical has allowed me keep my money all these years, while other family members haven't. If I stop being skeptical right now, then I think I should be, for lack of a better term at this point, freaked out."

"I've been freaked out since I stepped foot in this house."

"Beth, Elsa, look at this." Leslie turned the diary so both women could see the page she had just read. Leslie pointed to the middle of the page. "Read this. She is talking about yesterday, when we were in the studio alone, and we were able to speak to each other for the first time. See this. She said I asked her name, but she heard Mr. Todd coming and I disappeared before she could tell me." Leslie flipped back to another page. "Here, and see this?" She pointed to the open diary. "Here she is talking about hearing someone outside this room. I think this was when you and I were in the hall and the floor boards popped."

"How could a ghost keep a diary?" Beth asked.

"Perhaps she isn't a ghost," Elsa offered.

"Then what is she?" Beth asked.

"I haven't the slightest idea, love." Elsa put an extra emphasis on the word 'love.'

Leslie stood up, martini glass in her left hand and the diary in her right, and then began to pace across the floor. "What if she isn't dead?"

"What do you mean, 'what if she isn't dead'?" Beth turned and asked. Elsa, now sitting to Beth's back, leaned forward and rested her chin on Beth's shoulder. Beth felt a shudder go through her body; it was like electricity. It was a feeling she hadn't experienced with Angie in months.

"I don't know what I mean – I'm just thinking out loud. I've had too much to drink." Leslie paced across the room again. "What if she isn't dead in the past? What if..." Leslie's voice trailed off. "I don't know what I'm talking about." Leslie stopped walking and pinched the bridge of her nose for a moment, trying to focus her thoughts into one coherent image.

"Okay, Beth. You always tell me I'm the computer nerd and the science fiction nerd. Well, have you ever read anything on quantum physics?"

Beth rolled her eyes skyward, "Oh yeah, I keep a stack of books on the subject on my nightstand to read every evening before I go to bed."

Elsa leaned closer. Beth could feel the woman's breath on her cheek. In a soft throaty voice Elsa whispered, "I'd like to see what you have on your night stand." Beth breathed in deeply, as her body flushed with heat.

Leslie ignored the comment and continued, "In quantum physics, time is linear but there are alternate realities. For example, at nine o'clock I get in my car and leave the house and I make the green light at an intersection and keep driving, but behind me a car coming from the opposite direction runs the red light. In the alternate reality, something delays me, and I leave the house at say nine-o-one and I make the green light, but because I go through the intersection a split second later, the car that ran the red light broadsides me."

"Okay, so how does this explain that the ghost isn't dead?" Beth tried to concentrate on Leslie's words, but it was becoming more difficult with Elsa sitting so close.

"I've read some other things about time, and some people believe that time isn't necessarily linear. Time folds, and the past and present and future are all taking place simultaneously, we just aren't aware of it. This is a theory of why we sometimes have a feeling of déja vu. Our subconscious somehow taps into the future for a split second, and then when we catch up with it, we think we have been there before. And in essence, we have."

"Maybe it is just the alcohol, but believe it or not, I'm following you," replied Beth.

"So am I," Elsa said as she lightly touched Beth's hand again. "So love, you believe that this room is in someway a doorway to the past?"

"I don't know that it necessarily has to do with this room, but maybe it is because of the events that were played out in this room. Teenage girls have pretty intense emotions. Their minds and bodies are going through so many changes. Then, add the trauma of a mother's death, being locked up here alone, beaten up by a step-father. Maybe it's Cordelia's own emotions that are allowing us to see her and interact with her in the past."

"Interesting theory. So you feel that might be why neither of you have been able to find anything on her death?"

"I don't know. Edward Todd may be murdering her right now, as we speak, or perhaps he had already killed her and is disposing of her body. Or maybe I can stop him from killing her – if I can warn her in time."

"Assuming you have stumbled onto something, how are we going to warn her? There has been no pattern to her appearances," Beth reminded Leslie.

Elsa raised her hand to Beth's chin and turned Beth face to her own. "We could sleep in here and wait for her to materialize. I love a good adventure, don't you?"

"I think Elsa has a good idea. You and I could camp out in here for the next day or two and see if she shows up. Or we could take turns." Beth looked back at Elsa.

Leslie, annoyed, replied, "Elsa, I really don't think you want to experience the hours of nausea that accompany a first contact with her."

Elsa, still looking at Beth, smirked. "I'm sure I'm in good hands."

Leslie moved the desk lamp from her drawing table to the floor beside the futon. Then from the large linen closet on the second floor, she took two blankets and a pillow and carried them upstairs to her studio where she tucked herself into bed on the open futon. Leslie knew Elsa had not left the house, even though Elsa had said it was getting late and she should leave. Leslie liked her new friend, but she was angry with her old one for jeopardizing her relationship with Angie. But who was she to judge, she asked herself. She knew as well as anyone that sometimes, even what seems to be the best of relationships, can suffer from problems that are invisible to everyone except those living though them. Perhaps some of her resentment stemmed from a slight feeling of jealously. After all, she hadn't been involved with anyone for some time now. And secretly she was lonely, but not lonely enough to date the first man who came along.

As she lay there, waiting for Cordelia or Cordelia's ghost, she turned to the beginning of the diary and began to read each entry. There were passages about playing games with classmates, picnics with her mother and her mother's friends. She even wrote about a crush on a boy she knew. Leslie recorded his name in her notepad. It was possible that he could still be alive and might have some information on the girl who had been so enamored of him.

It was after midnight when Leslie finally fell asleep. She awoke only once during the night. It was a noise from somewhere inside the house, probably Beth, she thought. She wondered if Elsa was staying the night. Moonlight shown through the windows. Her eyes scanned the room; she was still alone. Leslie lay back on the futon, and then she drifted off to sleep.

47

"Good morning, sleepy head."

Leslie slowly opened her eyes to see Beth sitting on the edge of the futon, staring down at her and smiling. "Rise and shine, sleeping beauty."

Leslie rolled over and groaned. "Go away. You're the evil entity that makes people wake up too early."

"Too early? It's almost ten. I thought I better wake you before you sleep away the day. I only have today and tomorrow; I fly back Wednesday morning."

Leslie blinked and tried to better focus her eyes and rid them of sleep. "Ten. Why did you let me sleep so long? You should have woke me sooner?"

"Honestly, I haven't been up that long myself. Just long enough to have a cup of coffee and skim through the paper. Did you have any visitors last night?"

"I don't think so. I remember hearing a noise sometime during the night. I woke up for a minute and looked around the room, but it must have just been the house popping. Then I fell asleep again. I don't think I woke up any more until you came in."

Leslie adjusted her pillows then pushed herself up into a reclining position. "Where's Elsa?"

"Home, I guess. She left a little after midnight. She is going to stop by later today, if that's alright with you."

"That's fine. I like her."

An uncomfortable silence formed between Leslie and Beth. Beth hesitated then spoke. "I think I need to explain something."

"If you are talking about what was going on last night with Elsa, you don't owe me any explanations. You are my best friend, and I love you. It just surprised me and made me a little concerned. Over the years, I've seen both men and women, gay and straight, come on to you. And I know you liked the attention, but you never reciprocated, at least that I'm aware of. It just concerned me that you might do something to damage your relationship with Angie."

"Other than friendship, there isn't much left of my relationship with Angie."

Leslie sat up. "What! When did this happen? Why haven't you told me anything was wrong?"

"I did talk to you a little about how we were going in different directions."

"Well, a year ago, sure, but you never made it sound this bad."

"We have been through couples counseling, and we've talked about giving it another try, but I think we both realize it is over. I haven't talked about it, because I guess if I didn't talk about it, then maybe it would go away."

"You're like a sister to me. You should have said something."

"I know. Like I said, I guess I was playing ostrich and burying my head in the sand."

"Yeah, up to your ass. I can't believe you didn't tell me. I thought Angie was in the bedroom with you when I called the other day."

"She was. She had just walked in to get something out of the closet. We've been sleeping in separate rooms for the last two months."

"God, I can't believe this. The two of you were like poster children for great relationships. I would always look at the two of you and know that there was someone out there for me. All I had to do was just find him."

"We did have a good relationship, and she is a wonderful person. I can't say anything bad about her. We got together when we were in our twenties, and now that we have some age and hopefully, some maturity, we have grown apart. Me becoming actively involved in my father's company probably sped up the inevitable. But if it was going to happen, then it's better that it happen now, so we part as friends and move on. We don't want to end up hating each other."

"I'm so sorry for the two of you, but I still can't believe you didn't talk to me about it."

"I should have, but like I said, I believe my way of hanging on was to not talk."

"So, what are you going to do?"

"She is using these few days, while I'm down here, to get her personal things out of the apartment and into a place of her own. I told her to go ahead and take any of the furniture she wanted, but she is only taking one of the bedroom suites and the breakfast table. She said she didn't want me to come back to an apartment that had been cleaned out."

"When I get back, I'll arrange for movers to take most everything out and set it up for her, and then I'll go shopping."

"That's pretty big of you to not fight over anything."

Beth shrugged off the complement. "It really is the least I can do. She has a good job and good income, but since she is the one who elected to move, I just thought I should give her most of the furniture. After all, with my family money, I have pretty deep pockets. And you shouldn't praise me so soon, we haven't divided up the CD collection yet, and I'm asking for visitation rights with Geetz."

"I didn't think you liked cats."

"I've changed my mind. Geetz and I have bonded."

"I have another question. Are you interested in Elsa?"

"I don't know. She is here in Winchester, and I'm in Chicago. I doubt either of us would be willing to move. With me positioning myself to take over running the company, it would pretty much be impossible to leave Chicago. I guess we could meet halfway and rendezvous in Indianapolis. Honestly, I would predict we will have a little fling, and that will be the end of it."

"It seemed like she was pretty interested in you. Maybe the long distance fling thing will actually work for both of you. I should find someone to at least occupy my time."

"You need to get back out there. Not everyone is like Mike. Not every man is a jerk like he was."

"Let's get off the subject of me and onto something else."

"Very well. So what's on the agenda for today?"

"I thought that we could go back down to the courthouse and hook up with our old lady friend. Maybe we can get some more scoop on the Todd family. Then we can hook up with Elsa for a late lunch and have her introduce us to Robert Todd."

"Does she know how to get in touch with him?"

"She had a brunch date at the country club this morning, then she was going to make a couple of phone calls and get an address for us. She offered to go along and make the introductions. She said it might be better than two out-of-towners knocking on his door."

"Sounds like you have it all planned."

"Elsa and I talked last night after you went to bed."

Leslie narrowed her eyes. "Yeah, I bet you talked."

"What can I say? And she isn't as old as you think. The gray hair just makes her look older. She said if people think she is older than she is, then she gets away with more."

"So everything is still in working order?"

"So far as I can tell, but I didn't take it for a test drive, if that is what you are asking." The right corner of Beth's lips turned up to form a sly sideways smile.

"You are absolutely evil. I'm getting in the shower."

"You better save me some hot water."

48

When Leslie and Beth entered the courthouse, they were greeted by the elderly lady who had helped them the previous week. "You know, we forgot to ask your name last week," Leslie remarked.

"It's Hazel Norton. It was Hazel Price, but I married Claude Norton in 1947. I had been sweet on him in high school, when he went off to war. Of course, he was three years older than me and thought I was just a baby. I used to write him letters. Then, when he came back, he noticed me and said I had grown up real nice." Leslie and Beth watched as the old woman's face lit up as she spoke of her deceased husband.

"Now, you two were in here asking about the old Weatherly place?"

"Yes ma'am, we were. We would like to find out when it passed out of the Weatherly family's hands and who sold it. Also, if you could tell us anything else about the man who lived there, Edward Todd."

"Edward Todd. Now that was who I was trying to think of. That was his name, and I think his oldest boy's name was Edward, too. Now my sister, she was sweet on Robert, the youngest one. Edward Junior, he was too wild. He was just like his daddy, always drinking and getting into trouble."

"Tell us more about them?" Beth asked.

With long slender fingers, and joints that protested under attempts to make them bend, the old woman pulled her knitted heavy cotton sweater tighter around her shoulders. "I did some looking this morning. I thought you two might be back. You can come with me." Beth and Leslie followed Mrs. Norton to a ledger book lying open on top of a heavy oak table. The old lady pointed to the section she had marked with a small yellow Post-It note.

Leslie and Beth leaned over the volume, their heads touching as they read. "So according to this, a Mrs. William Miller sold the house in 1952 to Stephen and Rachel Sloan. Do you have any records of when she bought the house?"

"I couldn't find any in these books."

Leslie and Beth looked at one another. "I wonder if she was a family member?" Beth said, thinking out loud.

"We found no records of anyone with the last name Miller. However, everything we found in the attic stops sometime when Cordelia was a child."

"Mrs. Norton…"

"Oh, just call me Hazel."

Leslie felt uncomfortable using an elderly person's given name. It was in direct contradiction to what she had always been taught were good manners, but she complied with the old woman's request. "Hazel, do you remember anything about what Mr. Todd Senior did for a living."

"Now I was just a girl when all that was going on, but I do remember my daddy fussing about my sister liking Robert and saying Mr. Todd didn't have any money of his own anymore. Daddy said that he was living in that house, off his dead wife's money."

"How did he lose his money?"

"I think he lost it in the Depression. That was how most people lost it back then."

"What year was it, when your sister was dating Robert Todd?"

"They weren't dating like young people do today; they were just sweet for each other."

"Yes, I understand, but do you know what year it was?"

The old woman stared off into the open room. "Let me see, I was about eleven or twelve, so that would be about thirty-eight or thirty-nine. My sister was a little bit older than me."

"Is there anything else you can tell me about the family?" Leslie asked.

"I know Edward Junior was in the war, in the Army I think. Seems like I remember that. I'm not sure about Robert, but I think that he enlisted, too. I believe he was just there for the tail end of it, he being younger and all."

"What about the family? What happened to them?"

"Well now, I'm not sure. Like I said, we moved away for a while, and I lost touch with some of the people here in Winchester. I think Mr. Todd came to no good and Edward Junior didn't do much better. I'm not sure about Robert. I'll think on it some, and if I remember anything, I'll write it down so I don't forget to tell you."

Leslie reached into the pocket of her leather jacket and removed a brown business card case with her initials embossed in gold on the front. "Here, this is my card. It has my home phone number and my cell phone number. Call me anytime you like if you remember something."

Hazel took the card and held it out from her to better see the print.

"I'll do that, honey." She squeezed Leslie's hand.

Leslie and Beth left the courthouse and walked down the street to her car. "So, what do you think?" Beth asked, as she waited for Leslie to press the button on her key fob. Beth heard the lock trip, and opened the door and climbed inside.

Leslie fastened her seat belt and inserted the key in the ignition. "I think we need to find Robert Todd, and see if he knows anything about Mrs. William Miller. I'm guessing she is the key to what happened to the house and property Cordelia should have inherited. And we still haven't checked on the law firm that handled Elijah's estate."

"Likewise, Robert Todd could be the key to finding out what happened to Cordelia," Beth added. "Of course, he was only six when the mother died and, we suspect, when Cordelia was murdered. But there is always a chance he saw something, or in later years, his father let something slip. Maybe a death bed confession to clear his conscience?"

"Do you have Elsa's number with you?"

Beth smiled, "Do I have Elsa's number?"

Leslie laughed, "You are evil." Just as Leslie handed her cell phone to Beth, it rang.

"Maybe that's her now."

Leslie pressed the button on the phone to receive the call. "Hello, this is Leslie." There was a short pause.

"Leslie, this is Mark. I hope I'm not bothering you, and it's okay to call?"

"Mark! Hello. No that's fine, it's okay to call me. I just thought you were someone else."

"Remember Saturday? I said my girlfriend worked part time at *The Winchester Sun*?"

"Yes."

"I asked her to look up stuff in their database about your house and the owners, so we went to the office yesterday. She is really good on the computer and the Internet."

"Did she find something?"

"Yeah, the story is dated March sixth, 1952. It's about a guy named Edward Todd, who was living in your house back then. It says that when the police showed up to evict him, he was drunk and fired two shots at their cars. It says too, that his son went inside and talked him into coming out, and that he was arrested without further incident."

"Does it say anything about who had him evicted?"

"No, it just says the owner."

206

"Can you get me a copy?"

"I already did. Look, I got to go. I have to get back to class. I told my teacher I forgot and left something in the library, but I went to the restroom so I could call you. I'll drop by tonight and give you the copy if that's okay."

"Yes, that'll be great. Thanks, Mark." Leslie repeated to Beth what Mark had told her.

"Maybe we should go back to the courthouse and look for tax records, or maybe the police station and see if they still have any arrest records," Beth proposed. "Or, I had another thought. As far as we know, the only living members of the Weatherly family were Cordelia and Rebecca. Perhaps, after Cordelia died or disappeared or whatever happened to her, Edward didn't pay the taxes on the house and this Mrs. Miller bought it right out from under the son-of-a-bitch."

"It does sound like another trip to the courthouse, but I would rather check with Elsa first, then stake out my studio again, just in case Cordelia reappears." Beth dialed Elsa and from the moment Elsa answered, Beth's voice and demeanor changed. Her voice took on a softer quality; her fingers fumbled nervously with the corners of the notepad that was resting in her lap. Leslie listened intermittently while she drove.

"Good news. She has an address for us. Amazingly, she realized she knows his wife's niece and her husband."

"She knows Robert Todd's niece?"

"Yes, his niece by marriage. Elsa is meeting us at your house, then we are all going together to pay a social visit. She told them you had just moved here and bought the house Robert grew up in. And I was visiting from out of town. And that you were interested in the house's history."

Leslie smiled, "That's good. If he thinks we are trying to dig up dirt on the family, or drag his father's name through the mud, then he'll clam up and will never talk to us. I'm still holding onto the theory that Cordelia might still be alive in the past."

"Speaking of that, what did you do with the diary?"

"I put it back where we found it, and then put the tile back in place."

Beth lifted her sunglasses and rubbed her eyes. "I was just getting comfortable with the idea that I see dead people, and now the theory may be changing. If I stop and think about everything that has happened over the last few days, then I'll start freaking out."

"I thought we were already freaking out." Leslie pulled into her driveway and turned off the engine. Elsa was sitting in her car smiling and waiting for them. The three women went inside.

49

Leslie, with Elsa in the front seat navigating and Beth in the back seat, drove down the narrow winding country lane that led to Robert Todd's home. Leslie slowed her car and read the numbers on the mailbox aloud. "One-twenty-five, is this it?"

"It should be," Elsa responded, "if my directions and the GPS are correct."

As Leslie pulled into the drive, two medium-sized mixed-breed dogs quickly greeted her car. "I hope they're friendly," Beth remarked.

"I guess we'll know in a minute."

The house sat about fifty yards off the road and the long driveway, which led to the house, was bordered on both sides by an overgrown fence row. The house itself was a modest ranch. From the architecture, Leslie guessed it had been built sometime in the late 60s or early 70s. The gutters on one end were sagging under the weight of wet leaves, which were spilling over the edges. Every eve and windowsill needed a fresh coat of paint.

Leslie was the first to venture out of the car. The dogs circled around her, the smallest sniffing her hands. It suddenly jumped backward with a yelp and ran for the front door. Cautiously, Leslie, followed by Elsa and then Beth, walked up the cracked and uneven concrete sidewalk that led from the driveway to the front porch. As they reached the front steps the door opened, an elderly man wearing brown corduroy trousers and matching flannel shirt greeted them. "Can I help you?" The man asked.

Elsa stepped in front of Leslie. "Hello. Are you Mr. Robert Todd?"

"Yes."

"Hi, I'm Elsa Van Meter. I'm an acquaintance of your wife's niece, Ruby. My friend here, Leslie Newkirk, bought the old Weatherly place. She's trying to dig up some history on the house. We found out that you grew up there and just thought maybe you could tell us a little about it."

"Well, I don't know that I've got anything interesting to tell, but you can come on in. My wife said that she had talked to her niece and you all would be stopping by." Robert Todd held open the glass storm door, so the three women could enter. "Don't pay any attention to them dogs.

They won't hurt you; they just bark a lot when anyone pulls up. I think they might bite if they thought anybody was trying to hurt my wife or me, but other than that, they ain't much use as watch dogs. They let every animal you can imagine just walk right thorough the yard. I saw them out there the other day just lying on the sidewalk, while a raccoon was getting in my garbage can."

The three women seated themselves on the sofa, while Robert Todd slid down into his recliner. His wife, Joyce, joined them and positioned herself in an antique wingback chair to the left of the sofa.

"So what is it you want to know?"

Leslie knew she needed to proceed with caution when asking questions of the man. To her relief, Elsa started the conservation. "Mr. Todd, I've only been in the house a few times, but it's a huge home. I bet as a child it was fun to run around in there and play in all those rooms."

"Yep, my brother and I did a lot of playing in that house. Of course, Daddy never let us get too wild. You didn't want to make him mad."

"Did your mother keep you boys in check, too?"

"Well now, I don't remember that much about my mother. She died when I was six. I think we all grieved a lot after that."

"I'm sorry. What was she like?"

"She was a pretty woman, kind of small built. She would sing to us at night and make us say our prayers. That's about all I remember about her."

"How long did you live in the house?"

"I lived there up until I went off to the Army. When I came back, I got married and got a place of my own."

"Really? I'm surprised. With all that space in the house, I would have thought you would have lived there."

Joyce Todd now entered the conversation. "It's probably not my place to say, but his daddy was drinking a lot more by then, and if we were going to start a family, I didn't want the children growing up around all that."

"We are trying to track down some past owners. When did your family sell the house?"

As Elsa asked the question, Leslie saw the elderly man's face become hard and stern. "Daddy didn't sell it. It was stolen right out from under him."

"Stolen? I don't understand?"

"That was our home for all those years. Then some woman comes in from out of town and says she owns the house, and she throws daddy out

209

in the street. It wasn't like that man hadn't suffered enough."

"I'm so sorry. We thought he had sold the house. What happened?" Elsa's sympathetic demeanor encouraged the man to continue.

"I don't know everything that happened because Daddy never would talk about it much. We tried to get a lawyer to help us, but they just kept saying the house never belonged to us. The lawyer of the people that threw Daddy out said if we didn't shut up about it, they would charge us back rent for all those years. I tell you, it about broke his heart, having to move out like that. It wasn't like he hadn't suffered enough."

"Suffered? Was his health bad?"

"The drinking took a toll on him, but like a lot of people, he lost everything in the Depression; Mama's money paid for a lot of things. Then she died, and I thought she had left the house to Daddy, but them lawyers will find a way around everything."

"What ever happened to your half-sister, Cordelia?"

"Now that's a name I haven't heard in years. I'm not sure. Daddy promised Mama that he would raise her just like his own, and then she up and run off. I heard she was living up in Newport, Kentucky. Of course, Newport was a pretty wild place then. It had gambling halls and everything. If she was in Newport, on her own, then you can bet she wasn't living a proper life."

"Did you get along well with your sister?"

"Not really. I think all of those Weatherlys were kind of full of themselves."

"Are you sure she ran away? Other people seem to think she died young, perhaps not long after your mother died."

The old man thought for a moment. "Well now, I guess she could have, after she ran off. I just remember Daddy using some bad words and saying she was ungrateful to him for trying to take care of her, and he was glad she was gone."

The three women talked with Mr. Todd for a few more minutes, but it was obvious he knew nothing of the fate of his half-sister. After thanking him and his wife for their time, the three left.

50

"Now what?" Beth asked, as she snapped the buckle of her seat belt into place.

"We could check the tax records and see who paid the taxes on the house. Maybe that is how this Mrs. Miller got her hands on it," Leslie offered.

"If I were to leave my home and estate to a minor child, I would set everything up in trust and have the estate pay the expenses on the house. I would also have it pay for the care of the child until she was of age," Elsa remarked. "And, I'll add that I still haven't seen your ghost, so my vote is still pending."

Leslie put her car into reverse, then pulled into a gravel turn-about in the yard. She headed back down the driveway, toward the road. "I wonder if the law firm is still in business."

"It isn't," Elsa answered quickly.

"How do you know?"

"I called my lawyer. He was familiar with them. He said they closed their offices at least twenty or thirty years ago."

"I wonder what happened to their records?"

"I don't know, but I can find out."

"I still think Cordelia is alive."

"Alive now?" Beth asked.

"I don't know if she is alive now, but I believe she is still alive in the past. And if I can help her get away from her step-father, she won't die – well, you know what I mean."

The sun was beginning to shine from behind what had been a cloudy and overcast sky the last two days. Elsa removed her Ray Bans from her purse and put then on. Looking in the small mirror on the back of the sun visor, she adjusted a lock of her shimmering gray hair so it fell loosely around the frame of her glasses. Watching the older woman's every movement, Beth was captivated. Sensing Beth's gaze, Elsa turned and pursed her lips. Beth smiled and began mentally planning her next trip to Winchester.

"Turn here," Elsa directed.

Leslie turned without question. When she spent summers with her grandparents, she had learned the back roads around Clark County, but by now most of those memories had faded.

"I'm taking us out for cocktails. This is a short cut."

Elsa's short cut took them down a narrow road lined with limestone fences dating back to the early 1800s. With each curve and hill, Beth felt her stomach rise and fall. She was accustomed to the flat farmland of Illinois, not rolling pastures of central Kentucky. "How much further? I'm turning green."

Elsa turned around and placed her hand on Beth's knee. "Don't worry, it's not much further. I'll nurse you back to health." Beth tried to smile, but she was too nauseous.

Leslie drove across a bridge whose roadbed was just a few feet above the riverbank below. "The sign said Fayette County. I'm assuming that was the Kentucky River, and we are headed for Lexington."

"We aren't going into town; there is a little place up here on the left. It has a nice view of the river and great food and stiff drinks."

"I don't know if I can eat or drink anything," Beth moaned from the back seat.

"All you need to do, love, is get some food in your stomach and you'll be good as new." Leslie turned into the gravel parking lot and shut off the motor. Then Leslie and Beth followed behind Elsa and watched as she whirled into the restaurant, much the same as she had entered Leslie's house the night before. Everyone working in the restaurant knew her. The owner and chef came out from the kitchen, each giving her a hug and kissing her cheek.

"Tony, these are my friends. Leslie here just bought the old Weatherly house in Winchester..."

"Ah, the haunted house; I've heard of it."

Leslie's eyes widened, but she did not reply to the owner's comment. She simply shook his hand. "And this is Leslie's friend from Chicago, Beth. She's a very special friend of mine as well."

When Beth extended her hand to Tony, he wrapped both his large thick hands around hers and squeezed it gently. "I'm so happy to meet you. Ms. Elsa is a wonderful woman, and I'm so glad she brought you both to my restaurant."

Tony led the three women to Elsa's favorite table and seated them himself. He then gave each woman a menu; the wine list he presented to Elsa. He then recommended that the chef prepare something special for them, something not on the menu or the list of nightly specials posted at the hostess stand.

Dinner was flavorful and the wine poured freely. Elsa explained that she tried to eat at Tony's at least twice a month and she always brought friends who liked to spend money and tip well. She insisted that tonight's dinner would be on her. Throughout dinner, the conversation shifted from their next course of action in finding out the fate of young Cordelia, to local history, to art galleries in Chicago. After finishing off most of their second bottle of wine, Leslie noticed that it was starting to get late, and she wanted to get home and continue her stake-out of her third floor studio.

When they returned to Leslie's house, they noticed a light in the third floor windows. "Looks like you left the light on in your studio," Beth commented.

Leslie looked up as she pulled in her driveway. "I don't remember leaving a light on." She looked first at Elsa, then Beth. "I wonder if she's back." Leslie quickly exited the car and rushed up the steps of the back porch to the kitchen door. She fumbled with her keys, dropping them once. "Shit! I can't get the key to work!" No sooner had she said this than the tumblers in the lock turned and she flung open the door. Leslie raced through the kitchen, down the hall to the stairs, throwing off her leather jacket as she ran. She gripped the banister with her right hand, taking the stairs two at a time. Beth and Elsa, both several strides behind, rushed up the stairs as well. Beth was treading more cautiously than a few days before, when she had fallen and nearly broken her ankle.

Leslie stopped when she reached the door to her studio. The room was dark. No lights were turned on, not even her small drawing table lamp. "It was her. She was back." She spun around. "Beth, Elsa, look. All the lights are off. She was in here. She came back. Damn it, I missed her!" Leslie hit the side of the door facing with her open hand. "I should have been here. What if he killed her this time?"

Leslie walked inside her studio, turning around in circles as she called out, "Cordelia! Cordelia Weatherly, I'm back! It's me, Leslie. I came back to help you."

Beth and Elsa stood together watching her. "Maybe she didn't come back. It could have been something else causing the light." Beth tried to reassure Leslie, but she too feared that this time the little girl was truly dead.

"Her diary!" Leslie hurried to the fireplace and removed the tile. "It's here!" She turned to the last page. "There's a new entry, it's dated today," Leslie said as tears rolled from her eyes.

Elsa and Beth rushed to her side. The three women stood huddled together reading the latest entry.

October 20th, 1931:
I waited for a long time today, but the angels didn't come back. Mr. Todd was afraid to come up here. He was real drunk last night when he was hitting me, but he remembered the angels saving me. Today when I was scrubbing the kitchen, he pushed me into the wall and I hit my head real hard. It is getting to be almost every day now. I'm scared he really will kill me.

"Oh god, what if he did it. What if he killed her and I wasn't here to stop it?" Leslie's tears dripped from her cheeks, onto the pages of the open diary.

"Love, we don't know what the reality is in this situation. The poor little girl may very well be dead, and maybe she has been for the last eighty years. The intensity of her emotions may be allowing you to communicate with her, as if she were still with us. Didn't you both tell me the previous owners reported seeing her? That was why they moved out of the house?"

Leslie looked up from the diary. Elsa, seeing the distress and sorrow in Leslie's eyes, gently wiped the tears from her face. "I do believe you and Beth have seen this apparition. What it is, I'm not sure. It could be that this same scene will pay itself out year after year, and there is nothing you or any of us can do to change it."

Leslie wiped her eyes. "I just can't stand the thought of that little girl hurt and alone. I can't live in this house if I have to watch that over and over again."

Beth put her arm around Leslie. "Look at what she wrote. She thinks you are an angel sent by her mother to watch over her. You have given her some hope."

"But if I can't save her, what good is it?"

Neither Elsa nor Beth had an answer for Leslie. They too wanted to help the little girl whose spirit was trapped in another realm in the third floor room, but they were at a loss as to what to do. Elsa offered a suggestion. "Why don't you write a note or leave something for her to find?"

"Like what?"

"Write something in her diary. Tell her who you are. Tell her you care."

Leslie wiped her eyes and blew her nose on a tissue she had stuffed into her pants pocket. "I guess I could try."

"Would you like us to leave you alone, love?"

"For a minute, I guess."

"I'll show her some of the other things we found in the attic, and then we'll come back and check on you."

Leslie tried to smile, but her lower lip quivered with the effort. "Okay, thanks."

51

Leslie sat down at her drawing table and stared at the blank pages of the open diary. One of the pages still had little damp circles from her tears. She touched the crinkled spot on the paper. Silently, she asked herself how many times the child, Cordelia, sat with this same diary in her lap and cried while she wrote about the loss of her mother and the abuse she suffered at the hands of her stepfather.

Leslie picked up a pen and began to write:

Cordelia, my name is Leslie, and I am the woman you saw here on the third floor. I'm not an angel, but since seeing you for the first time, I have tried to watch out for you and find some way to protect you from the man who is hurting you. It is difficult to explain, but I believe that somehow I am from your future, eighty years in your future. I know there are people who love you and will help you. You must get to them as soon as possible, as I fear for your safety. If there was any way possible, I would protect you myself and love you and care for you, just as if you were my own daughter. I want you to grow up and be a strong and caring woman. Someday, please find me if you can. I want to know you are all right.
Love,
Leslie Newkirk.

Leslie started to close the diary, then stopped. She opened the small drawer under her drawing table and removed one of the business cards. On it was her name, address, phone numbers, and email, along with a list of the type of art in which she worked. Leslie wrote on the back: Some day, when you are older, look for me. Leslie stuck it inside the diary, then walked across the room and placed the diary back inside its hiding place. She then replaced the tile to cover the opening.

While Leslie was writing the note for Cordelia, Mark Rogers had come to the door with the 1952 news article about the eviction of Edward Todd from Wood Hurst and the stand-off with local police.

"Hi Beth. I have a copy of this article for Leslie, well, and you, too. It's the one I told her about today when I called."

216

"Oh yes. She's upstairs. Do you know Elsa Van Meter?"

Mark smiled and nodded. "Sort of. I saw you at the country club a few times."

Elsa extended her hand and shook Mark's. "Oh yes, you are the delightful young man who worked at the pool last summer. Your parents are Barbara and John Rogers, I believe."

"Yes, ma'am."

"So, I hear you've seen the ghost, too."

Mark's eyes widened, and he opened his mouth as if to speak, but he only stammered.

"It's okay. She knows. Actually, Elsa was helping us today. We were trying to track down some more leads on the family, which will hopefully help us figure out what happened to the girl who is haunting Leslie's studio."

"This is pretty cool. My parents would have a stroke if they knew you believed there's a ghost."

Elsa ran her fingers though her silky gray hair, pushing it back away from her face and letting it fall again. It was a gesture Beth loved to watch.

"So, I take it that your parents aren't open to the idea of ghosts?"

"I'll say. They thought the Andersons were crazy and a bad influence on me."

"Oh really? From what Beth and Leslie told me, they seemed quite nice. A little stressed obviously, but nice none the less." Elsa paused. "You know, when I was your age, one of my favorite pasttimes was giving my parents a stroke. And I still give my brother and sister a stroke on a regular basis. As a matter of fact, I believe your mother is friends with my sister."

Mark shrugged and rolled his eyes. "My parents are really into their country club friends, especially my mom. And my brother Thomas is going to be just like them. No offense though. I know you're on the board."

"None taken, and that's a pity. Not all, but many of those people are vapid. Even though they have no reason to be, they're often very self-absorbed. They don't know how to laugh at themselves and relax and have fun. And fun is very high on my list of priorities. It would be even if I didn't have money." Elsa looked at Beth. "Now, take Beth here. Her family has more money than most countries, and she is down here playing ghost hunter with her best friend."

Mark smiled. "My mom would freak out if she knew I was standing here talking to you."

"Oh my, don't tell me she thinks I'm a bad influence on teenage boys."

"No, she thinks you are it."

"It?"

"Yeah, she comes home from the country club and it's always, 'I saw Elsa Van Meter there today.' And she talks about what you were wearing and who you had lunch with. She volunteered for a couple of committees just because she heard you were going to head them up."

"Oh really? Well, we'll just have to have some fun with that won't we Mark? The next time I see you both at the club, I'll make certain your mother knows that you and I are fast friends."

Leslie, hearing the door chime and remembering Mark was stopping by, decided she should go back downstairs and rejoin Beth and Elsa. Then, just as Leslie turned out the light in her studio, she felt a heavy force against her right shoulder. The force was so great it knocked her off her feet and she fell against the wall. She was so disoriented that she slid down to the floor.

"Who the hell are you? And what are you doing in my house?"

Leslie looked up to see a man standing over her. He had thick shoulders and wore a white shirt, with a dark vest and trousers. She blinked and tried to focus her eyes, as light from the hall shown on his face. His eyes were large with rage, and his clenched teeth growled out at her from under a thick bristly mustache. Terror raced through her; she suddenly realized Edward Todd was standing over her.

Leslie scrambled to get to her feet, but he hit her hard again, pushing her further away from the studio door and safety. The entire left side of her face ached with an intense throbbing pain.

Edward Todd reached down and grabbed her by her shirt and pulled her up to her feet, slamming her against the wall. "I said, who are you?!"

"I'm an angel sent to take you to hell," Leslie spat back at him.

Leslie's head jerked to one side, as she felt the sting of a back-handed blow to her right cheek. He slammed her against the wall again. "How did you get in my house? Are you one of those Weatherly bitches?"

"This isn't your house, you son-of-a-bitch!" Again he landed another blow to her face. Leslie felt her legs weaken and the room begin to go dark. No, she told herself, don't pass out, not like this! He'll kill me if I go down.

Leslie felt his fist slam into her side. She gasped for air and fought to hold on to consciousness. As he slammed her head into the wall again, Leslie willed all of her strength to deliver a blow to Edward Todd. She knew it was her only chance. As she felt his hand go up around her throat, using the wall to brace herself, she thrust her knee up and into Edward's crotch. The heavy man shrieked with pain and, releasing his grip on Leslie, he doubled over and fell to the floor.

Leslie lost her balance and fell. She looked back at Edward Todd still lying on the floor writhing in pain. He was trying to get up and come at her again. Leslie struggled to her feet and staggered for the door. She was weak, and on the verge of collapse from the blows to her face and head, but she knew if she could just get through the door and into the hall that she would be safe.

Beth, Elsa and Mark were still in the foyer when they heard the noises and shouts coming from upstairs. Elsa saw a look of fear wash across Beth's face. "Leslie, she's in the studio alone." Beth broke into a run for the stairs. "God, I hope he didn't come back!"

Elsa fell in behind Beth. "God, I'm getting too old for this."

Mark, at first, wasn't sure what to do, but then he too broke into a run up the stairs behind them. He called out, "Who came back?"

Beth continued to race down the second floor hall. Elsa slowed only slightly and turned to Mark and replied, "Edward Todd; he killed the girl!"

Mark didn't stop long enough to think about what she had said. Instead he quickened his gait and ran past Elsa. He caught up with Beth just as she reached the stairs leading to the third floor. Side-by-side, they ran up the steps, Mark's long legs taking three steps to Beth's two. Just as he reached the top, he saw Leslie stretched out across the floor fighting her way to the studio door. Behind her was a man with his large thick hand tightly clasped around her ankle, cursing and struggling to pull her back.

Mark froze for just a moment, just long enough for Beth and Elsa to catch up with him. Elsa stopped, her hand over her mouth. She had accepted, as truth, what Beth and Leslie told her about an apparition haunting the third floor room, mainly because she wanted to believe, but seeing this for herself was beyond her wildest imagination.

"Leslie!" Beth called out. Leslie looked up to see her friends standing in the hall. Just as she did, her hand touched a vase that had been knocked off a table in the struggle. She grabbed it and swung it around, hitting Edward Todd across the top of his head. The man collapsed into a heap on the floor. Leslie sat up, breathing hard, her head spinning with pain. She turned to see Beth, Elsa and Mark running toward her. "Stop, don't come in yet. I'm afraid all this will disappear if you come in. I want to find out if she's okay, if Cordelia is still alive."

"What do you want us to do?" Beth yelled. Leslie looked up. She didn't know what to do next. Beth, now standing at the door with the others by her side, gasped. "Oh God, Leslie, your face. We need to get you to the hospital!"

"No!" Leslie felt on the verge of collapse, but she wouldn't agree. She struggled to get to her feet.

"We need to help you!" Elsa exclaimed, shocked by the beating Leslie had taken. Then she noticed the room. "My God, look at this room! It different. It looks like something from the turn of the century."

Mark's eyes quickly scanned the room. He was at a loss for anything to say; he just kept looking back at Leslie, wanting to help his friend. Suddenly the three, at the same instant, felt a sensation. It was like a static charge from touching a metal object. The sensation seemed to take the form of a force pushing past them. In almost the same instant, the girl, Cordelia, appeared in front of them. She was rushing toward Leslie.

Speechless, they watched as she knelt down beside Leslie and threw her arms around her. "Come on; let's get away from here before he wakes up. He'll be even worse after he wakes up." She helped Leslie to her feet and together, with Leslie leaning on her arm, they began to make their way to the door.

"Wait." Leslie stopped. "I have to tell you while there's time. I'm not an angel. You have got to get away from here. You have to go to someone who can help you get to your Aunt Rebecca in Cincinnati."

"You can help me!"

"No, you don't understand, and I don't know how to explain it. I'm not even sure myself, but I think I'm from your future. If I go out that door, I'll disappear or you'll disappear. Whatever happens, we won't be able to see each other, and I won't be able to protect you." Leslie began to lose her balance. Cordelia steadied her. "Promise me you'll run away from here. Go to your old housekeeper Jenny. She'll figure out how to help you."

"I promise I'll run away, but please, we have to go now."

Leslie's left eye was beginning to swell shut, and the blood running from a gash in her forehead was clouding her vision in the right. She blinked and looked directly at Cordelia. "I wish you could be my daughter. I'd love you and keep you safe, but it can't be. When you grow up, try to find me, so I'll know you're alright."

Cordelia began to cry. "I promise. I wish you could be my mamma, too." They heard a moan from Edward Todd. Hurriedly, they made their way to the door. Leslie felt herself losing consciousness. "Beth," she called out, as she and Cordelia passed through the doorway into the hall. Leslie collapsed into the arms of her friends. Cordelia was gone.

"Where did she go?" Mark asked. "Where's the ghost? She just vanished!"

"I don't think she can exist or materialize outside this room," Elsa answered.

"Mark, help me get her downstairs; she's in bad shape. We've got to get her to a hospital."

Following Beth's instructions, Mark lifted Leslie up into his arms. With Beth's help, Mark carried her down the stairs. Elsa paused to look at the room. There were no signs of a struggle, and like Cordelia, Edward Todd was gone. It was Leslie's studio once more. As Elsa turned to walk away, she saw a piece of broken porcelain lying on the floor. She picked it up and turned it over in her hand. It was part of the vase Leslie had shattered over her attacker's head, and there was blood on the edge. "She must have had it in her hand when she left the room." Elsa thought. She wrapped it in a tissue, and put it in her jacket pocket. She joined the others, who were now almost at the end of the second floor hall.

They put Leslie in Elsa's car. Beth sat in the back seat, cradling her friend in her arms. Mark went with them and rode in the front, watching for oncoming cars and police cruisers while Elsa drove her Jaguar like a demon, running red lights and passing everything in her path.

52

Leslie lay on an examination table in the emergency room of Clark Regional Medical Center. A doctor stitched the cut on her forehead, while Beth, Elsa and Mark stood along the far wall and watched.

Outside, a Winchester city police officer spoke with a nurse, then quietly entered the room. He looked at the three people lining the wall. "Is this the woman who was attacked?"

"Yes officer," Elsa answered. "Did someone report this to you?"

"Yes ma'am, hospital security called me. It's procedure. I need to get a statement from her."

"I don't know that she is in any condition to talk at the moment."

"I still need to try. This guy could go after someone else. Did any of you witness the attack?"

Elsa knew that, with her influence in the town, it would be best if she were the one to answer questions; questions they could not answer truthfully. "We were going to meet at Leslie's, Ms. Newkirk's, house this evening. She had been out, and when she arrived home, I suppose someone surprised her. We assume it was someone who was attempting to break into her home. He began beating her, and we pulled into the driveway as the attack was taking place."

"What about you?" The officer looked at Mark.

"Mark is the son of Ms. Newkirk's neighbors across the street. He has been assisting us the last few days. Ms. Newkirk bought an interesting old home, and we have been doing some historical research. Mark was due to come over this evening, and so he came across the street when he saw us pull in the drive."

Elsa put her arm around the tall teenager and hugged him tightly in a nurturing gesture. "Poor boy, he didn't know that he was going to walk into all this mess."

"Did you see anything? Did you get a look at him?"

Mark was frightened. He looked at Elsa and instinctively knew he should say nothing. "No. I just walked across the street to Leslie's house. All I saw was some guy run off down the street. I couldn't see what he looked like."

"What about either of you?"

"God, this is so terrible," Elsa said, as she put her hand to her mouth and looked again at Leslie.

"Yes ma'am, it is, but did either of you get a look at him?"

Still watching as the doctor examined Leslie, Beth replied, "He was Caucasian, average height. He seemed to have a stocky build, but that could have just been his clothes. Other than that, I didn't see anything. He ran away as soon as the headlights from the car hit him."

Elsa agreed, "Yes, that was all I saw, too, but if I think of anything we will call you immediately."

"Is there any chance this could be someone she knew? Former boyfriend maybe?"

Elsa again answered, "No, she just moved here from Chicago a couple weeks ago. Her family was from here originally. And correct me if I'm wrong, but I don't believe she has dated anyone in quite some time."

"Yes, that's right," Beth agreed.

"Let me just get your names and where I can reach you and, then I'll get a quick statement from Ms. Newkirk."

Beth gave the officer her name, phone number and address in Chicago, and then she stated that she was staying in Winchester for at least two more days, perhaps longer. Mark nervously gave his name, and those of his parents since he was still a minor. "And you, ma'am?"

"Elsa Van Meter."

The officer looked up from his note pad. "Oh, Ms. Van Meter, I'm sorry. I didn't recognize you. If you could just give me your phone number, if you don't mind, I'll try to hurry and not disturb you and your friends any longer than necessary."

"Certainly. You are being so kind." Elsa gave the officer her number, and he spoke with Leslie only briefly, but assured her he would investigate thoroughly and do everything in his power to identify and arrest her attacker.

After the officer left, the doctor took Beth, Elsa and Mark aside. "Your friend here is very lucky you pulled up when you did. She took some pretty hard blows to the face and head. You say he attacked her outside the house?"

Realizing Leslie had no grass stains or dirt on her clothes, Elsa quickly answered, "We, of course, haven't been able to talk with her much. She was barely conscious when we arrived here, but I believe she surprised him on her back porch, and then she ran into the driveway just as we pulled in."

"From the bruises on the back of her head and shoulders, it looks like he slammed her into the wall of the house. She also has bruises on her throat. He probably attempted to strangle her. She also has a cracked rib and a concussion. Like I said, she's lucky. I want to keep her here overnight for observation, but she should be able to go home tomorrow afternoon."

"Can we stay here with her tonight?" Beth asked.

"Sure. We'll get her settled into a room in a few minutes. I just need you to make certain she stays quiet. Head injuries like hers can become serious if she tries to move around too much."

"I need to call my parents," Mark said.

"Elsa, why don't you take Mark home and give them an explanation. I'll stay here with Leslie."

"I would like to stay, too," Mark offered.

Elsa put her arm through Mark's. "I know, love, but when your parents hear about the burglar, I'm sure they would prefer you to be safe and sound at home. And you do have school tomorrow. You can see her just as soon as you get out of class. I know she'll want you there."

Elsa drove Mark home and gave his parents the well-rehearsed story of the would-be burglar. Mark, of course, was praised by his father for helping thwart the attack, while Barbara hugged him and cried, saying over and over how grateful she was that he was safe. Mark hugged Elsa, and she gave him a kiss on the cheek as she left, which had the desired effect of impressing his mother.

53

Elsa stopped by Leslie's house and found sweatpants, a loose fitting button down shirt, and a cardigan sweater. She put them in a bag, along with a few toiletries. Then she did the same for Beth, sorting through her luggage until she found the items Beth had asked for. Just something to wear that would make her night at the hospital more comfortable.

As Elsa walked out of the guestroom, she looked down the hall to the stairs leading to the third floor. She hesitated, and then turned to leave. She was half way down the hall when she stopped and turned around, walking to the third floor stairway. Silently, she climbed the stairs, then, cautiously walked to the studio door. After seeing what had happened to Leslie, she didn't dare go inside alone. Elsa stood there, looking inside the room, taking stock of the easels, canvases, drawing table and painting supplies. Whoever would have thought that something like this – to have contact with and be affected by people who were either already dead or in the past – was possible? She looked at her watch; she hadn't realized the time. No wonder she was exhausted. She turned and left for the hospital.

* * *

Tuesday afternoon, Elsa and Beth took Leslie home from Clark Regional. Her head still ached, and with the cracked rib, every movement of her upper body was painful. They helped her into the house, and Elsa began cooking dinner in the kitchen, while Beth settled Leslie on the sofa in the parlor with a pillow and blanket. "Have you been upstairs? Up to my studio?"

"Elsa went up there last night, when she came back here to get us each a change of clothes. Why?"

"I was just wondering if she came back."

"You mean, Cordelia?"

"I don't want either of you to go in there alone, but I want to check the diary to see if she made any new entries."

225

"We'll check it later. Right now, I just want to get you settled. I'm going to stay a couple extra days."

"You really don't need to. You have probably stayed too long anyway. I know you need to get back to work. And Angie is moving out. You need to take care of that too."

"You need someone to take care of you for a few days."

"I'll be fine."

"I know you'll be fine, but you heard what the doctor said."

Beth looked up to see Elsa walk into the room. Beth noticed how tired Elsa looked, but even so, she was still strikingly beautiful. She knew, at that moment, that if Elsa were willing, she would most likely make many more trips to Winchester. "Beth, love, you need to listen to the girl. You shouldn't neglect your responsibilities at home."

Beth smiled. "Are you trying to get rid of me?"

"On the contrary, I'd love to tie you up and keep you here, but you do have responsibilities back in Chicago. Besides, I plan to watch after our patient."

"I appreciate all this, but listen, both of you, I'll be fine."

Before Leslie could protest further, the doorbell chimed. Elsa exited the parlor to get the door. When she opened it, Mark and his mother, Barbara Rogers, were on the front porch. Barbara had a pot of home-made soup and Mark carried a large arrangement of flowers in his arms. "Well hello there, Barbara and Mark, honey. So good to see you again."

Barbara craned her neck trying to get a look inside the house. Standing behind his mother, Mark smiled and rolled his eyes skyward, as if to say to Elsa that he was sorry his mother came along. "How is she? I called the hospital, and they told me she had been released."

Elsa opened the door wide enough for Mark and Barbara to enter. "She doesn't look well, but the doctor said she will be fine. She just shouldn't exert herself and should stay still for the next couple of days."

"I made this soup today. I thought, with everything that happened last night, it might be a help if you all didn't have to worry about making dinner."

"How thoughtful. Here, let me show you in. Then, I'll take this back to the kitchen."

"Leslie, love, you have visitors."

Barbara and Mark, with the flower arrangement still filling his arms, followed Elsa into the parlor. Barbara put her hand up to her face and gasped. "Oh, good Lord! This is terrible! Oh, you poor thing." Barbara sat down in a chair opposite the sofa, and she continued to shake her head as she stared at Leslie. Leslie's left eye was now almost completely swollen shut. Around her right eye was black and blue, her cheek was swollen, she had a cut on her lip and the stitches on her forehead were visible through the hair that was hanging down over her brow.

"I just can't believe something like this could happen in this neighborhood. John and I are going to call a meeting of the neighborhood association and get a watch started again. This is just horrible. You are so lucky that they pulled in your driveway when they did. Oh Lord, and then I think about Mark, and what if he had been the one to surprise the burglar. I didn't sleep at all last night."

Leslie's voice was weak and raspy, but she thanked Barbara for her concern and tried to reassure her that Wood Hurst had probably been singled out because it had sat vacant for so long. Barbara, however, was undeterred. After seeing Leslie's battered face first hand, she left more determined than ever to organize the neighborhood. Mark stayed with his friends for about an hour. He wanted to be near these three women, who, though much older then he, shared his experience with the ghost.

Later that evening, Mark returned, and he, Beth and Elsa removed Cordelia's diary from its hiding place. They checked for any new entries. There were none. Then, on Wednesday, they checked again. Nothing had changed. They didn't know if Cordelia had gotten away safely, or if she had been caught by Edward Todd and killed before she could leave the house.

That afternoon, Elsa drove Beth to the airport in Lexington, while Mark and his girlfriend stayed with Leslie at the house.

54

Two weeks had passed since the night Leslie fought Edward Todd, and in that time not only had her cuts and bruises healed, but the house remained still and quiet. There had been no more unexplained sounds, no more flashes of light, and no more appearances of the young Cordelia. The first week after the incident, either Elsa or Mark, and sometimes his girlfriend, were with Leslie almost constantly. They were afraid for her to be alone, and likewise, she was afraid to be alone.

As the days passed, and they all became more secure in the idea that the spirit or spirits, if that is what they truly were, had moved on. Leslie found herself spending more time alone in the house. For company, she adopted two cats from a local rescue group. A slightly temperamental female she named Chessie, because she had always liked the logo of the Chesapeake and Ohio railroad. The other was a black and white male, whose favorite pastime, she quickly noticed, was playing with a stuffed catnip mouse. She named him Axle.

It took both cats a few days to adjust to their new surroundings, but Leslie found they had no fear of her studio on the third floor, as the Andersons' pets had. Leslie took this as a good sign, but with the shadow of bruises still visible on her face, she was by no means ready to go into the room alone, or at least without someone standing watch at the door.

On one afternoon, she and Elsa scoured every antique shop they could find in three counties, finally locating a complete dining room suite that would fit beautifully in Leslie's home. Mark and his girlfriend helped Leslie hang the velvet drapes she and Beth had discovered in the attic. Then, on a particularly rainy and dreary Saturday afternoon, she, Elsa and Mark made a picnic lunch and ate in the attic under the sound of rain spattering on the roof top. After eating, they spent several hours sorting and cleaning items from the trunks and boxes, using them as accent pieces around the house.

Leslie bought white wicker furniture and placed it on the front porch of her house. She thought it gave the big Victorian an inviting look, and weather permitting, she began sitting on her porch every afternoon, watching neighbors come and go while she sketched or read.

Leslie's parents had scheduled a visit from Florida in three weeks. She felt that would allow enough time for her to furnish a couple more rooms, and by then, any telltale signs of cuts and bruises would have completely vanished. Leslie let her mother make arrangements with their other family members, who still lived in and near Winchester, to bring a dish and join them for dinner one afternoon during their stay. She knew her parents wanted to show off their daughter's house, and Leslie wanted to reestablish connections with some of her cousins.

Leslie was on the front porch waiting for Elsa, when she saw a red BMW convertible drive down her street and then slow as it passed her house. The windows were tinted, so she wasn't able to see the driver. She watched the car until it reached the end of the street. It turned left, then disappeared around the corner. At first she thought it odd, but she decided the driver was probably just admiring her home.

A few seconds later, Elsa pulled up in her Jaguar. "Are you ready?" She yelled out the window of her car.

"Sure, just let me double check the door." Leslie put her key in and made certain it was locked. "Where are you taking me today?"

"We are going to Versailles. There is a shop that has an antique desk, and if what they told me is accurate, it is nearly one hundred years old, in perfect condition and would be beautiful in your study." When they arrived at the shop, they found the desk to be everything the shopkeeper had described it to be. It was a nine-drawer, made of English walnut with a hand-tooled leather writing surface. Each drawer was triple band-ed around a central inlaid panel; the back sides and knee hole were also banded. It was fifty-nine-and-one-half inches wide and thirty-five inch-es deep. Leslie needed a large piece to begin filling the large room. She looked around the shop and selected a lamp table, then wrote a check for both items.

Leslie made arrangements for delivery the next day, then she and Elsa left. "Have you spoken with Beth lately?" Leslie asked.

"Actually, we talked for almost an hour last night."

"Really? I spoke with her night before last. She said the two of you were going to make plans to spend some time together?"

Elsa smiled. "Yes, we did."

"She is very taken with you, you know," Leslie added.

"I assure you, love, the feeling is mutual. But these long distance things never work well. At least not after some time passes, and the in-fatuation wears off."

"So what are you planning to do?"

"Enjoy it one day at a time, and see how it plays out. And speaking of how things play out, have you checked Cordelia's diary lately?"

"Yes, as a matter of fact, I have. Mark and his girlfriend Jamie stopped by last night for a few minutes, and I had them stand watch at the door while I went inside and checked. That's terrible isn't it? I'm still afraid to go into a room in my own house."

"Considering the beating you took, of course it isn't. It would be foolish to go in there without someone present to help you if anything happened."

Leslie watched the scenery along US 60 as Elsa drove. "Everything from that night is still so fuzzy. Sometimes I think I remember something, but I'm not sure that I didn't create the memory."

"Do you have an example?"

"I thought I put a business card in the diary."

"Why did you put a card in the diary?"

"Just on the outside chance that Cordelia survived and grew up. I thought maybe she would try to find me. Of course, she would be about 90 by now, and I think she would have tried to contact me years ago."

"I seem to recall some cards lying on your drawing table, but we didn't find one in the diary when we checked."

"See, that's what I mean. Maybe I thought about putting one in the diary but didn't. I wish I could remember things from that night more clearly."

"It might come back to you in time. A positive way to view this would be to think that your interaction with Cordelia. Whether she was a restless spirit or the emotional imprint of a traumatized girl, or even a doorway to the past. Somehow brought about a resolution or closure to the events of the past."

"I guess you're right. I may never know what happened to her, and I have to accept that and move on."

"That's the spirit. Sorry, I didn't mean to make a pun. Now, how about stopping off in Lexington for a glass of wine before we go home."

Leslie looked at Elsa and smiled; she liked her new friend. No matter where Elsa went, a party, large or small, would soon follow. "Sure, I'm up for a drink. I haven't had one for days."

55

At home the next day, Leslie nursed a headache, the result of a night out with Elsa and the entourage that congregated around the woman. On the phone she spoke briefly with Beth and made plans for her next trip down. Then the two discussed the positioning of the desk in the study, along with the new chairs Leslie had ordered. The chairs were upholstered in leather, in an overstuffed contemporary design. She thought the lamp table would look good sandwiched between them, but where in the room? Leslie still hadn't made up her mind about the purchase of a billiard table. The room was certainly large enough. Leslie's father would love the idea, but she really didn't play. Then she thought, why should she care? She could decorate the house in any way she saw fit. After all, she was buying a piano when her own skill level was barely above playing "Chop Sticks."

As Leslie took another long drink from her glass of water, she heard the doorbell chime. She knew it was either a neighbor, Elsa, or the deliveryman with her desk. Leslie, smiling, opened the door wide, expecting a familiar face or a delivery truck on the street. "Oh, hello," she said, surprised to see a dark haired man standing on her porch.

"I'm sorry. Am I interrupting something?" The man asked.

"No, I was just expecting a friend of mine or a delivery person. Can I help you?" Leslie asked, as she looked past the man and saw a red BMW convertible parked at the curb.

"Are you Leslie Newkirk, the artist who bought this house a couple months ago?"

"Yes, why do you ask?"

"My grandmother and I came across some of your work, and we were interested in seeing more of it. Possibly purchasing a piece or two?"

"You want to buy some of my work?"

"Yes, perhaps. But we can come back another time if this is inconvenient."

"Wow. I mean, I sell pieces, but not a lot. It's more of a hobby. How did you come across some of my work?" Leslie remembered a painting Elsa had admired, and Leslie had made a gift of it to her. "Are you friends of Elsa? Elsa Van Meter."

"I'm acquainted with her, yes."

Leslie hesitated. "Tell you what. You can come in, and I'll take you upstairs to my studio to look at some pieces, but if the delivery man shows up I may have to leave you alone for a minute while I take care of him."

"That will be fine. I'll get my grandmother out of the car. She is elderly, and I didn't want her out in the cold, walking up the steps unnecessarily if you weren't home."

"My studio is on the third floor. That may be too much for her. I have a portfolio with photographs of my work that I could bring down. The two of you could look at those."

"I'll ask her. She usually likes to view the original work. She's a little fussy like that sometimes." The dark haired man smiled.

"I'm sorry; I didn't get your name."

"I'm sorry, how rude of me. My name is Clay, Clay Montgomery, and my grandmother, you can just call her Mrs. Lyle."

"Clay? What a coincidence. A former owner of the house was named Clay."

"Interesting," the man smiled. "Actually, my grandmother Lyle named me." Clay Montgomery removed his dark Ray Bans, revealing beautiful liquid blue eyes.

Leslie tried not to stare, but she found herself lost in the blue of the man's eyes. "If...if you like, you can pull your car under the porte-cochere and your grandmother won't need to walk as far."

"That would be nice, thank you."

Leslie stood in the doorway, watching the dark-haired man, Clay, go down the walk to his car. His movements were strong yet smooth and graceful, as if he could float on air. He walked to the passenger side of the car and leaned over, apparently speaking to his grandmother. When he stood up, and Leslie saw him beside the car with his dark hair and the long dark overcoat, she realized that he was the man from the cemetery. He was the man parked along the drive who appeared to watch as she and Beth searched the Weatherly family plot.

Clay pulled his car under the porte-cochere. As Leslie waited, Clay helped his grandmother out of the car, then held her arm to steady the old woman as they climbed the porch steps.

"Can I help you?"

"No, we're fine. Grandma Lyle usually gets around very well; it's just sudden weather changes like this cause the arthritis in her knees to flare up."

The old woman was very neatly dressed, like the old money matrons Leslie often saw in the theaters and art museums around Chicago. Even for her apparent age, the elderly woman didn't seem at all frail. "This is my Grandma Lyle."

Leslie extended her hand. "It is nice to meet you, Mrs. Lyle."

The old woman took Leslie's hand in her right, and then cupped her left on top, gently patting the back of Leslie's hand. "So you are the artist. Well, it is so nice to meet you, honey. Did my grandson tell you I collect art?"

"No, not exactly, but I assumed."

"Well, I do. I like to buy art from all the new young artists. I always tell them that I'm going to hang onto their work until they are famous, then I'm going to resell it for a fortune. They like hearing that. It makes them laugh."

Leslie smiled broadly. "I don't know that you will ever be able to resell any of mine for a fortune, but I'm certainly flattered that you want to buy something. Why don't both of you come inside out of the cold."

Leslie led Mrs. Lyle and her grandson into the foyer, and then she closed the door behind them. She watched as Mrs. Lyle stood motionless, taking in every detail of what she could see of the house.

"Beautiful old house. I bet it is almost as old as I am."

"I would say a bit older."

"Do you mind if I look around these rooms. I'm nosy; my grandson will tell you that."

"Please excuse my grandmother. She is nosy and very forward. I think she uses her age to get away with murder."

"I guess that is one of the advantages of old age." Leslie paused and thought for a moment, then asked, "Did I see you at the Winchester cemetery a couple weeks ago? It was on a Sunday afternoon."

"You may have; I take my grandmother there occasionally to put flowers on some of the family graves."

"I was there with a friend of mine from Chicago. She came down for a visit and helped me do a little historical research on this house." Leslie noticed Mrs. Lyle running her finger tips across the intricate carvings of the stair rail. She quickly returned her attention to Clay when he spoke.

"Seems that I do recall that now; I assumed she was your partner."

Leslie was caught off guard by the comment. "Partner?"

"Yes, your significant other."

"Ah, no, we're just friends."

"I'm sorry, I'm being too forward. I guess I inherited that from my grandmother."

"Along with her eyes, the two of you have the same eyes."

"Yes. So does my mother. Strong gene pool, I guess. You know, I walked through this house when it was on the market. I thought seriously about buying it for myself. I'm glad to see someone got it that cares about preserving it."

"Thank you. I'm glad you decided not to buy. I fell in love with it the first time I pulled in the driveway." Leslie looked again at Mrs. Lyle, who was now walking around in the parlor. "Why don't we join your grandmother?"

Clay followed Leslie into the parlor. "If the two of you would like to have a seat, I can go upstairs and get my portfolio. Then, if there is anything you are interested in, I can bring it down for you to view in person."

"You don't need to go to all that trouble," Mrs. Lyle answered.

"It's no trouble, really. I don't want you to have to climb all the stairs."

"Well, if you don't mind. My knees are acting up today."

"I don't mind at all. I'm expecting a delivery, so the doorbell might chime, but I can answer it from the intercom upstairs. I just had it installed; the house is so big I needed it. Also, a friend of mine is coming over, and she has a key, so if I don't answer right away she will just open the door and come in. So don't be startled if you hear her. Just have a seat and I'll be right back." Leslie hurriedly climbed the stairs to the second floor, and then rushed down the hall at a quick walk.

When she reached the door of her studio, she stopped. She could see her portfolio lying on a table across the room. Not since the night Edward Todd attacked her had she entered the studio alone. Leslie contemplated her options. She could wait for Elsa, but she wasn't sure what time her friend would arrive. She could go downstairs and make some excuse for why she needed Clay to accompany her. Leslie breathed in deeply. Or she could simply overcome her fear and enter the room.

Leslie put her hand on the door facing and felt the smooth polished surface of the varnished wood under her fingertips. Her gray cat, Chessie, curled around her legs and then walked into the room from behind her. "You aren't afraid, are you girl?" Chessie meowed and jumped on top of the drawing table. "Here goes," Leslie said to herself. She took another deep breath, then stepped into the room. Leslie grabbed the portfolio, picked up Chessie with her other hand, and then, looking around her quickly, left to rejoin her guests downstairs.

"Here you go," she said as she walked into the parlor. She flipped a switch and turned on the overhead chandelier, giving Mrs. Lyle better light for viewing the photographs. Clay leaned close to his grandmother and together they reviewed Leslie's work, pointing to details of each and making quiet comments to one another. Leslie sat patiently in a chair opposite them and continued to stoke Chessie, who was contentedly lounging in her lap. "If you would like me to tell you about any of them, just let me know."

Clay looked up at Leslie. "Thank you, we will." Then he returned his attention to his grandmother.

After they had viewed each image, the old woman asked, "There are two in here that have caught my eye. Could you come here and tell me about them, please."

"Certainly," Leslie stood and placed Chessie in the seat of the chair. Then she joined her guests on the sofa. "Oh, you like this one? It is one of my favorites, too. It's oil on canvas, and it is a street scene in Paris."

"I thought I recognized the location. My second husband and I liked to travel. We made several trips to Paris when we were younger. Clay's grandfather, my first husband, didn't like to travel." She put her hand on top of Clay's and squeezed it gently. "I always told people that the only way to get him out of Ohio would be to put a firecracker up his behind." The old woman laughed, and then returned her attention to the photograph of the painting.

"That's funny. I like that expression."

"Grandma Lyle has lots of expressions like that. And not all of them can be repeated in public."

"Don't listen to my grandson. So tell me more about your painting. Did you paint that while you were in Paris?"

"No. I did it from some photographs I took while I was there. My father was in the Army, and we traveled a lot. I sort of lived all over, but my family is originally from Winchester. That's how I ended up here." Leslie looked up and noticed Clay studying her face.

Leslie wasn't sure why, but it made her uncomfortable. It was almost as if the man was searching for something.

"Now, tell me about this one," the old woman asked pointing to an impressionistic landscape. "I love the colors in this one. It reminds me of the sunset over the fields by my house."

Leslie began explaining the background information on the work. When and where it was painted, the style, and any other little facts she thought Mrs. Lyle would be interested in hearing.

When there was a short pause in the conversation, Clay interrupted, "Excuse me, and you can tell me if it is none of my business, but I couldn't help noticing the shadows of some bruises on your face. Were you in an accident recently?"

Leslie was surprised by the question. While her face was healing, most people just stared and most likely assumed she was beaten by an abusive husband or boyfriend. Leslie stammered but gave the rehearsed response, "Ah, no, I ah, came home one night and found someone trying to break into my house. Instead of running off, he turned on me. I was lucky a neighbor and some friends of mine pulled up when they did. I guess it could have been worse."

"That's terrible. I bet it was frightening."

"I was pretty shaken up by it."

Mrs. Lyle looked into Leslie's eyes. "Do you live here alone?"

"Yes, but I have a good security system, and I'm much more careful about going in and out at night."

"Do you have a special someone in your life?"

Leslie didn't like the woman asking questions about her personal life, but she was so surprised by the question she answered without thinking. "No, not at the moment, but I do have my two cats."

"Neither does my grandson. I want him to find a nice woman like you."

"Grandma, please." Clay looked up at Leslie, his blue eyes sparking in the light from the chandelier. "I'm sorry. I apologize for my grandmother. She likes to embarrass me."

Leslie, frowning, stood up. Taking one step back she crossed her arms. "All right, I think there is more to this visit than just wanting to see my paintings and drawings. Why are you here?"

"Grandma, I think it's time." Turning now to Leslie, Clay smiled slightly, "My grandmother wanted to get to know you."

Mrs. Lyle patted her grandson's knee, then said, "I met you once years ago. You were with your grandparents, sitting at that little dairy freeze eating chili dogs. Clay is about three or four years younger than you, and he was hungry, so his mother and I stopped to get him something. The two of you played across the street on the headstones in the cemetery.

"Were you friends with my grandparents?"

"No. That was the first time we met. Your grandmother and I ran into each other maybe two more times after that, but that's all."

"So you tracked me down because I played with your grandson however many years ago?"

Clay put his arm around his grandmother's shoulder. "Grandma Lyle."

"It's okay, sweetie." The old woman opened her purse and removed a small billfold. From it she took a plastic bag, which contained a single piece of paper. With trembling hands, she extended it to Leslie.

Leslie took the plastic bag. "It's one of my business cards."

"Look at it," Clay directed.

"Okay, it's a pretty tattered business card. It looks like it was run over by a bus." Leslie turned the card over to look at the back. On it, in her own handwriting, was a scribbled note. It simply read: *Some day when you are older, look for me."* Leslie felt a chill run through her body, and she gasped as if the air had just been sucked from her lungs. "Where did you get this?"

"It was inside my diary. You put it there nearly 80 years ago."

Leslie looked at the card again. The paper was yellowed with age. The corners of the card were worn and frayed, and the ink in which the note was written had faded slightly.

"Cordelia?"

"My friends and family always called me Cordy. You didn't get those cuts and bruises from a burglar. My stepfather Edward Todd did that to you. That was the night you told me to run away. You gave me the courage to run away."

Leslie sat down in the chair opposite the sofa. She looked first at Mrs. Lyle, and then at Clay, searching their faces for some hint that what they were telling her was – or wasn't – real. "Tell me something else. Tell me something, so I'll know this is true."

"That night, I ran into the upstairs room, and my stepfather was lying in the floor. You broke a vase over his head, and you were hurt very badly. You told me you weren't an angel, and I needed to get away and go live with my aunt."

Leslie closed her eyes and rubbed them with her fingertips. She began to recall her words to Cordelia. "What else?"

"When we went through the doorway, you vanished and I was left there alone. I called out for you, but you were gone. I went back into the room. I was going to get my diary and some things, but Mr. Todd started to wake up. When I pulled the diary out of the hole in the fireplace that card fell out. Then Mr. Todd moved. I guess it scared me, so I put the diary back. I saw your card lying on the hearth, so I just grabbed it and ran."

Leslie stood up and walked to the elderly woman. Tears began to fill Leslie's eyes; she bent down and hugged her. "Since the first time I saw you and realized what was happening, I wanted to help you. And now you are sitting here." Leslie wiped her eyes.

Clay took Leslie's hand in his. "I was named after my great-grand-father Clay Weatherly, whom my grandmother never got to meet. My name is Clay Weatherly Montgomery and my grandmother has told me about you for years. Most of the family didn't believe her; they dismissed it as memories created by a child to deal with abuse and death. I always believed her; I always knew you were real."

"Why didn't you contact me before now?"

"We didn't want to risk changing the series of events. We didn't know what would happen."

"I understand." Leslie wiped another tear from her face. "I told you I wanted to take care of you like you were my daughter. Now I see you and …I'm sorry. This is pretty overwhelming."

"Now I'm old enough to be your grandmother."

Through her tears Leslie laughed. "Yes, old enough to be my grand-mother."

"I think you and Clay would be nice together," Mrs. Lyle said.

"Grandma Lyle! Please. I'm sorry, she has been talking about fixing us up for the last two weeks, ever since we were sure it was safe to contact you and everything had finally come full circle."

Leslie felt like her head was spinning. "Tell me what happened after you left that night, after you ran away."

Cordelia Lyle leaned back against the back of the sofa. "Well, there is a lot to tell in so many years. I went to Jenny, our old housekeeper, just like you said to do. She kept me hidden in her house until my Aunt Rebecca could come down here to get me. It was a long trip back then. I remember taking the train back with her. Aunt Rebecca was a good woman, and her husband Jim was a good man. They raised me and loved me, just like I was one of their own."

"I'm so glad. It's good to know that."

"Why didn't you take the house? I found the will. The house, the money, everything was left to you."

"Edward Todd, he was a slick one. He couldn't get his hands on the money, but he had some crooked lawyer draw up papers so everyone would think he had control of the house. It took some time, but I got everything, the house, all of it. My first husband William Miller, was a big help to me."

Leslie's eyes widened. "You were the Mrs. Miller who sold the house and threw Edward Todd out in the street!"

"The day I showed up on the door step, Edward Todd took one look at me and knew who I was. He knew why I had come back. You see, I was using my husband's name then, and I don't think Edward ever told anyone who I was. He was afraid, too; he was afraid people would find out what he had done."

"Why didn't you live here?"

"They always say home is where the heart is, and my heart just wasn't here back then. So I just sold it. Edward had walled up the attic. Probably because he was afraid something proving that I owned everything would get out. When I sold the house, I just left it like that. I didn't know all those things were still in there."

"All of your things, the things from your family, I'll give them to you. They belong to you."

"Now, there are some things I want to stay with the house, and I want you to have. The rest of it Clay should have. To hell with the rest of them. They never believed me, and all they want is money anyway. My grandson here is the one who really cares about our history."

Leslie raised her left eyebrow and smiled. Clay patted his grandmother's hand. "Grandma has always been very blunt."

Epilogue

Over a month had passed; Beth was in town for another visit and staying with Elsa. With the exception of one upstairs bedroom, which Leslie had reserved for exercise equipment, Wood Hurst was now fully furnished. Leslie and Clay rushed to get Christmas decorations hung before their party the following weekend. They had decided to decorate in the Victorian style, and open the house to the neighborhood and their friends.

Leslie's parents were planning another trip to Winchester at Christmas, so there would be another party for them and the two families. Cordelia Lyle was a frequent visitor, and now that Clay was living with Leslie, Cordelia made a gift of her mother's grand piano to her grandson. Cordelia Lyle's father, Clay had given it to Elizabeth as a wedding gift. The elderly woman wanted to hear music in the house again, just as she had remembered from her childhood, before her mother had fallen ill.

There was a fire in the fireplace and Cordelia sat close by; the heat helped relieve the pain in her knees. Elsa, singing a Christmas carol and with Beth in tow, breezed into the parlor with a silver serving tray filled with brandy snifters and a crystal decanter full of her favorite brand. Clay was on the ladder, putting the star on top of their ten-foot tree, when the doorbell chimed. Leslie, brandy in hand, answered the door.

Barbara Rogers, with Mark and his girlfriend standing behind, smiled at Leslie. "I just wanted to get an early peek at your decorations. I hope you don't mind. And I have been baking all day. I made a fruitcake for you." Barbara held up a pedestal glass cake dish, and thrust it into Leslie's free hand.

"Barbara, Mark, Jamie, what a nice surprise."

"Mark said he was coming over, so I just came along with him to bring the cake."

Leslie smiled at Mark, who rolled his eyes skyward as usual. "We just finished the tree. Why don't you come on in and join us for a brandy. Everyone is here." Leslie knew Barbara had seen Elsa's car in the driveway. "And thank you for the fruitcake; believe it or not, I actually like fruitcake. And since you made it, I know it's delicious."

***

Upstairs, on the third floor in Leslie's studio, sheets of paper fluttered off the drawing table and fell to the floor, pencils rattled on a desk top, and there was a flash of light.

The Third Floor
by Leigh M. Rose
P.O. Box 902
Clay City, KY 40312

www.ingramcontent.com/pod-product-compliance
Lightning Source LLC
Chambersburg PA
CBHW071309250626
47159CB00004B/1361